Praise for the Family Skeleton

"Dr. Georgia Thackery is smart, resourceful, and determined to be a great single mom to her teenager. Georgia is normal in every respect—except that her best friend happens to be a skeleton named Sid. You'll love the adventures of this unexpected mystery-solving duo."

—Charlaine Harris, #1 *New York Times* bestselling author

"Adjunct English professor Georgia Thackery makes a charming debut in *A Skeleton in the Family*. Georgia is fiercely loyal to her best friend, Sid, an actual skeleton who is somehow still 'alive.' When Sid sees someone he remembers from his past life—who later turns up dead—Georgia finds herself trying to put together the pieces of Sid's past as she works to hunt down a killer. Amateur sleuth Georgia, and her sidekick, Sid, are just plain fun!"

—Sofie Kelly, *New York Times* bestselling author of *Faux Paw*

"No bones about it, Leigh Perry hooked me right from the beginning. An unusual premise, quirky characters and smart, dry humor season this well-told mystery that kept me guessing until the very end. It's too bad Perry's sleuth is fictional—I'd invite Georgia over for dinner in a heartbeat."

—Bailey Cates,
New York Times bestselling author of *Magic and Macaroons*
on *A Skeleton in the Family*

"A delightful cozy with a skeleton who will tickle your funny bone."

—Paige Shelton,
New York Times bestselling author of
If Onions Could Spring Leeks on *A Skeleton in the Family*

"An effortlessly narrated, meticulously crafted cozy mystery."

—*The Big Thrill* on *A Skeleton in the Family*

"I had a grand time reading this fresh, original novel peopled (and skeletoned) with enchanting characters and a warm, engaging story. The undercurrent of the gift of love and loyalty between friends and family members gives this book a burnished glow of strength and peace. I totally loved every page and want to visit with Georgia and Sid again and again."

—*Criminal Element* on *A Skeleton in the Family*

"This newest in the Family Skeleton Mystery series is absolutely terrific. Yet again, Perry has come up with a fantastic concept that has never been done . . . Such a fun read . . . and because Perry has, yet again, come up with a barrel of surprises it's a good bet that there will be more tales of Sid and family in the not too distant future."

—*Suspense Magazine* on *The Skeleton Takes a Bow*

"The book [is] very funny, and Sid is a great character. Not to slight the humans. Georgia, Madison, and Deb are fun, too, but it's Sid who steals the show. If you like a good cozy, this is one to look for."

—*Bill Crider's Pop Culture Magazine* on *The Skeleton Takes a Bow*

"This fun cozy paranormal mystery provides a unique look at the investigative process when one of the sleuths has been distilled down to bare bones—literally . . . The characters are fun and the wacky situations escalate nicely to the exciting climax."

—*Night Owl Suspense* on *The Skeleton Haunts a House*

"Leigh Perry does a marvelous job utilizing the humorous aspects to full effect as there are more than a few laugh-out-loud moments. However, the sense of family togetherness is what truly makes *The Skeleton Haunts a House* perfect . . . each and every aspect of *The Skeleton Haunts a House* is a true delight."

—*Fresh Fiction*

THE SKELETON STUFFS A STOCKING

LEIGH PERRY

DIVERSION
BOOKS

FAMILY SKELETON MYSTERIES

A Skeleton in the Family

The Skeleton Takes a Bow

The Skeleton Haunts a House

The Skeleton Paints a Picture

The Skeleton Makes a Friend

Diversion Books
A Division of Diversion Publishing Corp.
443 Park Avenue South, Suite 1004
New York, New York 10016
www.DiversionBooks.com

For more information, email info@diversionbooks.com

First Diversion Books edition September 2019.

Paperback ISBN: 978-1-63576-647-9

eBook ISBN: 978-1-63576-643-1

1 3 5 7 9 10 8 6 4 2

To my husband and alpha reader, Stephen P. Kelner, Jr.

I dedicated a book to you before, but that was twenty-five years ago, so I think you're entitled to a new one.

Chapter One

I saw my teenaged daughter Madison standing on the sidewalk in front of our house as I pulled into the driveway.

"Mom, have you seen Byron?" she asked.

"Did he get out of the yard?"

Madison made a face. "One of G-Dad's grad students let him out the front door."

"Seriously?" That meant another awkward conversation with Mom. Unfortunately, I couldn't complain too strenuously about her letting people overrun the house, since it did belong to her and my father. Madison and I—and Byron—were taking advantage of their generosity even more than the grad students were. "How long has he been missing?"

"I don't know! All I know is that Byron didn't meet me at the door when I got home from school a few minutes ago, and when I asked the crew in the living room if they'd seen him, the guy who needs a haircut said he saw Byron sneaking out when somebody didn't close the door all the way. Then he just shut the door without even telling anybody that Byron was loose. Do I have permission to cuss?"

Madison didn't use profanity often, at least not around me, so that told me how furious she was, and I didn't blame her. "Later. Did anybody see what direction Byron went in?"

She shook her head.

"Okay, you go right, and I'll go left. Have you got your phone?"

She waved it at me and took off down the sidewalk, calling "Byron!" as she went. I went the other direction and did the same. I'd been hunting for ten minutes or so when my cell phone pinged.

MADISON: *Good news! Found him.*

GEORGIA: *Great!*

MADISON: *Also bad news. Meet you at home to explain.*

I jogged back to the house, worried about what she meant. My first thought was that Byron had been injured, but if he'd been seriously hurt, Madison would have wanted me to come to her. My next thought was that Byron had hurt somebody—a child or a smaller dog—but, though Akitas are known for aggressiveness to other dogs, Byron had always been even-tempered. Next up was wondering if he'd found a lady dog and they'd decided to make puppies together, which had me wondering if we'd be liable for the resulting vet bills, which could put a dent in my Christmas shopping budget.

That was as far as I'd taken my fretting when I got to the house and saw them on the front porch. Madison had Byron by the collar with one hand, and in the other, she held a bone.

A large bone.

A bone I was ninety-nine percent sure was a human femur.

Some people might think it odd that an English professor would be able to identify a human femur so quickly, but when your lifelong best friend is a walking, talking skeleton, you can't help but pick up a basic knowledge of bone structure. I'd aced every test on the skeletal system in high school biology. Fortunately, those tests hadn't included questions about ambulatory skeletons because I think the teacher would have had a hard time with my answers. Then again, Sid's continued existence was more a matter of philosophy than science.

Madison said, "Sid is going to be so mad."

"How could this have happened?" I asked.

"I don't know! Maybe the attic door was left unlocked and one of the grad students opened it for some reason."

"Did Byron hurt it?"

Madison looked more closely. "It's dirty, but I don't see teeth marks."

That was a relief. Sid was going to be angry enough without having visible damage. "Do you want me to go talk to him?"

I could tell she was tempted, but she took a deep breath and said, "No, Byron is my responsibility. I'll do it."

"Do you want me to go with you?"

For a minute I thought she was going to say no again, but she weakened. "Would you mind?"

"No, of course not." Byron might be Madison's dog, but I was her mother, which gave me a share of the responsibility. "We better go straight up."

As soon as we got inside, Madison let go of her dog, who headed for the kitchen. We could hear voices from in there, and Byron likely realized that if people were in the kitchen, food might be available too. It was just as well. Under the circumstances, Sid was not going to want to see him.

We went upstairs and paused at the door to the attic to make sure no random grad students were around. My parents, both lifelong English professors with a taste for mentoring, had always made their house available to their grad students for working, meeting, eating, and occasionally sleeping. The students weren't supposed to go upstairs, but I'd seen enough evidence in my bathroom to prove that they ignored that rule fairly often. Sid kept the attic door locked for just that reason.

Madison used her phone to text Sid that we wanted to come up, and a moment later, we heard a click as the door unlocked. My sister Deborah, who was transitioning from a locksmith to a security consultant, had installed a remote-control lock so Sid didn't have to clatter down the stairs to let people in. She'd wanted the chance to troubleshoot a system, and he loves gadgets, so it was a win-win. I had no idea how Byron or a grad student could have bypassed the system, but that was a worry for another time.

Madison went up the stairs, holding the femur tightly, and I made sure the door was locked behind me before following her.

"Hi, Georgia! Hi, Madison!" Sid said. His attic room was much nicer than it used to be. The whole family had pitched in to move the storage boxes to the basement to make room for a secondhand but still comfortable couch, several bookshelves, a worktable with chairs, and his desk. There were even pictures on the wall: a mixture of family photos and movie posters.

Sid was sitting at his desk, which was no surprise. After all, Madison was holding one of his femurs.

Sid can do many things, most of them highly unlikely. In all honesty, his whole existence was the pinnacle of unlikelihood, and the fact that I've known him for most of my life didn't make it any less so. But while he can move his bones independently if the need arises, sheer geometry would have made it difficult for him to stand for very long without both of his femurs.

"What's up?" Sid asked.

Madison started talking as fast as she could. "Sid, I'm really sorry. I don't know how Byron got up here and got outside with your bone, but I don't think he left any marks, and I'll clean it up right away, and I'll make sure he never does it again, and—" Unlike Sid, my daughter needs to breathe, which meant she had to stop to inhale.

Sid looked confused, an expression that should have been impossible for a bare skull, but no more so than the rest of what he did on a daily basis. "Madison, what are you talking about? And what's that?"

Now Madison looked confused too. "Your femur. Or is it a tibia? I get them mixed up."

"That's not all you've got mixed up." Sid came out from behind his desk, walking on two boney legs that were equipped with the usual number of femurs and tibias. "That's not mine."

Chapter Two

"Let me get this straight," said Sergeant Louis Raymond of the Pennycross police. "You found your dog carrying a human bone, and you brought it inside the house?"

We were in the living room, talking quietly because of the grad students in the kitchen. I'd told my mother what was going on, and she'd distracted the students with freshly baked pizza bagels.

"We couldn't be sure it was a real bone," Madison said.

"And when we decided it was, I thought it was from the skeleton in the attic," I said. Between one thing and another, it was known to quite a few people in town that we had a human skeleton, though not how active it could be. Louis, one of my sister's boyfriends, had seen Sid playing the part of a typical, nonambulatory skeleton on Halloween. We'd dialed him directly instead of 911 because we thought it would be moderately less awkward to explain the situation to somebody we knew. I added, "We called as soon as we realized that it wasn't from ours."

Technically, Madison had washed her hands three or four times first, then applied most of a bottle of hand sanitizer. Even I'd washed mine, though I hadn't actually handled the nasty thing. We were used to touching Sid, but that wasn't the same as some random stranger's bone, which Louis was holding with the stained oven mitt we'd used to keep from having to touch it again. Needless to say, we intended to throw away the mitt afterward.

"And you don't know where Byron got the bone?" Louis asked.

"I found him near the intersection of Thatcher and Broadway," Madison said.

"How long was he gone? That might help us figure out how far he went."

Madison started to explain why we didn't know, but I thought of something. "The porch cam!" I said. As another part of her endeavor to master the latest tech, Deborah had installed a camera above the front door that showed the porch and down the walk to the street, in case of package thieves. It was still new enough that I hadn't thought of it when we were searching for Byron. "I can access it from my phone and see when he left."

"Let's see what you got."

I pulled my phone from my pocket and opened the app, then backtracked on the feed until I saw the front door left open for ten solid minutes before Byron hesitantly ventured outside and started down the sidewalk. Only then did a grad student come to shut it. "Two forty-five." I was going to have a stern talk with my parents' students. Heating a house as big as ours wasn't cheap. I kept watching until the video showed Madison arriving after school and then going back outside to look for Byron. Adding the ten or fifteen minutes it took Madison to find him, I said, "He was gone about half an hour."

"That's something to go on." Louis put his notepad into his pocket and pulled on his coat. "I'll head toward Broadway and see what I find."

Madison said, "Do you want us to come and bring Byron along? If we take him back there, maybe he could lead us back to where he found it."

"Is he trained to follow a trail?"

"Not really," she admitted.

He didn't look enthusiastic, but said, "I guess it's worth a try. Let's get going. It'll be dark soon." While he called for more cops to assist in the search, Madison got Byron on his leash, and I picked up the bag I used for special occasions. It wasn't technically a pocketbook, though I used part of the space for my wallet and other necessities. It had started out life as a purple bowling bag, and then my crafter mother had decorated it with a Día de los Muertos style sugar skull. Though it was striking, I didn't carry it for fashion. I used it to bring along Sid's skull. His consciousness resided in it, even when separated from the rest of his bones, and Mom had installed eye holes so he could see what was happening. Naturally Sid had wanted to listen in on our conversation with Louis, and also to be ready to accompany us in case we went skeleton hunting.

Madison and I bundled into our coats, scarves, and gloves before going outside. The temperature had dropped like a rock since we'd gotten home, which was only to be expected in December in Massachusetts. At least it wasn't snowing, but when I said as much to Louis, he pointed out that it might have been easier to track Byron if it had been.

We kept a brisk pace until we got to the intersection where Madison had spotted Byron. A quick glance around didn't show us open graves or other obvious skeletal parts strewn across the grass, so Madison let Byron lead the way. He didn't seem to be in any hurry.

A Pennycross squad car pulled up as we made our way down the sidewalk, and Louis told the officers inside to drive down the nearest side streets to see if they could spot anything important while we kept hoping Byron wasn't just enjoying the walk. Akitas are a lot fonder of cold weather than I am.

Finally, when I could tell from Louis's expression that he was about to give it up, Byron led us away from the street and diagonally across somebody's lawn.

"Good boy, Byron," Madison said. "Show us where the bone came from."

We kept going past the house, across the backyard, and to a border of trees dividing the lot and the one behind it. I wondered what the homeowner would have thought if she'd spotted us following the dog across her nicely tended lawn.

Beyond the tree line was a messy, overgrown lot, and Louis pulled a flashlight from his belt to help us avoid the worst of the clumps of weeds and rocks as we continued to follow Byron. He sniffed around for a while, then stopped just past an elderly oak tree with deep hollows between the exposed roots gripping the ground. There was a depression there, and Byron started pushing leaves around with his snout.

"Pull him back," Louis said, and as Madison obeyed, there was a flash of white in the fading daylight as a display of Christmas lights came on from the house behind us. They'd used so many bulbs that it was nearly bright enough to read by, and there was more than enough light to see the tangle of faded red cloth that Byron had uncovered. The bones were even easier to spot.

Unlike Sid, this skeleton didn't move.

Chapter Three

Louis called for more cops and various forensics experts and had one of the uniformed officers give Madison, Byron, and me a ride home while they got to work. I could feel my phone vibrating in my pocket and knew Sid had to be bursting with questions from inside the sugar skull bag, but my hands were so cold I didn't want to remove my gloves to text with him. Madison was shivering too, and though we both knew it wasn't just the frigid weather that was affecting us, we huddled with Byron to try to warm up during the short drive back to the house.

My father, who I'd called Phil since I was young, had arrived while we were gone, and he and Mom must have chased off the grad students because the house was blissfully empty. They herded us into the living room and onto the couch and whipped out a pair of afghans to cover us. After making sure the curtains were all drawn, I pulled out Sid's skull, and a minute later, the rest of his skeleton clattered down the stairs to grab it, put it where it belonged, and squeezed in between Madison and me on the couch.

"Are you two okay?" he asked.

"No," Madison said. "I'm freaked out."

"You're not alone. Sorry I didn't respond to your texts in the car, Sid," I said.

He waved it away. "I was just checking on you." He put one bony arm around each of us.

It was a testament to the oddity of my life that I found the embrace of a human skeleton comforting after the shock of finding a human skeleton.

A minute later, Phil brought in mugs of hot chocolate, complete with the pastel marshmallows Madison preferred, and insisted we take a few sips before telling them what had happened.

"My gracious," Phil said when Madison and I had finished tag-teaming our way through the story. "And you don't know who the poor deceased person was?"

"All I saw were bones and what I think was an item of clothing, maybe a shirt," Sid said. "Louis got us out of there pretty quickly."

"And rightfully so!" Mom said, looking at Madison.

"Oh, absolutely, Mrs. Dr. T," Sid said. "Believe you me, I wanted Madison out of there as fast as possible."

"Okay, stop talking about me like I'm made of china," Madison said. "I'm fine."

"Of course you are," Sid said. "You're a fine brave girl, even if you do have an impressive hot chocolate mustache."

Madison *thunked* him on the skull loudly. It had taken her a while to learn how to do so without hurting her finger, but she had it down pat.

"You say it was on Thatcher Street?" Mom said.

I said, "Technically the street that runs parallel to Thatcher. We went off the sidewalk in front of that blue house with white shutters. You know, the one that goes a little overboard with Christmas lights."

"The Lupton's place," Mom said.

"If you say so. Right behind their backyard is a vacant lot. I didn't know there was any empty land in the middle of town." Pennycross wasn't a big place, but it was old and, as the street signs said, thickly settled.

"There used to be a house there, a big Queen Anne place," Phil said. "Unfortunately, the woman who lived there was a hoarder, and after she passed away, the place was found to be in such bad condition that it was torn down."

"Wait, are you talking about the Nichols house?" Madison asked.

"Yes, Margo Nichols was the owner. Why do you ask?"

"I heard it was haunted."

"Seriously?" Sid said, and I could tell he'd have been raising an eyebrow if he'd had one. "Since when do you believe in ghosts?"

"Present company excepted?" Mom said.

"I've told you, Mrs. T., I'm not a ghost. For one, I'm corporeal, and for another, I don't haunt. I cohabitate."

"An interesting distinction," Phil said. "Yes, Madison, there were rumors of mysterious lights and sounds from the Nichols house, but I'm surprised you've heard of it."

"I hadn't thought about it in years, but one summer when I was visiting, I had a play date with Jo Hensley, and she loved telling ghost stories. She tried to get me to sneak out to come see the place at midnight once."

"You fell asleep before midnight, didn't you?" I said.

Madison grinned. "Yep. Anyway, Jo's family had moved away by the next time we came to visit, so I missed my chance."

"I never have understood the whole 'go visit a haunted house at midnight' thing," Sid said. "Haven't these people ever seen a horror movie? No good ever comes of visiting a haunted house at midnight."

"I thought you didn't believe in ghosts," I pointed out.

"There's no reason to tempt fate."

A buzzer went off in the kitchen, and Phil said, "That must be the macaroni and cheese. I thought serious comfort food was called for tonight."

There are disadvantages to living with one's parents as an adult, but when one of those parents cooks as well and as enthusiastically as Phil, it makes up for a lot. Madison and I usually set the table, but this time Mom insisted that we should continue to warm up while she took care of everything. By mutual decision, we decided not to discuss the discovered skeleton over dinner.

Sid was at the table too. Though he doesn't eat, of course, he does like joining us for family meals whenever possible. Once dinner was over, I wasn't at all surprised when Sid gave me a nudge before saying in an overly loud voice, "Well, I've got something I need to do." He looked at me, and if he'd had eyebrows, I felt sure he'd have waggled them a time or two to make sure I got the hint. "Up in the attic."

I dutifully followed him up to his attic. "What's up?" I asked, though I already knew the answer. Somehow Sid and I had become immersed in what he called murder cases. Okay, I guess they were murder cases, but it still felt both pretentious and silly to say it that way. Naturally I assumed he was going to want to jump right on the case of the remains we'd discovered.

One of the reasons I find it hard to accept our odd avocation was that I get things wrong so much. This was another one of those times.

Sid said, "I've got a line on some manga for Madison's Christmas present. Brand-new, hot titles, won't be officially released until after Christmas, but the guy at Wray's Comics says he can get them for me early. The problem is that there won't be time to ship them, so somebody would have to pick them up at the store on Christmas Eve. Can you help an elf out?"

"Yeah, sure. No problem."

"Excellent! Don't forget!"

I waited a minute, thinking he'd segue into a less festive conversation, but he'd pulled up what looked like a Christmas spreadsheet and was muttering to himself under his breath. Or under what would have been his breath if he actually breathed.

Though Halloween was Sid's favorite holiday because it gave him a chance to get out of the house and interact with other people while in costume—usually skeletal-themed costumes, for obvious reasons—Christmas had been a close second when I was growing up. Then after Madison was born, there was a long period when Madison hadn't known about Sid, making family caroling around the Christmas tree impossible. This year was only the third since that situation had changed, and since my parents hadn't been around for the first and I'd been preparing to move out of town on the second, Sid was determined that this year's celebration would be the best Christmas ever.

Still, I had expected him to say something about finding a body. "Anything else you want to talk about?" I asked.

"Do you have any ideas about what to give Deborah? She's so practical that it's hard to find anything really creative for her."

"When it comes to shopping for Deborah, I gave up on creativity years ago. I got her a couple of sweaters exactly like the ones she usually wears."

"That's no fun." He started flipping through web pages at an almost alarming rate. I think having no eyes or eyelids saves Sid time—he doesn't have to pause for blinking. "How about these?" he said, showing me a picture of skeleton key earrings.

"I think she'd like those."

"Yes!" He pushed the buy button. Since Sid can't work, I give him a stipend so he has money of his own. I used to call it an allowance, but he objected.

"So that body we found," I said. "I wonder if it was murder."

"Probably," he said. "It didn't bury itself there."

"Good point." I paused for him to speculate further.

"And maybe a sweater with a key embroidered on it. What size does Deborah wear?"

"Either medium or large, depending on how it's cut."

"Got it." He kept flipping.

"Sid, are you messing with me, or are we really not going to talk about that murder?"

"What's to talk about? The police got to this one first, and I don't think there's anything we can add unless you know something about the body that I don't."

"Nope, nothing."

"Okay then."

"Okay. Good. We don't have to get involved this time." We discussed other ideas for Christmas presents, and then Sid chased me off, saying he knew I had student papers to grade. I did, but

I was pretty sure he wanted to do some online browsing for my Christmas present.

I was really quite relieved that for once we weren't going to be sticking our noses into places that they didn't belong. I was an academic, not a detective, and Sid was…Sid was Sid. We had better ways to spend our time. Yes, I was definitely relieved.

Despite my overwhelming relief, I was restless, and instead of getting any work done, I spent the rest of the evening watching TV with my parents, even though they'd picked shows I don't particularly like.

I stopped to peek in on Madison on my way to bed to make sure she hadn't been upset by finding a body, but she was sleeping soundly, with Byron keeping watch beside her. I was drifting off myself when I saw my own bedroom door open just a crack. Mom and Phil were checking on me the same way I had Madison.

Chapter Four

It was Friday night when we found the body, and I was so relieved about not being involved that I didn't even think about it over the weekend other than to check the Pennycross news site repeatedly to see if there was any new information. Which there wasn't. It wasn't until Monday afternoon that I had a good excuse to be interested.

I was spending the year teaching at Bostock College, a place I'd never expected to work. Even though the pay for an adjunct English professor was as good as it was anywhere—which is to say, not very good—and the school's location outside Pennycross made it extremely convenient, I'd never been able to get a job there. The problem was that Bostock had a laser focus on teaching business, and preferred that even their English professors have some sort of business background, making a lifelong academic like myself a tough sell. But over the past couple of years they'd beefed up their core curriculum, which meant they needed more people to teach expository writing. A former student of my mother's—one who worked at a different business college—had put in a good word for me and helped me get the job. In fact, I was getting enough hours that I didn't have to work at multiple campuses or teach any online classes, which was a bonus.

I'd finished teaching my classes for the day, had gone back to my desk to check email and take care of some paperwork, and was packing up to go when there was a knock on my office door. Well, calling it an office was stretching the point, and the door was a figment of my imagination. Like the rest of Bostock's adjuncts, I had a four-foot-tall green-cloth-covered cubicle with a desktop, a lap drawer, a file drawer, and two shelves fastened to the cube walls. If they'd been able to figure out a way to attach my desk chair and guest chair, I suspect they'd have done so. I'd had worse office space in the past, so I only complained about the slanting desktop once a week.

I turned to see a set of helicopter parents who'd been making my life interesting since their son started taking my class. I pasted on a professional smile. "Good afternoon."

"Hello, I don't know if you remember us, but we're the Gleasons. Reggie Gleason's parents?" Mrs. Gleason always did the talking while Mr. Gleason stood by and looked concerned. She was a curvy blonde who invariably wore a dark blue pantsuit with either a white or a light blue blouse. Her husband was taller, balding, and wore a suit with the air of someone who'd be a lot more comfortable in khakis.

"Yes, I remember you, Mrs. Gleason."

"Is Reggie doing all right in your class?"

"I'm sorry, Mrs. Gleason, but as I told you before, I can't share any information with you. The FERPA regulations are very strict." I'd reminded them about the Family Education Rights and Privacy Act which forbad me from sharing their student's records at least once a month since September. I wouldn't even have acknowledged that Reggie was in my class if Reggie hadn't introduced them to me himself.

"Oh, we didn't mean his grades," she said, then smiled winningly. "Though of course, if there's anything you can tell us..."

I said nothing, though had I done so, she'd probably have been more worried than she already was. Reggie had been late with several papers, and once he did get them in, they were marginal at best. It was a toss-up as to whether he'd do well enough to pass.

She gave a tiny sigh of disappointment, but went on. "The reason we came by is that we're wondering how the strike is going to affect Reggie's assignments. Will he get some extra time because of the disruption, or will final papers be canceled entirely?"

"I'm sorry, I don't know what you're talking about."

"Oh, there's no reason to try to keep it quiet. It's all over the Bostock Parents' Facebook page."

"Then you guys have better sources than I do." I'd always suspected as much. "I haven't heard anything about a strike."

"Really?" she said, sounding as if she didn't completely believe me. They looked at one another and had one of those silent married-couple conversations before she said, "Speaking hypothetically, what effect would a strike have on your course requirements?"

"That's really not something I've ever had to address." I pointedly looked at my watch. "I'm sorry, but I do have an appointment. If I hear anything about anything that would affect Reggie's class, I will let *him* know." I didn't really think my emphasizing *him* would work, but it was worth a shot.

"Well, thank you for your time," Mrs. Gleason said, and they left, no doubt heading for one of Reggie's other instructors. I beat a hasty retreat before they came up with any more hypothetical questions.

In an ironic twist for somebody who'd just chased off a set of helicopter parents, my appointment was for a late lunch with my parents. I wasn't sure if that made me a helicopter daughter.

Bostock has a sprawling campus, and my classes and office were in a building that was about as far as possible from the parking deck. Fortunately, there were shuttle buses available for students and faculty, even adjuncts. I only had to wait for a couple of minutes outside the Core Center, where the core curriculum classes were taught, before a Bostock green-and-gold shuttle pulled up. When I climbed on board and flashed the ID attached to the lanyard around my neck, I saw David Chaudoir at the wheel. Though I'd ridden with all the shuttle bus drivers by that point in the semester, David's choice of T-shirts had shown me early on we had more in common than mere transportation.

I said, "Valar morghulis, David!"

"Valar dohaeris, Dr. Thackery."

The other passengers were all students, none of whom I knew. While I hadn't intended to eavesdrop as the shuttle hit several stops on the way to the parking deck, I did hear the words *faculty strike* repeated. Maybe the Gleasons really did have cause for concern.

I was meeting Mom and Phil at a very different campus. McQuaid University is in the center of Pennycross and is much more compact. Both my parents have been tenured faculty for decades, so I knew my way around the place long before my stint as an adjunct there. Though I'd gladly have stayed, my extracurricular murder-related activities had kept me from getting invited back. I told myself that was another reason I should be glad that Sid wasn't dragging me into another case.

I joined Mom and Phil at Hamburger Haven, one of the on-campus restaurants, and we shared gossip over our cheeseburgers. Neither of them knew anything about a faculty strike brewing at Bostock, but Phil had heard that the faculty union's contract negotiations were not going well.

From there we moved on to the best way to get a research grant, since I had a project I was hoping to get a grant for. If adjuncts aspire to tenure track position, they need publications, but the Catch-22 is that there isn't much financial support for adjunct research. My parents had a few ideas, and I took notes, meaning to go back home and do some preliminary work. I was on my way back to my car when I saw our favorite Pennycross cop Louis Raymond standing in front of one of the campus map boards McQuaid has erected around campus.

"Hey, Louis. Are you lost?"

"A little. I'm trying to find Easton Hall, and according to the online map, it should be right there, but…" He looked over at the fence that was surrounding the latest on-campus renovation project, which was the building he was looking for. "This map wasn't much help." The laminated notice taped at the top had a list of changes, starting with *The 3rd Floor of Easton Hall has been temporarily moved to the 2nd Floor of Savage Hall.*

"I see your problem. They've got people scattered around campus until they finish rebuilding Easton. Which department are you going to?"

"Physical anthropology."

"Hang on, I'll call the department and ask where they're living now." It took a bit of telephone tag, but I finally got directions from the departmental secretary. "Okay, what you have to do is go to the computer science building, but not the main entrance because physical anthropology is camping out in the basement. So you need to go around to—" I noticed the look on his face. "Or I could just show you the way."

"I would appreciate it."

I knew all the back routes, so it didn't take us long to get to the department Louis was looking for. "Are you going to be able to find your way out again?" I asked.

"Eventually," he said, not very confidently.

"Or I could wait until you're done and walk you out again."

"That would be great, but I don't know how long I'll be."

"I've got time."

"You might be interested anyway. I'm working on the case involving the skeleton your dog found." He gave me a sideways look. "I don't know how much interest you're taking in this one." This was his way of acknowledging that I'd been involved in unofficial investigation in the past. I wasn't sure if he approved or if he only accepted it because he was dating my sister.

"Did you identify the person? Was it a McQuaid employee or student?"

"No, and I don't know. I'm here because the coroner did what he could with the remains, but he doesn't have much experience with remains in this condition."

"Meaning a skeleton?"

He nodded. "We normally work with Dr. de la Cova on bone cases, but she's at a conference, so she recommended we consult one of the other faculty members."

"I'm not faculty," a voice from behind us said. "Merely a lowly adjunct."

I turned and saw a young woman with azure hair shaved nearly to the scalp on one side, and hanging down to her shoulder on the other. She was wearing a lab coat over leggings and a sweater that was the same color as her hair.

"You here to talk bones?" she said.

"Dr. Jacobs?" Louis said hesitantly.

"Yo," she responded, and led the way into the lab.

Louis looked at me for reassurance.

"Yolanda Jacobs, PhD," I confirmed. "Yo for short."

I'd met Yo when I'd taken Sid to be analyzed in hopes of finding out more about him after decades of having him around the house. That's when we'd learned that he'd been murdered. The last time I'd seen her, she'd been finishing up her dissertation and had been confident that she'd never end up as an adjunct. Then again, becoming an adjunct wasn't usually anybody's career path.

Still looking doubtful, Louis followed Yo into the lab, and after only a moment's hesitation, I went along too. Surely Sid would want to hear about what Yo had found in her examination.

Even though it had been moved to a different building, the lab looked much as it had the last time I'd seen it. We were surrounded by battered metal shelves holding plastic bins filled with the bones and skulls that made up the department's reference collection. Any available wall space was covered with anatomical charts and photos of bones, with and without meat. A rolling cabinet held a wide selection of scales, measuring gadgetry, and sharp objects whose use I didn't care to think about too carefully, and in the center of the room were two body length tables covered in black, inert laminate. The jointed cardboard skeleton rescued from a post-Halloween discount bin was missing, but had been replaced by a stand-up of Jack Skellington. A word balloon was taped to his mouth with the cheerful invitation, "Let's get boned!"

The table closest to me held a skeleton I deduced was the one

Byron had found, though I couldn't be sure. Sid was the only skeleton I recognized on sight.

It looked as if the worst of the dirt had been brushed off, and it was no longer covered by the bits of fabric we'd seen. Seeing it lying there gave me mixed feelings: familiarity, because it was a skeleton; sadness, because it had been a person; and creeped out, because it was a dead skeleton.

Yo said, "What we've got here is a female, who was approximately five-foot-six when standing. The age is a little tricky. From the epiphyses, I can tell she was above thirty, in the thirty-five to fifty year range, but given the wear on the teeth and other areas, I'm going to guess on the younger end of that range, thirty-five to forty. She was in good shape, though she could have used a trip to the dentist—she had a cavity that does not look as if it had been filled."

Louis was scribbling rapidly in his notepad. "Could the filling have fallen out?"

"Maybe, but you'd expect signs of dental drilling around it if that had happened, and I'm not seeing it."

"Any idea about cause of death?"

"Strangled."

"You're sure?"

"Mostly sure. The hyoid bone is fractured, which is usually indicative of strangling, either manually or by ligature."

"It couldn't have been postmortem?" I asked.

"Not likely. Postmortem fractures tend to splinter and show color differences, which I'm not seeing, and it wasn't antemortem because there's no sign of regrowth. That only leaves perimortem. It's possible that the blunt force trauma that broke her hyoid didn't kill her, while something else did immediately thereafter. But since I've found no bullet holes, knife marks, or other blunt force trauma, my money would be on strangulation.

Louis nodded. "What about the time of death?"

"I'd say between 3 and 4 p.m. on Friday, March 6, 2009."

"Really?"

She rolled her eyes. "Don't write that down! This isn't *CSI*. I'll be doing well if I can get you into the right decade!"

"I was wondering," he said, but I saw him scratching out something in his notebook.

"The body wasn't in a container or plastic wrapping or anything like that, right?" Yo asked.

Louis consulted his notes. "We found what looks like a blanket, but that's it."

"Then she was in the ground for at least eight years—that's how long it would take a body in our environment to decay down to the bones. I'd guess she was probably in the nine to fifteen year range—a specialist in forensics might be able to be more precise. You might also get something from her clothes, which I assume you've sent elsewhere for analysis."

"How did you know that?" he asked.

"Cotton fibers stuck in some of the joints, some dark staining on the legs. That is information it would have been good for me to know beforehand, by the way."

"Sorry. Working with skeletal remains is new territory for me." He jotted a note. "Can you tell me anything else?"

"This is more speculative, but I've got a couple of thoughts. See these bony ridges on the wrists?" She pointed them out. "This tells me that she worked with her hands. I'm also seeing signs that she was on her feet a lot. When she was still alive, that is."

I'd intended to stay quiet but couldn't stop myself from asking, "Couldn't that have been from exercising?"

"Possibly, but a runner or a walker presents differently, and even the most enthused walker doesn't usually have this much wear and tear at this age. There's more osteoarthritis than typical in a woman this age, and her feet were going flat. Plus, there's something about the spine that makes me think she bent over a lot." Yo shrugged. "It's just the impression I get, so don't get aggravated if it turns out she had a cushy desk job."

"I won't hold you to it," Louis said, slipping his notepad back into his pocket. "Should I arrange to have the bones shipped back to the morgue?"

"Let me keep her around for a few more days while I write up the formal report. I want to triple check my measurements, and I'll poke around some more and see if I notice anything else."

"You've already given me a lot more than I had before," Louis said. "Appreciate it."

Yo waved away his thanks. "Doing actual science beats the snot out of teaching freshmen the difference between a femur and a finger bone."

"Thanks for letting me sit in," I said.

"It's the same rate for one or two," she said. "Speaking of which..."

Louis said, "I'll get the paperwork in as soon as I get back to the station. Accounts payable should cut you a check tomorrow, next day at the latest, and get it into the mail ASAP."

"Good deal. I hate to be mercenary, but Georgia can tell you how little adjuncts get paid."

We left her glaring at the skeleton as if she, too, was a troublesome student or a stingy college administrator.

Chapter Five

Fortunately for my credibility as a native guide, I was able to get Louis back to the building's side entrance without any wrong turns. When we got outside, we found a sandy-haired man in a McQuaid security officer uniform waiting for us.

"O'Leary," Louis said stiffly.

"Raymond," Oscar O'Leary replied just as stiffly.

I sighed. I really hated being with both of them at the same time, especially when Deborah wasn't around. The problem was that both of them were dating her. It was all above-board, with no guilty secrets. They knew about one another, and she'd been honest that she wasn't interested in being serious with either of them and that they could either accept it or move on. Neither of her beaus was entirely happy with the arrangement, but they'd stuck around. I just hoped it was because their affection for Deborah was that strong and not because they'd gotten caught up in their competition.

"Hi, Oscar," I said, hoping to cut some of the tension. "How's it going?"

I got a smile. "Pretty good, Georgia. I still hate that you aren't teaching here anymore."

"It's all part of the happy-go-lucky adjunct lifestyle," I said.

Oscar turned back to Louis. "I heard you were on campus. Anything I need to know about?" Oscar was head of McQuaid security, and even without personal issues, turf wars often crop up between campus cops and town cops.

"Just consulting one of your scientists about a murder case.

It's a police investigation, nothing for campus security." He didn't quite make *campus security* sound like kids playing dress-up.

Oscar turned to me. "Are you helping him out, Georgia?" I wasn't sure if this was intended as a compliment for me, which I might then tell Deborah about and earn Oscar a brownie point, or an insult to Louis. Or both.

I said, "Right now, I'm only leading him through the current campus maze."

Back to Louis, sans smile. "Let me know when you're on campus again, and I'll provide an escort. In fact, I'll show you the way back to your car now."

"I was going to—" But one look at the expression on Oscar's face showed me that he was going to direct us no matter what I said. The idea of spending another ten minutes between them did not appeal, but luckily, Yo came out the door behind us. I said, "You two go ahead. There's something I want to talk to Yo about."

Louis paused long enough to say, "Thanks for your help, Georgia," then hurried to catch up with Oscar. Neither of them wanted to be behind the other, so each kept trying to go faster. I suspected they'd be sprinting by the time they got to Louis's car.

"What's up with them?" Yo asked.

"Testosterone."

"Best thing about skeletons? No hormones. What did you need to talk about? Or was that just an excuse?"

"Just an excuse." It had been an excuse, and while I'd have made up a polite fiction with most people, Yo preferred people to be as blunt as she was. "It is good to see you."

"Yeah, ditto. You want to get some coffee?"

"Sure."

We had to take a detour or two to reach McQuaid's Coffee Corner but were soon seated at a table with our caffeine fixes.

"So here you are tied up with another skeleton," Yo said. "Is this like a fetish for you? I mean, I don't judge. I've run into other skelesexuals."

"Skelesexual? Are you making that up?"

"Why bother to invent stuff when the real world is weird enough? I don't care what people do with consenting inanimate objects as long as they don't try to raid my lab's reference collection to introduce themselves to new special friends."

"That's very open-minded of you. Anyway, no, I am not sexually attracted to bones, though our dog Byron has a certain fondness for them. He brought home one of those femurs, and we helped the police find the rest of the skeleton. So I can't help but be curious."

"Yeah, I hear through the adjunct grapevine that you can't help but be curious in a lot of odd cases."

I started to deny it but realized there was no reason to. If it was so thoroughly imbedded into adjunct lore, the tale would travel with me wherever I went in academia. As Madison would have said, I might as well start owning it. So I said, "It's a hobby. What's going on with you?"

"You don't have to dance around it, Georgia."

"Dance around what?"

"My job. Don't you want to know why I didn't get a real job instead of working as an adjunct?"

I'd really just been making small talk, but I shrugged and said, "I figured it was for the same reason as everybody else. Not enough permanent and tenure track jobs available because schools would rather pay adjuncts chump change and not worry about those pesky contracts and benefit packages."

"Or maybe I decided I didn't want to be trapped by a system that chains academics to the never-ending treadmill of publish-or-perish."

"Is that what happened?"

"Nah, you nailed it. I'd love a good set of chains, and I haven't given up on getting a set padlocked on. Which reminds me, I kind of remember dissing you for being an adjunct back before I realized how things were. Sorry about being a jerk."

"No worries. I used to be a jerk about adjuncts myself. My

parents made it sound like anybody who couldn't get a tenure track job just wasn't good enough or trying hard enough. That may have been true in their day, but it hasn't been that way for a long time."

"A long time in a galaxy far, far away," Yo agreed. "I bet they never have nightmares about having to teach on three different campus in the same semester just to pay the bills."

"That's definitely the worst."

"Speaking of other campuses, what's the latest on the Bostock strike?"

"You are the second person to mention a possible strike to me today, but I don't know a thing about it."

"What rock have you been under? Where are you teaching this semester anyway?"

"Bostock, as a matter of fact."

"Then maybe you ought to be paying more attention to your living colleagues and not dead people. No offense."

"Actually, that's pretty offensive."

She considered it. "Yeah, I guess it is. Sorry again. So they're talking about something happening in the next couple of weeks."

"This late in the semester? That'll cause no end of problems." Like many colleges, Bostock's fall semester culminated with exams right before Christmas break, only a few weeks away.

"I bet that's part of the union's strategy. Which isn't bad, as far as it goes. Anyway, Bostock administration has been sending out feelers to see which local adjuncts would be available to cover extra classes if the tenured faculty does strike. I haven't heard if they need any physical anthropologists, but if they do, it'd be a sweet way to get some extra bucks."

"Would you cross a picket line?"

"Why the heck not? The tenured faculty is all, 'We're in this together,' and 'loyalty to your peers,' but a month ago, they barely acknowledged my existence. Or is it different at Bostock?"

"Not so much. Of course, that might be because I'm in English, not in anything business related."

"Yeah, sure. I heard that the union bozos want Bostock adjuncts to strike, too, even though the contract doesn't mention you guys because they won't let adjuncts into the union! And, yeah, the union will give financial aid to striking faculty, but I bet they won't offer adjuncts a lousy McDonald's discount coupon. Why should we tighten our belts so they can get better pay and insurance?"

"You're not wrong," I admitted. "But what about after the strike is settled? Some of those people whose picket line you crossed might be the ones you're hoping to work with some day."

"Sure, maybe, but I can see it going either way. If the strike goes on long enough, administration might hire some of the so-called scabs long-term. All I know for sure is that making some extra money while I've got a chance would help me keep up with my student loan payments."

"That's fair."

"And not to sound overly selfless, because I'm not, I'm also thinking about the students. They're not going to be happy if their semester schedule gets scrambled."

"I can only imagine the helicopter parents circling if that were to happen."

"Like choppers of doom! And I don't blame 'em—if the schedule means their kids have to go an extra semester to make up for the mess, that means a whole lot more money."

I nodded. Madison would be looking at colleges all too soon, and the thought of her future tuition bills was already giving me heartburn.

"I've already got all the hours I can handle," I said, "but I'll keep an ear out to see if they need anybody in your field."

"I appreciate it."

Yo had to head to her next class, and we parted amicably.

I brooded about the strike on my way home. There had been many semesters when I would have been tempted to take extra work, even if it meant crossing a picket line. The fact was, Yo was right. I'd never been on a campus where the faculty union represented adjuncts, whereas I had been on several where the tenured and contract faculty treated adjuncts with poorly concealed disdain. Why shouldn't Yo take an opportunity to make some extra cash? Why shouldn't any adjunct?

Still, I had a hunch that most of the tenured professors I knew would have a different opinion, including my parents. I just hoped that the strike would be forestalled and that the question would remain academic.

Chapter Six

I didn't bring up the examination of the skeleton during dinner because past experience had told me that discussing the nittier and grittier aspects of crime investigation wasn't good for my parents' digestion. Besides, Andrew, the grad student who needed a haircut, was eating with us, stowing away chicken and broccoli stir-fry as if he hadn't eaten all semester. While my reputation might already be permanently tainted by playing detective, I didn't think my parents' needed to be.

Instead we talked about Andrew's dissertation. At least, he talked about it. We listened. Madison was openly bored, and the only thing that kept me from showing my own complete lack of interest was remembering how obsessed I'd been with my own doctoral research. I just hoped my table manners had been better.

After the dishes were tended to, Phil and Andrew went into my parents' study, Mom settled onto the couch with a book, Madison retreated to her room for homework and online gaming—hopefully in that order—and I headed for the attic to visit Sid.

I expected that he'd be fascinated by what I'd learned about the discovered remains, but instead he rushed me through the explanation so he could run some more Christmas shopping ideas by me.

I didn't stay with him long. Instead I told him I had work to do and went to my own room, where I spent more time wondering how the woman we'd found had died than I did marking up grammatical errors. I only made it through a handful of papers before calling it quits and going to bed.

Once I'd finished my next day's classes at Bostock, I checked my email again, and since I still hadn't received any official communication about the supposed strike, I took the shuttle bus to the faculty lounge to see if I could dig up somebody who paid more attention to such things. My friend Charles Peyton was there chatting with somebody from the history department, but when he saw me, he excused himself and came toward me.

"Georgia, just the person I was hoping to encounter."

"Hi, Charles."

Charles was another adjunct, and our job paths had crossed enough times for us to become good friends. This semester, he was teaching classes at both Bostock and McQuaid.

"Georgia, are you free for lunch?"

"I am, actually. Where would you like to go?"

"I was thinking of the Stock Pot. It's tomato basil soup day."

"That sounds great."

The Stock Pot was a student-run business, like many of the Bostock services, and since it was in the same building as the faculty lounge, we didn't have to catch the shuttle bus again. The place was decorated in what I think of as American pub, meaning what Americans think an English pub looks like: dark wooden booths and tables, dart boards, and neon Guinness beer signs. They serve mostly soup and sandwiches, and their tomato soup is one of their best.

We found a table, and Charles helped me with my coat before holding the chair for me.

With most men, this would have been a romantic gesture, but Charles treated all women that way. He was a historian with a specialty in the Pax Britannica, 1815 to 1914, and I've never been sure if his formality in manners and attire was a result or if he'd picked that period because he liked formality in manners and attire. That day he was wearing one of his tweed suits with a waistcoat and freshly shined shoes.

Once we'd given the waitress our orders, Charles said, "I'm delighted that you could come on such short notice."

"Actually, I wanted to pick your brain about something." I lowered my voice. "Have you heard anything about a strike on campus?"

"Sadly, yes. The new core curriculum requirements are causing a ripple effect of greater workloads, and to make matters worse, insurance costs have taken a sharp rise, and the college is trying to pass some of those costs on to the faculty."

"Ouch. Giving them more work and cutting into their paychecks is a bad combination."

"Agreed. Contract negotiations are nearly at a standstill. Having all this happen so close to the holidays is particularly unfortunate."

The waitress brought our tomato soup and grilled cheese sandwich combos and we dug in.

I was about to ask if Charles knew anything about Bostock hiring more adjuncts when he said, "I must confess that I invited you under false pretenses. Not that your company isn't always a pleasure, of course, but I have something to ask you about."

"Ask away."

"I heard talk of your unpleasant discovery last week."

"The adjunct grapevine is swift, and in this case, accurate."

"I was wondering if you'd be willing to tell me about the remains you helped the police locate. Not, of course, if it would upset you to talk about it."

"No, it's fine." I was just surprised Charles had asked. He was usually so unwilling to intrude on other people's privacy that he never asked about anything unless he was sure that the topic would be welcome. I told him about Byron bringing home the bone, though of course I left out the part about us thinking it had been Sid's, and then how the dog had led us to the rest of the skeleton.

"You saw nothing else? Nothing at all?"

"Just some fabric," I said, remembering what Sid had said. "It looked like a shirt, but the police hustled me away before I could see much."

"Was the shirt a dark red, by any chance?"

I blinked. "It was faded, but I think so. How did you know that?"

In another departure for Charles, he didn't answer. Instead, he reached into his suit's breast pocket to pull out a street map of Pennycross. "Could you show me exactly where the body was?"

"Sure." With my finger, I followed the path we'd gone that night and pointed to the lot. "Right there. I understand there used to be a house there."

"Yes. There was." He put the map back into his pocket and stared into space for a long moment.

"Charles?"

He shook himself. "I must again apologize. It's just that I am very much afraid that I know the identity of the woman you found, and when I disclose this information to the police, I may very well be arrested for murder."

Chapter Seven

"Charles!" I said. "There's no way you'd murder somebody."

"I appreciate your faith in my character, and I assure you that I did not kill her. I just don't know that the police would accept my innocence." He took a swallow of his tea. "Georgia, you have long been aware of my unusual living arrangements."

I nodded. Like most adjuncts, Charles didn't make much money and, unlike me, didn't have parents he could live with. So he'd given up on buying or even renting a home. Instead he squatted. Sometimes he took up residence in a vacant classroom or office, or stayed with a friend, or even shared a trailer at a carnival. I'd given him a room a few times in the past, but he refused to stay more than three days. Since squatting in campus buildings could have gotten him fired, I'd carefully kept his secret. I'd never even told Madison, though Sid and two of my former boyfriends knew.

He said, "Some ten years ago, when I was first teaching at Pennycross, I learned that the Nichols house had been left vacant, and after careful investigation, I moved in."

"I heard the previous owner was a hoarder."

"So I understand, but I didn't take up residence there until after her heirs had cleared the place out. They had not cleaned it particularly well, but that was easily remedied." He made a face. "Well, not easily, given how long it had been since the owner had maintained it properly, but remedied just the same. There'd been talk of the house being torn down, but since there was pushback from the community, I thought it would be safe to inhabit for a few weeks. There was even running water and electricity, though I used as little as possible of either since I didn't want to take advantage of those paying the bills.

"I set up in the cleanest of the upstairs bedrooms. It had dark curtains, so I wouldn't be seen from the outside. Since my last few homes had been quite small, it was a pleasure to have room to spread out for a change. Other than having to pack my effects into a closet each morning, park my car elsewhere, and arrive after dark to avoid being seen, it was ideal."

Only Charles would think that sneaking into a dirty house every night was ideal.

He went on. "I'd been staying there some three weeks when I came home and realized somebody else was in the house. My initial thought was that it was the owners, so I was trying to get to my room to gather my belongings before I was discovered. That's when I came across her."

"Her?"

"Rose. That wasn't her real name. I never knew her real name, but Shakespeare gave me the idea. 'That which we call a rose by any other name would smell as sweet.' Excuse me, I'm getting ahead of myself. One night I returned to the house and found a woman sleeping in what I had considered my room.

"She later told me she didn't know anybody was living there and only chose that room because it was the cleanest in the house. As I stared at where she lay wrapped up in her coat, feeling like nothing so much as Baby Bear finding Goldilocks in his bed, she woke up and screamed. The next few moments were confusing, as you might imagine. She understandably feared that I meant her harm, and I was trying to quiet her to keep from alerting the neighbors, who would then contact the police.

"Eventually we both calmed down enough to discuss the situation. I told her why I was there, and though she was not as forthcoming with her explanation, I felt sure that she had good reasons for her discretion. After some discussion, we agreed that there was no reason we couldn't both stay in the house, at least for the night, since neither of us had anywhere else to go. Naturally, I loaned her my sleeping bag and let her keep that room while I made do with an extra blanket in another room."

"Naturally," I said, amused by his unfailing chivalry.

"The next day was Saturday, so I didn't have to work, which gave us time to become better acquainted and to negotiate arrangements. The house was large enough to accommodate two squatters as long as we were careful to avoid being seen, and she assured me she would be. As a matter of fact, Rose rarely left the house at all."

"And you don't know why?"

"I do not. She was obviously afraid of someone, but I never learned more than that."

"I take it that you didn't spend much time with one another."

"On the contrary, we became constant companions. We took turns with meals and cleaning, though we did have to use my equipment and supplies since she was inadequately prepared for squatting. All she had was what she was wearing, including appropriate outerwear, her purse, and an overnight bag in which she carried a change of clothes, some toiletries, and a few books. She told me she'd left her phone behind so she couldn't be traced. She did have some money and insisted on paying for her share of the food, though she did ask me to do the shopping.

"At first our cohabitation was a convenience, but as the days went by, it became something more. We read, watched movies on my computer, and talked so late into the night I was barely keeping up with my work. Though Rose avoided any topic that might lead to her identity, she was open about more important matters of philosophy and thought. I cannot express how much it meant to me to have a companion to share my evenings with." He smiled in a way I'd never seen him smile before.

"You weren't just friends, were you?" I said softly.

"No, Georgia, we were not just friends."

I realized he was tearing up and scrambled in my purse for a tissue to hand him. "What happened?"

"We had over a month together, from just after Thanksgiving to the day before Christmas, but then I read in the paper that the owners of the house had resolved their issues with the town and were planning to demolish it right after the new year. We discussed the situation but made no definite plans. That night I came back to the house intending to ask Rose to allow me to make a permanent home for her. For both of us. But she was gone."

"She didn't leave a note?"

"Nothing. Her belongings were gone as well. There were no overt signs of violence, so I hoped that whomever it was she'd feared had not found her, but I couldn't be sure. I was distraught, as you might imagine, but I had no way to find her. By her own desire, I knew almost nothing about her, and in all fairness, I had no claim on her. An obvious conclusion was that her attachment to me had not been as profound as mine to her.

"Still, I stayed up all that night, hoping she would return."

"On Christmas Eve? Oh, Charles!"

He shrugged it off. "I had no work because of the holidays, so for the next week, I never left the house. It was foolish of me, because of course she knew my cell phone number and could have called at any time, but I only abandoned my vigil on New Year's Day because the house was scheduled for demolition the next day. That night, I gathered up my belongings and found a new place to squat. I never heard from Rose again." He smiled sadly. "I know it sounds impossible in the era of frequent selfies, but I don't even have a photo of her."

"I'm so sorry. Maybe the body…Maybe the person we found wasn't Rose."

"As heartless as it sounds in regard to that poor person, I have been hoping that ever since I heard the news, and of course, that's why I wanted to speak with you. But you may have confirmed my fears. You see, Rose didn't have many items of clothing and refused my offers to purchase more for her. Most of the time, she wore a particular shirt. A dark red shirt."

"What about this?" I gave him a summary of the information Yo had given Louis about the body.

"That, too, fits Rose," he said sadly.

There didn't seem to be anything I could say to that other than to repeat, "I'm so sorry."

He wiped his eyes again. "Under the circumstances, I would like some advice. Do you think it would be better to call the officer in charge of the case directly or just to go to the station and present myself?"

"What are you talking about?"

"Obviously I need to tell the police what I know. Fortunately, I have no classes this afternoon, so I won't need to find a substitute. If I'm held overnight, I'll see about informing the administrators here and at McQuaid."

"Charles, you can't go to the police!"

"How can I not? It is the least I can do for Rose."

"So you're going to tell them that you squatted in an abandoned building?"

"Of course. Admittedly I broke the law, but I doubt they'll prosecute under the circumstances. If they do arrest me, then at least that will temporarily resolve my housing problem." He smiled wryly.

"Charles, if you go down there, the police are going to think you killed Rose yourself."

"I realize that, but I can only hope that my lack of a motive will reassure them. I had no reason to kill Rose. Quite the opposite, in fact."

"They won't believe that. They'll think she was going to leave you, or you wanted to take her money, or you made a pass and she turned you down. They'll come up with all kinds of reasons."

"Since none of them are true, they won't be able to find any evidence to that effect."

"That won't stop them from digging into every corner of your life. Are you living on campus these days?"

"I've got a cozy broom closet in the adjunct building at McQuaid."

"What do you think will happen when that comes out? It's almost certainly going to cost you your job. Both your jobs."

He stroked his chin. "That had not occurred to me. Still, it must be done. If the police are to find Rose's killer, they must have all the information available."

"What information can you give them? You said she never told you anything about herself. Do you know how old she was? Was she married? Was she from Pennycross or somewhere else? Who was she hiding from? Who had a reason to kill her? Telling them what books and movies she liked won't help them solve her murder, and it could cost you your career."

"Georgia, I have to do something. I failed to protect Rose before. I can't fail her now."

"You're not going to. We're going to search for her killer ourselves."

"We?" He raised one eyebrow.

"Well, me, but with your help." By *we,* I'd actually meant me and Sid, but I was willing to let Charles be on the team, too, as long as I could keep him away from my real partner. "Look, you know I've been a..." I couldn't say *detective* with a straight face, and *sleuth* sounded even worse. "You know I've been involved in murders before. I don't see why I can't get involved in this one on your behalf."

"Georgia, I could never ask you to do such a thing."

"You're not asking. I'm offering. In fact, I'm telling. Charles, I want you to promise me that you won't go to the police until I've done everything I can to find out what happened to Rose. If I can't do it, you can always talk to the police then. It's been ten years. Waiting a couple of weeks won't make a difference."

"I suppose that's reasonable. If you're sure."

"I'm sure." Sid would, of course, be delighted.

Chapter Eight

"You told him what?" Sid said, his eye holes wide in defiance of both biology and geometry.

I'd rushed up to the attic to tell him the news as soon as I left Charles at Bostock. "I told him that we'd investigate. Well, that I would, since Charles doesn't know about you."

"Without consulting me? You didn't think that maybe I'd have better ways to spend my time this close to Christmas, that maybe I'd had enough with death and danger and…" Then he burst out laughing. "Ha! I had you going there, didn't I?"

"Sid!" I *thunked* him on top of his skull.

"Of course we'll investigate. I've been ready to get started ever since we found the body."

"What about 'oh I've got gaming and Christmas shopping to do' every time I tried to discuss the case?"

"Ha! You called it a case!"

"All right, all right. I admit it. I like playing detective with you."

"Playing detective?" He waggled a finger bone at me. "Must I point out that we have successfully detected more than once in the past?"

"Yeah, but it was…Okay, you're right." Then I had a thought. "Sid, were you trying to make a point? Was that why you kept pretending you weren't interested?"

"No. Yes. Sort of. I just wanted to make sure you really did like doing this stuff. The first time we got involved, it was because of my murder. The second and third times were because of something I knew but couldn't tell the police. I dragged you into the fourth because I was afraid you were a suspect, and the fifth time was because of a friend of mine. This time there is no particular reason we needed to get involved, and I thought maybe you'd prefer it that way."

"The fact that I'd been trying to give you background information didn't convince you that I was interested?"

"Yeah, okay, I've been messing with you a little." He grinned, which technically he did all the time, but sometimes it was more emphatic than others. "It was fun watching you try to lure me into the murder."

"You ossifying piece of sacrum!"

He just snickered.

"What would you have done if Charles hadn't pulled us into the case?"

"We'd have found a link somehow. A murder in our neighborhood? A haunted house? A skeleton? How could we resist?"

"Fair point. I guess we know who was doing the haunting now."

His eye holes widened. "Do you think the spirit of Charles's girlfriend couldn't rest?"

"Some skeptic you are. What I think is that the neighbors heard Charles and Rose moving around a supposedly vacant house and thought it was a ghost."

"That makes more sense. I'll add that to the file."

"You've already got a file?"

"Of course I've got a file. Not that there's much in it so far. Now we know a whole lot more."

"It's not that much more. Charles doesn't know the victim's real name, where she lived, or anything about her."

"But we do know an approximate timeline for her death, and that'll make it easier to figure out who she was. From there, it won't be hard to find out who killed her."

"You're pretty sure of yourself, Bone Boy."

"Team Supreme," he said, holding his fist up for a bump.

I couldn't leave him hanging, so I returned the gesture. "By tomorrow, I should have more for the file because I gave Charles homework. He's going to try to remember every single conversation he had with Rose to see if there are any clues to who she really was."

"Wouldn't that work better with you questioning him?"

"I don't think so, Sid. I think this is something he needs to do by himself. He got very emotional when he was talking about Rose. He nearly cried."

"Wow. Yeah, that's not like Charles. He's usually so reserved."

"I know. Gracious and warm, but kind of restrained."

"Who'd have guessed he had a romantic tragedy in his past?" he said.

"Sid, you've never met Charles."

"I have, however, hidden in the armoire to eavesdrop on your conversations with him a number of times."

"That's true." If there was an Olympic competition for eavesdropping, Sid would take the gold.

"Plus I'm taking his class," he added.

"Excuse me?"

"I'm taking one of his online classes from McQuaid—your mother got me in for free. I watch him on video, but I told him I've got bad internet so we can only interact by voice and text. He's an excellent teacher, you know. He was talking about the Christmas Truce of World War I today, and it was riveting."

"He is good, and he's a great guy, too. So even if I didn't like playing detective…"

Sid waggled a bony finger at me.

"I meant to say, even if I didn't like investigating, I'd do it for Charles. It can be a Christmas gift for him."

Sid turned back to his computer. "Now I want you to go through his story with me in detail and let me make sure I've got it all. And you better tell me about Yo's examination of the remains again. When you told me before, I was distracted by pretending not to care, so I might have missed something."

I did so, barely having to pause as I went because he typed so much faster than I did. He was having a great time, and had I been pushed, I would have admitted that I was enjoying myself, too.

Still, I did wonder if Sid and I had been able to do other things together, like going out to dinner or a movie without having to sneak in his skull while the rest of him stayed behind, would we have wanted to investigate murders? Maybe not, but I sure wouldn't have traded having him as a friend for ordinary activities.

Once I'd given Sid all I had, he said, "Let's recap. According to Charles, Rose had some money, so she wasn't just homeless, but she didn't seem to be prepared to squat the way he was."

"Right. She didn't have any of the proper supplies. Charles said she'd run away from someone and was hiding, but he doesn't know who from or why."

"Okay then." He drummed his finger bones noisily against the table. "Let's run down the possibilities and then figure out how we can investigate them."

"My first thought was that she was running from an abusive spouse or partner."

"Couldn't she just go to the police?"

"Sid, you read the news. How many times have women been beaten or killed when they tried to escape abusers?"

"You're right, unfortunately. You should check with Charles to see if she had any scars or bruises. Assuming he saw her without clothing, that is."

"Given the way he spoke about her, I think that's a safe assumption. What else?"

He tapped his jawbone speculatively. "What if she was hiding from the police?"

"You don't think Charles would fall in love with a crook, do you?"

"Lots of people do. Crooks can be excellent actors. Or maybe she wasn't that bad of a crook, just got in over her head and made a mistake. She could still be a basically decent person even if she was in trouble with the law."

"Okay, I'll accept that as a possibility," I said. "How can we test it?"

"I could go through news sites for people who went missing after being arrested or tried."

"We don't know where she was from."

"Charles said she didn't have a car, right?"

I nodded.

"Then it probably wasn't from too far away. I can start with Pennycross and expand the search as necessary. And yes, I know it's a needle in a haystack, but it's something. Next idea."

"She could have been running away from home."

"She was kind of old for that, wasn't she?"

"Not necessarily from her parents, but what if she had a house full of children, or was the caregiver for an ailing relative, or was just feeling overwhelmed?"

"Georgia, tell me you never felt that way."

"I've only got one child, and I've got a good support system with you and my folks, but not everybody is that lucky. Anyway, I don't know how we could check that one. I'm not sure how we could check any of them."

"Well, if she was hiding, she must have thought somebody was looking for her. If they were looking for her ten years ago, I should be able to find a trace online. Maybe a newspaper or a police report or even something on social media. Having a date to start with puts us way ahead of the cops, but it still sounds like a long and tedious job of going through countless web pages in hopes of finding some small crumb."

"You can't wait to get started, can you?"

He cracked his knuckles. "Nope!"

"I'm going to leave you to it. I've got papers to grade."

Sid didn't respond. He was already cheerfully typing away.

I might have been fooling myself about getting a kick out of investigations, but Sid had no such illusions.

Chapter Nine

Though Mom and Phil hadn't invited any grad students to dinner that night, we did have an extra person at the table. My sister Deborah had come over to make sure that her latest security gadgets were working as intended, and it hadn't taken Phil long to talk her into staying for baked ziti.

"I changed out the backup batteries," she said between mouthfuls, "so everything should be up to speed. Just remember to monitor the front door camera. There are a lot of package thieves out and about this time of year."

"They better not grab any of my Christmas boxes," Sid said indignantly.

"I wasn't sure the camera was necessary," Mom said, "but it did come in handy the other day. Georgia used it to track Byron and help the police find that body."

"Louis told me all about it," Deborah said. "They still don't know who the dead woman is—she doesn't match any of the open missing person reports from the area. By the way, he wanted to know if Georgia is going to be sticking her nose into this one. Are you?"

Madison snickered. "As if you had to ask."

I really hated it when my entire family knew something about me that I'd just barely concluded for myself.

"Our investigation is indeed underway," Sid said loftily. "It seems that we have sources the police do not."

Deborah made a face. "Whatever. Just don't make Louis look bad, okay? He's up for a performance review."

"We'll be careful," I said.

"It's so odd, a body being found on that lot. It's like a bad luck magnet," Mom said. "First Professor Nichols's death, then his wife Margo's mental issues after he died, and now a body. It sounds like something out of Poe, doesn't it?"

"Did you know the Nichols?" Sid asked.

"Not well, just enough to pass the time of day when we ran into each other at the grocery store or around town. We used to see the two of them at campus events now and then, and they seemed nice, but we didn't really have much in common. Professor Nichols was a physicist, and Margo had been in business before their marriage, marketing or management I think, and they both said that they didn't read fiction at all." She shook her head sadly at what the two of them had missed. "After her husband died, I invited Margo over here for dinner a few times, but she always reciprocated with restaurant meals. After I heard about her affliction, I realized that she must not have wanted to have anyone in her house, but at the time I just thought that she didn't like to cook. I wonder if the hoarding began before her husband died or after."

"And Sid, before you ask, Professor Nichols died of a heart attack," Phil said. "There's nothing there for you to get excited about."

"Probably not. Wait, how long before her death did he die?"

There was some discussion back and forth while my parents tried to figure it out. They finally decided there had been six years between the deaths.

"That's enough time for her to have done some serious hoarding," Sid said.

"The house was bad when I saw it," Deborah said.

"I didn't know you knew Margo," said Phil.

"I didn't. This was after she died. The executor hired me to help out when they were clearing the place out. It turns out that in addition to everything else, Mrs. Nichols collected locks: padlocks, combination locks, knob locks, even some Rabson locks. Those are the best." Her voice turned wistful. "It wasn't just modern stuff either—she had some antique decorative locks that were just amazing. Things I'd never seen outside of pictures." Then she was back to practical. "Of course, those things are easy-peasy to pick. I just wish I could say the same for all her modern padlocks. She'd locked everything—room doors, the cabinet doors, pretty much anything that could be locked. Plus there were lockboxes of all sizes and descriptions, and one honest-to-God safe I had to call in a specialist for. And not a key or combination to be found. I don't think they ever located those, or if they did, it was after I was done. I spent a week at that place."

"A whole week of picking locks?" Madison said. Since she worked part-time with Deborah, she took a professional interest.

"It wasn't just dealing with the locks. It was getting to them. It was a big house. Full basement, full attic, and I don't know how many rooms. And most of it was packed ceiling to floor with stuff. At least the living room had a path through it, and the couch was clear."

"What about her bedroom?" Mom asked.

"There wasn't an accessible bed in the place. As far as we could tell, she slept on that living room couch. I think she ate there too."

"The kitchen? The bathrooms?" Phil said. "Or should I not ask?"

"You sure shouldn't ask at the dinner table," Deborah said. "Anyway, there was a crew sorting and cleaning, and whenever they found anything portable that needed unlocking, like a jewelry box or a lockbox, they'd bring it to me. We had a staging area outside in the driveway because there was nowhere inside to work. I'd open the boxes as fast as I could without damaging them, but sometimes there'd be half a dozen of them stacked up waiting for me. Then, when they cleared enough stuff to create a path to a locked door or cabinet, they'd call me into the house." She made a face. "I had to wear a hazmat suit."

"What did she hoard?" Sid asked.

"What didn't she hoard? Newspapers, books, pizza boxes, tote bags, shipping boxes, clothes, shoes, old toys, brand-new toothbrushes still sealed up, magazines, makeup, records, tacky little figurines, dog food."

"She had a dog in there?" Madison was horrified.

"Nope. Just the food. Which was even weirder. Though probably the weirdest was this bureau that was stuffed with meticulously folded paper bags. There was nothing in the bags, mind you, not even a spare receipt. Just four drawers of empty paper bags."

Phil said, "What kind of items did she have in the lockboxes?"

"My job was to unlock, not to peek inside," Deborah said loftily.

We all just looked at her.

"Okay, I peeked in some of them, but it was mostly junk. Cancelled checks, coupons, photos, rolled pennies… There was no rhyme or reason why any of it needed to be locked up. Her tax records—which you'd expect to be put away somewhere—were in a clothes basket along with a bunch of singleton socks."

"The whole house was like that?" Mom asked, and when Deborah nodded, she said, "What a shame. It was a lovely house, at least from the outside. I was surprised when they tore it down rather than fix it up."

"Had it just been the mess, they could have renovated it, but even basic maintenance had been neglected, probably since before Professor Nichols passed away. The roof leaked, the appliances were all junk, there were mold issues, the plumbing and electrical systems were shot…" She shrugged. "Everywhere we looked was another problem that would have cost big bucks to fix. The executor was talking about breaking up the lot or building condos. I guess the heirs thought they'd get more money that way."

"They might have if the town hadn't stopped them," Phil said. "I remember reading something in the *Gazette*. That area is zoned for single family housing, and since the head of the zoning board lives next door, they won't be getting a variance any time soon."

"Who was the heir?" I asked, theorizing that he or she could have found Rose living in his or her newly acquired house and turned violent.

"There were no children," Mom put in.

"You know this was ten years ago," Deborah grumbled, but thought for a minute. "That's right—that's part of what made it complicated. The house and the land went to some cousins of the late Professor Nichols—that's who wanted to build the condos or sell the land for condos. The contents of the house went to Mrs. Nichols's alma mater." She waved a fork in my direction. "Which was your new stomping grounds, Georgia."

"Bostock?" I asked.

"That's right," Phil said. "There was some vexation at McQuaid at the time. As a longtime employee, Professor Nichols had said there would be a bequest for the school, but after his death, Margo changed the will to benefit Bostock instead."

"If you ask me, they didn't miss out on much," Deborah said. "Not that that stopped the squabbles. I remember one endless argument over whether a built-in china cabinet counted as furniture or as part of the house? I don't know how they resolved that one. Since I had no dog in the race, once I unlocked it, I left them alone to slug it out."

We were finished with dinner by then and broke apart for the evening. I offered to give Sid a hand with research, but he turned me down, saying he could do it faster on his own.

It was just as well. With the end of the semester looming, I had plenty of papers to grade before bedtime.

Chapter Ten

When I opened the door into Sid's attic after I got home from work the next day, for a moment I thought I was in the wrong room. The place was spotless. Not that Sid is normally overly messy. His flesh-free lifestyle means he doesn't have to deal with dirty dishes, towels, or clothes, but he does like books, movies, comic books, and video games, all of which are usually scattered around. Plus he's gotten hooked on action figures and has several shelves jam-packed. But now everything was organized within an inch of its life. He'd even arranged the action figures by fandom and, within that, alphabetically.

"Whoa!" I said.

"Looks good, doesn't it?" he said, looking inordinately pleased with himself. "I even snuck down to borrow the vacuum cleaner while everybody else was out of the house."

"What brought this on?"

"Research."

"Come again?"

"I started looking through missing person reports but didn't get anywhere. So I switched to hunting for dirt about the Nichols family."

"Like what?"

"No idea. I just thought that since the body was found at their house, they might be connected."

"I never thought of that."

"You didn't miss anything. The only dirt I found was the literal kind, meaning several news stories about the condition in which the house was found after Mrs. Nichols passed away. That got me started reading up on hoarding disorder and watching the show *Hoarders: Buried Alive*. After two episodes, I couldn't stand it anymore and started cleaning up my space."

"You're not a hoarder, Sid."

"Most hoarders don't realize that they're hoarders."

"Seriously?"

"Okay, the bad ones do, but most people kind of slide into it over time, with a small amount of stuff, then some more, a little more, and then boom! Hoarder! I wanted to make sure I wasn't starting to slide down that slope."

"I'm impressed." I also told myself I was going to have to do some decluttering of my own when I got a chance. I used to move so often that I never had a chance to accumulate much detritus, but Madison and I had been at my parents' house for long enough that the amount of stuff I owned had been slowly increasing.

Sid said, "Another big part of hoarder symptomology is hiding and shame. They'll do just about anything to keep people from knowing."

"Which explains why Mom never knew how bad the Nichols house had gotten."

"Exactly. Psychologists used to think hoarding disorder was an offshoot of OCD, but now they consider it a separate disorder. They don't know what causes it. It seems to be genetic with some people, but for others, it seems to be a response to emotional trauma."

"Like maybe Professor Nichols's death?"

"It could be."

"So what does all this stuff about hoarding have to do with Rose's death?"

"Don't get caught up in the details, Georgia. It's early days yet."

In other words, he didn't know that it did.

"Did you talk to Charles?" he asked.

"I called him, and he didn't have time to meet with me today, but he left a letter in my faculty mailbox."

"Why didn't he just email it?"

"Security?" I said.

"As if leaving it in a mailbox was more secure," Sid scoffed. "Anyway, what did the letter say?"

"I haven't opened it yet." I waved a thick envelope at him. "I thought you'd want to read it with me."

"You are the perfect partner," Sid said. I took a seat on the couch, and he plopped down next to me as I opened the envelope.

"Oh my spine and femur," I said. "It's handwritten. That's why he didn't email it. And look at the writing. Sid, he used a fountain pen."

"I know you adore the guy, Georgia, but he is nuts."

"Sometimes I think he should have been born in a different era."

The first page was a note to me.

Georgia,
I find it easier to express my recollections about Rose in writing. I trust this does not hinder your investigation. Feel free to ask for more information if needed.

With warmest regards,
Charles

He'd labeled the rest of the pages "Clues to Rose's True Identity" and created a bulleted list.

- *Rose was approximately five and a half feet tall. I didn't measure her, but in comparing her height to my own, I feel reasonably confident in my estimate.*

- *I'm a poor judge of age, but from her appearance and the things she said, I gathered that she was my age or a year or two younger. I was thirty-seven at the time.*

"That matches what Yo determined in her examination, doesn't it?" Sid said.

I nodded, and we continued.

- *Rose's eyes were dark brown. Her hair was a rich chestnut shade that hung to her shoulders. (It was her natural color—there was ample time for her roots to begin to show.) Her coloring was Caucasian, neither pale nor tanned, but a rosy peach.*

- *Though not classically beautiful, she was very attractive, and her smile transformed her face.*

- *Rose's build was what is often known as full-figured or curvy. I would describe her as having a classic hourglass figure.*

"Charles was really smitten with her," Sid said.

- *Since Rose was in hiding, given the way in which women are often mistreated, my first thought was that she was escaping an abuser of some kind. However, I never saw any physical signs of this. Of course, even after our relationship deepened, I could have missed injuries or they could have healed before I had an opportunity to observe them, but she never showed any signs of experiencing pain.*

- *Rose didn't say where she was from, but her accent was that of a New Englander.*

- *Rose had no car that I ever saw.*

- *Rose was a strong woman, so I doubt she was a desk worker of any kind. Her hands, though entirely feminine, showed signs of good, strong labor.*

"That is the sweetest way ever of describing callouses on a woman's hands," I said.

"Smitten."

- *I suspect Rose was college-educated. Her knowledge was strongest in history, particularly European, and she knew a great deal about art. She seemed less well-versed in literature and never mentioned math or any of the sciences. Her knowledge of philosophy was less indicative of formal study than of a person making her own observations.*

- *Rose said her parents died early, and she had no siblings. She never mentioned any other family connections.*

- *Rose made vague references to a checkered past. I believe her exact phrase was, "I'm no angel, Charles." I disagreed.*

- *Rose had no pets.*

- *Rose was right-handed.*

- *Rose's cooking was, I fear, not outstanding, though some allowances must be made for our limited equipment.*

- *During the times when I was away from the house, Rose spent her time reading and sketching. She was shy about showing me her work, but from what I remember, she was quite talented. Though I confess that I could be biased.*

"No kidding!" Sid said.

"Don't make fun. He was in love."

- *As far as I knew, Rose had no plans for the future. And in truth, I did not push her. Our sojourn together seemed timeless, and the world outside our walls unimportant. Had we not learned that the house was to be demolished, I almost believe we could have lived there forever.*

- *The events of our last days together may be of particular interest, so I will describe them in some detail.*

  On the morning of the twenty-third, I went out to get us a hot breakfast, and I picked up the Pennycross Gazette as well. That's when we saw the announcement that demolition was imminent. We were both quite concerned, but I had to put worry aside. I was teaching at McQuaid that semester, and thanks to spending time with Rose, I'd fallen behind in my teaching duties. Since I still had papers to score and grades to post, I had to leave her alone while I worked on campus. When I came back, she seemed calmer and said that perhaps things would work out after all. I should have pressed her for more information, but I was mulling over a decision.

  Georgia, I shall never forgive myself for not telling Rose that I would have been honored to make a home with her, but in my defense, I had nowhere to take her. I was up all night considering my options, and by the next morning, I'd decided to damn the torpedoes, as it were.

  I left her at the house to do some Christmas shopping, and again, was gone most of the day. By the time I returned, she was gone.

Sid said, "Do you think he went to get a ring for her?"

"I can't imagine what else he would have rushed off to buy at a time like that." I folded up the pages and put them back into the envelope. "I feel so bad for him. They had that one month together, and then he spent ten years wondering what had happened. Now he finds out she's dead."

He patted my shoulder. "We're doing what we can for him, Georgia, and maybe it did him good to talk about it, even on paper."

"I hope so."

"So what did he tell us that might help us?" Sid said, making a steeple of his hands in his favorite time-to-detect pose.

"One thing stands out. How did Rose know the Nichols house was vacant?"

Sid said, "There may have been something in the news. I can check that online."

"I don't think it would have been reported anywhere other than locally. So that might mean Rose came from this part of the state, at least."

"That leads to another thought. No matter how she found out about the Nichols place, why did she go there?"

"She was on the run and needed a place to hide out," I reminded him.

"That's what she said, but maybe she wasn't really on the run. Maybe she was searching for something hidden in the house."

"Deborah said it was cleared out."

"The cleaning crew could have missed something. Hoarders are all about hiding stuff."

"That's something to consider. Though if it is true, I don't want to be the one to tell Charles she was at the house under false pretenses."

"Maybe she came for a MacGuffin but stayed for love."

"I think Charles could accept that," I said. "Suppose Rose was making one last hunt for the MacGuffin when she was caught and killed by a competing thief. Or she did find it, and the competing thief found out and killed her to get it."

"Or somebody came to buy the MacGuffin and decided it was cheaper to kill her and steal it."

"Whatever it was, if it exists."

"Which it may not," Sid concluded. "We know that she didn't have a car. How far do you suppose she could have walked?"

"It depends on how cold it was, how much snow there was, and how physically fit she was. For me, on a good day, a mile or two.

Madison could walk further, but cold bothers her more. Deborah could go for miles."

"I'll check the weather and the bus schedules for that date. Of course, I won't be able to track her if she hitched a ride."

"I doubt she'd have hitchhiked. She was about the age I am now, and I wouldn't hitchhike if I had any other choice. Given that she was on the run, I think she'd be even less likely to rely on the kindness of strangers."

"That makes sense. Still, I've got a few things to look for online: weather, bus routes, MacGuffins, and more missing person reports."

"How are you going to look for a possibly nonexistent MacGuffin?"

"It requires mad search engine skills that are far too sophisticated to explain to the layperson."

I just looked at him.

"Okay, I'll probably skip the MacGuffin and go on to the missing person reports. Which are really depressing, by the way."

I patted his scapula in sympathy. "Why don't you take the night off. We haven't watched *Rudolph the Red-Nosed Reindeer* or *Olive the Other Reindeer* yet this year."

"And *The Grinch Who Stole Christmas*? The animated short, of course."

"Absolutely!"

Between dinner with the family and our Christmas DVD orgy, we managed to shake off my sadness about Charles and Sid's about all the missing people, but I was sure that Sid would go right back to work as soon as I went to bed.

Chapter Eleven

The next day was a busy one thanks to classes and meetings with students to help them fine-tune their final papers. I felt more than a little guilty when I got home, and after greeting Madison and my parents, I headed upstairs. I was sure Sid had been working on the case nonstop, and I hadn't so much as texted him to see how it was going.

Then I got upstairs and found him playing a computer game.

"Hang on," he said without looking up. I waited for him to finish his game of Bejeweled Blitz, expecting him to stop when he was done. Instead he started a new game. And a third one after that. Sure, they were only one minute long each, but he knew I was standing there.

"Should I come back later?" I said with a certain sense of irritation.

"Sorry," he said, but he still finished his game. When he turned around, I noticed his bones weren't attached as tightly as usual. Since Sid is held together purely by attitude, if for some reason he is feeling unsure of himself or worried, his bones become looser. During rough times, they barely hang together at all. His current condition wasn't that bad, but it wasn't good either.

"What's the word?" I asked.

"Weather's supposed to be cold tonight, but there's no snow in the forecast. They've got sleet down in Boston this afternoon, and the traffic is a mess, but the storm won't make it this far."

"That's good. But I was talking about—"

"Of course, it would be great to have some snow on the ground for Christmas. It makes everything look Christmas-y." He actually hummed the first bars of "White Christmas." "Don't you think it would be odd to have Christmas in Australia where it's summer in December? Do they put up fake snowflakes and stuff like they do in Florida and California?"

"I have no idea."

"Speaking of Australia, I found a slew of great videos of quokka. I thought it was pronounced to rhyme with rock-a, but it really rhymes with mocha. They are such cute animals and so friendly. I'll send you some links." He started to type on his computer.

"Sid!"

"Hmm?"

"Did you find out anything about Rose?" I asked.

"Maybe. I don't know. It probably doesn't mean anything."

"The way you've been avoiding talking about it tells me that (a) you think it does mean something and (b) you don't want me to know."

"It's not that I don't want you to know. It's just that I don't want to be the one to tell you. I should also remind you that coincidences do happen."

"I know that. What coincidence did you find?" I remembered his list of tasks from the night before. "Was it something to do with the weather, bus routes, or missing person reports?"

"No, though I did check all those out. The weather was cold, but there wasn't much snow, and there are a lot of buses that come into Pennycross, so when you factor in connections, she could have come from anywhere in New England. The bus depot is less than a mile from where the Nichols house used to be, and she could easily have walked that far. In other words, I got nothing useful. So I went back to the missing person reports, and despite working my fingers to the bone—literally—I had no luck." He started popping his fingers off, then putting them back on.

"And? Don't tell me you found a MacGuffin."

"Of course not. I have too much sense to waste time on that."

"Then what are you upset about?"

"I wish you couldn't always tell when I'm upset."

Normally that would have called for a joke about being able to see right through him, but I didn't think the timing was right. I settled for, "I have known you a long time."

"True. I'm the kind of guy who'd wear my heart on my sleeve if I had either a heart or sleeves."

"I can also tell when you're stalling."

"A bit. To continue, after I ran out of things to try, I went back and reread Charles's letter to see if we'd missed anything."

"Had we?"

"One tiny thing. He said that the day before Rose disappeared, they read the newspaper and found out that the house was going to be demolished, which made them both super stressed. Charles went to work, but by the time he came home, Rose seemed calmer. So what happened in those few hours?"

"She could have just pulled herself together, or maybe she suddenly got a brilliant idea."

"Brilliant ideas require inspiration. She wouldn't have had a cell phone or a computer handy because Charles would have taken his with him, so the only things in the house that might have sparked an idea were their books, her sketchbook, and that newspaper Charles had just bought."

"I'm guessing it was the newspaper."

He nodded. "The *Pennycross Gazette* has online archives dating back decades, so it wasn't hard to find the right issue, but I did have to go through it several times before I spotted what Rose saw. Or might have seen. I don't know for sure, Georgia, but it's the only thing in that newspaper that hinted at where Rose might have come from or where she might have gone. But maybe you'd rather look for yourself. I can access the archive again."

"Sid, just spill it."

He sighed heavily, or at least made a heavy sighing sound for effect. "North Ashfield had a big Christmas Festival that year."

"Okay."

"With Santa, decorative lights, a parade, and a carnival."

"So you think Rose was a carney?"

"It would make sense, wouldn't it? Say she got in trouble with a local and had to get away. Or somebody at the carnival itself was after her. Or she'd decided to join the carnival to get away from town."

"All reasonable possibilities, and some of them would explain why there was no police report. I just don't know why you were so worried about telling me." Then I realized what he was getting at. "Which carnival was it?"

"It was Fenton's." He showed me a printout of the ad, which included a familiar logo.

Fenton's Family Festival was the carnival where I'd first encountered Sid, but the reason Sid hadn't wanted to tell me was because it was owned and managed by the parents of my ex-boyfriend Brownie Fenton, who still worked there part of the time. No wonder Sid's bones were loose.

I was on good enough terms with most of my ex-boyfriends that I would have had no hesitation in reaching out to them. It was different with Brownie. For one thing, we hadn't broken up that long ago, and for another, the circumstances were more awkward than usual.

Even if I were best buddies with Brownie, it would still have been ticklish having to get in touch with his parents. I had no reason to believe that they would be any happier with me than I was with the boy who'd dumped Madison back in September.

So rather than acting like an adult and bowing to the inevitable, I spent the next hour going through that back issue of the *Gazette*, trying to come up with something else that would have given Rose hope for a new sanctuary. But unless a last-minute sale at Building 19 had attracted her, there was nothing else there.

By the time I went to bed, I no longer felt guilty about Sid doing all the investigative chores. Uncomfortable or not, I had to go talk to the Fentons.

Chapter Twelve

Sid had already found out that Fenton's was providing rides for a zoo lights gig at the Atwood Zoo, which was about forty-five minutes away from Pennycross. Their being nearby wasn't as big a coincidence as it sounded. Fenton's was a small carnival and pretty much stuck to stands in and around our part of New England.

To save time, I packed Sid's skull, right hand, and cell phone into the sugar skull bag the next morning and carried him to work with me. If my students wondered why I kept the bag on my desk during classes, they weren't curious enough to ask, and I didn't volunteer an explanation. Sid always says he enjoys watching me work, so I tried to do a good job despite being nervous about the afternoon's plan.

We left Bostock right after my last class, and I drove through a McDonald's for lunch so Sid could keep me company while I ate in the car. In a different time, I'd have been self-conscious about apparently talking to myself in the car, but with ear buds and speakerphones everywhere, most people would assume I was on the phone.

As soon as I finished eating, we hit the road again. I can't say our conversation was scintillating. I was anxious about seeing Brownie's parents, and possibly him as well, and Sid was nervous about revisiting the place where he gained consciousness in his current skeletal form. Granted, the idea of him losing that consciousness by returning to the scene of his first waking moments made no sense, but since nothing about Sid made sense, that wasn't much comfort. It didn't even help that the carnival had been in a different location that day. A carnival feels the same no matter where it sets up.

Our mutual fretting resulted in a ridiculously intense argument over which movie better expressed the Christmas spirit: *Miracle on 34th Street* or *It's a Wonderful Life.* Toward the end I think we both realized that we were just filling the time before we arrived at the zoo, and we declared it a draw just as I pulled into the parking lot, even though it was plain that *Miracle on 34th Street* was the obvious choice.

I'd halfway expected that I'd have to pay admission to get to the Fentons, but the carnival was set up in the parking lot, not inside the zoo's fence. Presumably at night, they'd have people watching to make sure nobody got to the rides without paying, but the handful of people out and about didn't even blink as I ducked under the red-and-white rope outlining the carnival grounds and headed for the backyard, meaning the area where the cook shack, business trailer, generator truck, and those other less scenic show necessities were arranged. I went straight to the green trailer marked *Office.*

"The show looks smaller than usual," I whispered to Sid as we walked.

"Who's going to want to go up in a Ferris wheel in December?" he whispered back. "That would make even me cold."

I hadn't called to let the Fentons know I was coming because I wasn't sure what kind of reception I was going to get, so I thought it would be better to take them by surprise. Though I'd never been sure how happy they were with their son dating a towner, that didn't mean that they'd be happy about my ceasing to date him. I knocked on the door, and when I heard Dana Fenton call, "Come in," I took a deep breath and went inside the trailer. As I shut the door behind me, I could almost feel the Fentons glaring at me.

Dana Fenton, whose father had founded the carnival, was a sturdy-looking woman with short silver hair and eyes just like her son's. She glared at me while continuing to type on her computer.

Her husband, Treasure Hunt Mannix, had a wiry build and wispy gray hair and looked neither welcoming nor hostile, only curious.

The trailer was filled with the equipment you'd expect to find in any office: two desks, computers, filing cabinets, a storage cabinet doing double duty as a printer stand, a mini-fridge, a coffee maker, a time clock, and a couple of desk chairs. The small safe was less common, but not entirely unheard of. The only signs that this wasn't your average business were the compact size and the colorful carnival posters and photos on the walls.

"College Boy ain't here," Treasure Hunt said. *College Boy* was his nickname for Brownie. I'd always thought the point of a nickname was to be shorter than the formal version, but Treasure Hunt believed that a carney without a nickname wasn't a true carney. Once he gave somebody a nickname, he stuck with it.

"That's all right." I'd come as early as I had in hopes of missing him, but I wasn't going to tell them that. "I actually wanted to talk to you two."

"Ready to give up teaching and join the show?" Treasure Hunt said. "We can use another backyard boy. Excuse me, backyard person."

I was pretty sure I'd been dissed but didn't bother to ask in what way. "No, thanks. I'd actually like to talk to you about a case." I'd practiced saying *case* without choking on it, trying to make it sound natural. From Dana's reaction, I don't think I succeeded.

"Is that what you call it?" she said, frowning. "Brownie told us you like to nose around things. Of course, that was back when you were dating, so I didn't know if you were still at it."

I know my face went red, but I didn't respond to the dating part of her remark. For one, it had only been a couple of months, and for another, I was defended by an unexpected source.

"She's not so bad," Treasure Hunt said. "She may be a towner, but she's not as bad as a cop."

Dana sniffed, which I took as permission to continue.

"I don't know if you two have seen anything in the news, but a woman's skeleton was found in Pennycross a few days ago." When their only reaction was to shrug, I went on. "The police haven't been able to identify her yet, but I found out that she disappeared from Pennycross on Christmas Eve ten years ago."

"You think she hitched a ride with Santa Claus." Treasure Hunt snickered at his own joke.

"Actually, I was wondering if her disappearance had something to do with you guys. You were working a Christmas Festival in North Ashfield that year."

Now it was Treasure Hunt's turn to frown. "Maybe you are as bad as the cops. Anything happens when a carney is around and it has to be our fault!"

I would have politely explained, but my nerves were on edge. "Oh, cut it out!" I snapped. "How long did I date Brownie? How much time did I spend with him and both of you? Do you think that after all that I'd have some stupid idea that all carnies are crooks and killers? I'd rather be a towner than a chump!"

Treasure Hunt gaped for a second, but when Dana burst out laughing, he joined in.

That lightened the mood considerably, and when they quieted down, I said, "Here's the deal. While you guys were in North Ashfield that year, a woman broke into a vacant house and holed up there for nearly a month, hiding from somebody or something."

"You got a name?" Dana asked.

"She never said." I went on to describe Rose, using terms considerably less poetic than the ones in Charles's note.

Dana gave me a long look. "The only way you'd know this tale is from somebody who was hiding out with her."

"That's right," I said because it was obvious, though I wasn't going to tell them who it was. "My source said she left on December twenty-fourth, and until the body was found, he thought she'd left town on her own hook. The body seems to match the woman's description, but I can't find a corresponding missing person report. So I wondered if she might have been a carney."

"That's not completely stupid," Treasure Hunt said. "The police don't care when one of us goes missing, so there wouldn't be any reports. Are you thinking that a towner killed her?"

"All I know is that we've got a dead woman without a name. Maybe your show being in town that week is just a coincidence, but I don't have any other leads. I take it nobody like that left the show around then."

"He doesn't know," Dana said. "Neither do I. You have to realize that not everybody is cut out to a carney. You get people who stay for seasons and some who get sick of the show after a month and take off without warning. Depending on how long the person had been with it, we might not take special notice. When did you say this was?"

"Ten years ago."

Dana scratched her chin. "Nobody is springing to mind, but I suppose I could go through our files and see what I can find. Might be nothing, of course."

"I sure would appreciate it." After that, they relaxed enough to offer me a cup of coffee, but I begged off in order to head back home. Once I made sure that Dana had my cell phone number and email address, I said goodbye, and Treasure Hunt even wished me a good day. At least I think he did. His love for old-time carney slang rivaled Sid's affection using bone names in place of profanity, but while I know bone names, I frequently have no clue what Treasure Hunt is saying.

I made it back to my car, relieved that I hadn't run into my sometime-boyfriend after all. That is, of course, until I saw Brownie leaning against the hood of my car.

Chapter Thirteen

Dr. Brownlow Mannix, known as Brownie to everybody other than his father, was just as good-looking as I remembered. He had reddish brown hair, dark blue eyes, and a tiny little cleft in his chin. When he wasn't working with his family's carnival, he was a fellow adjunct, specializing in American Studies.

"Hey," I said. It wasn't a cool or sultry reading of *Hey*. It was more like *Hey, I'd hoped to get out of here without seeing you, and now I feel like a complete idiot.*

"Hey," he responded, leaving me to consider interpretations of his greeting. "I thought I recognized your car, so I figured it was worth waiting around to see for sure."

"Your mother emailed you that I was here, didn't she?" I said, remembering how Dana had kept typing after I came into the trailer.

"She might have mentioned it. What brings you out here? Something skeleton related?"

He thought he was joking because I'd first encountered him when trying to track down Sid's origins, so he was taken aback when I said, "Actually, yes. I found another dead body, and I thought your parents might know something about it."

"Excuse me?"

"It will probably sound less insane if you let them explain it."

"I was hoping you'd tell me. Hence my standing out here."

"You could have waited for me at the trailer. It's a whole lot warmer there than it is out here."

"But not as private. Since you're all too accurate about the cold, can I buy you a cup of coffee? There's a Starbucks about half a mile away."

"Make it hot chocolate and you've got a deal."

I could feel Sid vibrating from inside the sugar skull bag, and I had a hunch he was laughing at me.

It was easier for us both to go in my car, since we were standing right next to it. I started telling the story on the way, going into a little more depth than I had with Brownie's parents. Since he knew about Charles's living situation, he guessed instantly who'd been sharing the Nichols house with Rose. That meant he understood why I hadn't let Charles go to the police with the information.

By the time I finished, we were at Starbucks with steaming cups of hot chocolate in front of us.

"If you don't mind my saying so, the connection with my family's show seems kind of tenuous," Brownie said.

"It defines tenuous, but I've got to start somewhere."

"Well, let me know if there's anything I can do to help. I like Charles, and I've always been curious about how you do the things you do."

"You realize most people think I'm nuts for having this hobby." There was a sharp nudge from the sugar skull bag, which I'd placed on the floor by my feet so I could at least pretend to be alone with Brownie, but Sid's hearing is as sharp as he wants it to be. "Maybe not so much a hobby as an avocation."

"That's their issue. My parents think I'm nuts for working as an adjunct because the money is so bad, and my fellow academics think traveling part-time with a carnival is nuts because it's not intellectual enough."

I was quickly remembering why I'd enjoyed spending time with him.

"What's next with the investigation?" he asked.

"I'm really hoping your parents can dig something up, but until then, it consists of looking at missing person reports to see if I find one that matches Rose."

"That sounds time-consuming."

"I squeeze in what I can." Or rather, Sid did. "It helps that I'm teaching five sections of the same class, and it's one I can nearly teach in my sleep."

"How is life at Bostock? I've been hearing about the imminent strike."

"Word is definitely getting around. I still haven't heard anything official, but we've got an adjunct faculty meeting next week, and I suspect it'll be discussed then."

"I got a call from a friend of mine asking if I was going to apply for a temporary position, should one become available."

"What did you say?"

"I'm not sure. Crossing a picket line makes me uncomfortable, but..."

"But," I agreed. Though Brownie had another income stream, that didn't mean he didn't understand what it meant to be an adjunct.

By then the hot chocolate was gone, and I realized how late it was getting. I drove Brownie back to the carnival lot, and before he got out of the car, we shared a quick kiss. It would have been just about perfect if he hadn't said, "Maybe we can see each other over the holidays."

I stiffened just a touch, but I think he noticed, and I'm sure he noticed my lame response of, "Sure, let's stay in touch."

He looked perplexed as he got out of the car, and I couldn't blame him. I drove out of the parking lot without looking back.

For once, Sid hadn't picked up on the subtext, mainly because I'd put his bag in the backseat.

"Hello!" he called from behind me.

"Wait until I get to a red light," I said, and at the first opportunity, pulled him into the front seat. Since he had his hand, he unzipped it for himself so he could get a clearer look at my face.

"Well, well, well," he said with more than a hint of insinuation. "I think somebody's got a crush."

"One does not have crushes on someone one has dated."

"Then why did one sound like a junior high school student when encountering someone one has dated?"

"One did not!"

"One did so!"

"One did not!"

"One did so!"

"One…I mean I didn't. Nor do I have a crush on Brownie Mannix. Look, I like him. We've had a few laughs together. That's it."

"So why did you stop having laughs with him?"

"I don't know, Sid. It just didn't…We don't have…Just no spark."

"It seems to me like you two spark just fine."

"Well, he doesn't seem to agree. Until today, I hadn't heard from him since October."

"Did you two fight?"

"No. He asked me out one time when I was busy, and I guess he was upset that I wouldn't change my plans. Or maybe he started seeing somebody else. I don't know, Sid. Don't make more of it than it is."

"If you say so," he said.

He sounded suspicious, but I preferred suspicious over guilty, which is how he'd have felt if he knew the whole story.

Though Brownie and I had never made our relationship formal, we had certainly enjoyed spending time together whenever our schedules meshed. Unfortunately, they didn't mesh all that often. He both traveled with the carnival and relocated for adjunct jobs, and I'd been teaching outside Pennycross for a while. Still, when I'd come back to town in the fall, Brownie had made it plain that he wanted us to pick up where we'd left off, and at first, it had been great.

Then Brownie asked me to come to Dana's birthday party, even including my parents and Madison in the invitation. I liked Dana and I really hadn't had an excuse to refuse.

Except Sid. I'd promised to take him to a Halloween carnival that same night, and he'd already bought a costume. I couldn't exactly tell Brownie that, and I'd gotten flustered enough that my excuse for turning him down had obviously been an excuse, and he'd been understandably annoyed. At least I assumed he'd been annoyed because that was when he'd quit calling. That had annoyed me, so I hadn't called him, either.

I'd dated a reasonable number of men over the years, but Brownie was only the second I'd considered a long-term relationship with. The first had been Madison's father, and we'd been engaged when I found out I was pregnant. Shortly thereafter, he'd told me that he didn't want children—at least not anytime soon—so I had to choose between him and my baby. It had been a surprisingly easy decision, which made me wonder just how seriously I'd taken the relationship. I'd always been grateful that I hadn't told him about Sid.

That was the problem. Sid was a big part of my life. Therefore, I couldn't be entirely open with a man until I told him about Sid, and I couldn't tell anyone about Sid until I was sure he was going to accept him. Which I couldn't know until I told him. It was the most vicious circle I'd ever been trapped in.

"Do you think Dana will find anything in her files?" I said, firmly changing the subject.

"I'm not feeling hopeful," Sid said. "And I'm out of ideas unless I can somehow find the right missing persons report."

"You want to listen to music?"

"Christmas music?"

"You bet." I let him play his favorites all the way home, and he sang along to them all, including my least favorite, "The Christmas Shoes."

We got home just in time for dinner. Andrew, Phil's poorly groomed grad student, was already at the dining room table, so I took the sugar skull bag up to the attic and let Sid reassemble himself up there. Sometimes he listens in on dinners even if he can't sit at the table for some reason, but he was no more interested in Andrew's dissertation than Madison or I were. Unfortunately, I was hungry and couldn't think of a way to avoid the ordeal, so I went back down just as Phil brought out the fixings for tacos.

As I'd feared, Andrew almost immediately started sharing tidbits from his dissertation research. It's not that I don't enjoy discussing literary scholarship—we English professors live for that stuff—but I've never been a fan of Nathaniel Hawthorne and had only moderate interest in the Transcendentalists. Even a well-thought-out thesis about them wasn't going to enthrall me.

When Andrew finally stopped to take a big bite of taco, Madison kicked me gently under the table and gave me a significant look to let me know that she was counting on me to save her from dying of ennui. I didn't want to talk about our investigation or Brownie, so I went with the first thing that came to mind.

"So Mom, Phil, what's the McQuaid buzz on the looming Bostock strike?"

Mom said, "It seems to me that the union has reason to be unhappy."

"It's hard to imagine academics walking a picket line," Madison said.

"I hope it won't come to that," Phil said.

"If it does," Andrew said, "a lot of us McQuaid grad students are planning to offer our support. You know, bring them coffee and donuts. We academics have to stick together!"

Madison asked, "What are they striking about? More money?"

"It's more about healthcare and workload," Mom said. "The administration is trying to cut costs."

"Yeah, at the faculty's expense," Andrew said. "And you know what I heard? If the strike happens, they're going to hire adjunct scabs to teach the classes because they know adjuncts won't respect the picket line. It's all about the bucks for some people."

"People like my mom?" Madison said icily. "The adjunct sitting next to you?"

His eyes widened. "I didn't realize you were an adjunct, Mrs. Thackery."

"That's Doctor Thackery," Madison snapped.

"Right, I meant Dr. Thackery." He started stuffing taco into his mouth.

"Is this true, Georgia?" Phil said, looking troubled. "Are adjuncts going to assist the administration?"

"Possibly. Bostock may be looking for adjuncts to hire if the strike takes place, and I've talked to a couple of my fellow adjuncts who are considering it. No, they're not thrilled with crossing a picket line, but some people actually need their paycheck to put food on the table. You can't make tacos with solidarity." I pointedly didn't look at Andrew.

"What do you think, Mom?" Madison asked.

"Honestly, I'm not sure. On one hand, I think the union has raised points that need to be addressed, and if the administration won't listen, the union is justified in going on strike. On the other hand, Bostock's union doesn't allow adjuncts, so why should adjuncts support a strike that won't benefit us? On the other hand, if the union loses power, colleges and universities might increase their reliance on adjuncts, meaning most adjuncts will never have a chance to get permanent jobs. On the other hand—"

"Mom, you don't have that many hands."

"Sorry. If I did, I'd be waving that last one on the students' behalf because they've paid their tuition—or their parents have—and they're entitled to their classes." I shrugged. "It's complicated."

My parents nodded thoughtfully because, unlike many tenured faculty, they understood the complications.

"You know, some of my best instructors have been adjuncts," Andrew put in. "There's nothing wrong with taking that route instead of going in for more serious scholarship."

Now he had three Thackerys' worth of glaring. Not only had Madison turned her irate gaze back on him, but Mom and Phil had joined in.

"Actually," Phil said in a quiet voice that told me how angry he was, "many adjuncts are just as devoted to their research as their tenured counterparts, and their contributions are just as valuable. The difference is that adjuncts get no support from their colleges, meaning that they have to work twice as hard."

"Well, yeah, I mean not all adjuncts—"

Phil interrupted Andrew, something he almost never does. "Enough of that. Andrew, since you've finished eating, I'm sure you'll want to head back to your apartment to start in on those rewrites I suggested this afternoon. I'm afraid I didn't have time to prepare dessert."

Andrew drew back the hand that had been reaching for yet another taco shell. "I just hope my noisy neighbor isn't blasting his music the way he usually does. It can be really hard to concentrate on my work."

"I'm sure you'll manage," Mom said with a devastatingly sweet smile. "After all, Georgia had a baby to tend to when she was completing her dissertation, and she did a remarkable job."

"Really?" he said, wiping his mouth and getting up from the table. "That must have been a challenge."

I didn't say anything. In fact, none of us said anything as he packed up his backpack and put on his coat. "Thanks for dinner," he said, reluctantly walking toward the door.

"About that noise problem at your apartment," Phil said.

"Yes, Professor?" he said hopefully, meaning that he was hoping for an invite to stay and maybe crash on the sofa as he had half a dozen times before.

"I have some earplugs that might help. Let me get them for you."

"Yeah, earplugs. That would be great."

Once Andrew had slunk away, Phil said, "Sometimes I forget that your academic career has obstacles mine did not, Georgia. Let me say once again how much I admire your perseverance." He clapped his hands together. "Now, who wants ice cream?"

“I thought you said you didn’t make dessert,” I said.

“That’s true. I didn’t make anything. However, I did pick up a quart of dark chocolate at Arturo’s this afternoon.”

“I’ll get it,” I said, stopping to kiss both my parents on the way to the kitchen. And on the way back, I smooched Madison, too. Andrew could keep Hawthorne and the Transcendentalists. I had my family and dark chocolate ice cream.

Chapter Fourteen

Sid kept reading missing person reports all weekend, expanding his search more and more as he tried to find somebody whose description matched Rose's, but every time he found a possibility, something in the description ruled the person out.

When Deborah came for dinner Sunday evening, she told me that the police weren't having any better luck. I didn't know if I should be cheered by that because it gave us an open field or depressed because if a case was beyond their professional capabilities, what chance did an English professor and a skeleton have?

I had just finished my last class on Monday when my cell phone rang. "Hello?"

"Georgia? Dana Fenton here. I've got some information for you about your mystery woman. Or about a mystery woman, anyway. Not sure if it's the one you're looking for, but—"

"Anything could help. What can you tell me?"

"I'd rather not get into it over the phone. Are you free today?"

After a quick check to make sure I didn't have any meetings scheduled, I said, "I've got time."

"Then can you ride back out to the zoo this afternoon? Say around one-thirty?"

"I'll see you then." If I didn't have to wait too long for the shuttle bus, I should be able to run by the house to pick up Sid and still make it on time. Luckily, Phil was working at home with no graduate students around, so he had Sid's skull, hand, and phone loaded into the sugar skull bag before I arrived. He even ran it out to the car to save me time, and being Phil, had also packed a ham sandwich and a can of soda because he knew I'd be missing lunch. With Sid helping out, I was able to eat and drink along the way.

People swear by their cup holders, but there's nothing as convenient as having a disembodied skeletal hand help hold your food while you're driving.

It was just short of one-thirty when I pulled into the parking lot at the zoo, and I went straight to the carnival's business trailer. Dana must have been watching for me because she opened the door before I had a chance to knock. Treasure Hunt was sitting on the couch next to a woman I didn't recognize.

"Georgia," Dana said, "this is Sue Weedon. Sue, this is Georgia Thackery, the one I told you about."

Sue was between Dana and me in age, maybe ten or fifteen years older than I was, with short gray hair and the tan of somebody who worked outside a lot. Her denim overalls and red flannel shirt were liberally spotted with bright splotches of color, but she'd somehow kept her wire-rimmed glasses clean. I couldn't say the same for the hand she offered, and when she noticed me looking, she said, "Don't worry—the paint is dry."

As we shook, Treasure Hunt cackled. "You should have told her it was the latest in manicures. You could make a few extra bucks airbrushing towner hands in between rides."

I tried for a polite smile, but Dana and Sue just exchanged a knowing glance. Apparently Sue was used to Treasure Hunt's sense of humor.

"Have a seat, Georgia," Dana said, nodding at a chair.

I put Sid's bag on the floor next to my feet, aimed so he could see and hear the conversation. "You said you have some information about the dead woman I found?"

"We might," Dana said. "After you came to see me, I did some hunting in my files. We didn't have any employees go missing during those dates you gave me, but I did remember something that happened that week ten years back.

"A woman came to the show one day looking for work. I

knew she was a towner who'd seen too many old movies because she thought she could sign on without giving me her name or her Social Security number. You know, like she was running away to join the circus, which doesn't happen like that anymore either. We get that a lot.

"I explained that she had to fill out an application, just like anywhere else. She left a lot of the fields blank—like her address and phone number—but we get a lot of that, too. I didn't squawk because she gave me enough information that I could do a background check to see if she had a record.

"I spoke to her for a few minutes, and she seemed okay. Like I said, she'd never been with a show, but she said she'd do anything we wanted her to do. I told her I'd let her know, but since she didn't have a phone number to give me, she said she'd call the next day for an answer. That afternoon, I spoke to the only reference she'd given me and had decided to hire her on a probationary basis. Only she never called."

"Do you still have her application?"

"After ten years?" She waved her hand at the trailer. "I've got two file cabinets, Georgia—I have to clear out the deadwood every few months."

"Oh. I don't suppose you remember her name?"

She gave me a disgusted look. "Of course not, but lucky for you, I do remember who I called for a reference because it was another carney." She gestured at Sue Weedon. "It took me a while to track down Sue here—she's been doing a job in Windsor Locks."

"I'm a show painter," Sue put in.

"I'm sorry, but I don't know what that is," I said.

Treasure Hunt guffawed.

"Shut up, Treasure Hunt," Dana said. "Why would Georgia know about that?"

"I paint rides and signs for carnivals and amusement parks," Sue explained, "especially carousels." She waggled her fingers. "That's why the paint. I've got to use good quality stuff, and it's the devil to get off. I don't bother to do a thorough job unless I'm going to have a couple of days off, and since I'm doing a rush job restoring horses for a restaurant—"

"She doesn't care about all that," Dana said impatiently.

"Nobody cares about all that," Treasure Hunt muttered. "Most shows have their maintenance crew do their painting. They don't have to wait until Rembrandt here has time in her schedule, and it's a heck of a lot cheaper, too."

"And pictures from those shows end up on Fail blogs and bad fairground art pages on Pinterest," Dana retorted. "Meanwhile ridership on our carousel went up ten and a quarter percent after Sue repainted it, which more than made up the extra cost."

Apparently Treasure Hunt didn't dare argue with Dana's numbers because he just shrugged.

Dana said, "Go ahead Sue, tell Georgia what she wants to know."

"I don't get called for references that often, so I remember the name of the person who Dana called to ask me about. It was a woman named Annabelle Mitchell."

"Annabelle Mitchell," I repeated. "What can you tell me about her? Had you worked with her?"

"No, Annabelle was my college roommate. We met when we were assigned to the same dorm room and hit it off right away. Neither of us had any close family living, and we bonded over art, books, movies, and just about everything. We were so much alike that some people thought we were sisters." She sighed sadly. "Unfortunately, we lost touch after graduation. Well, after she graduated—I dropped out. Then I wandered around a few years before ending up in show painting, and she went back to college."

"You mean for an advanced degree?"

"No, she worked at Bostock College, not far from here."

I blinked, startled to hear the familiar name. "She was a professor?"

"I'm not sure what she did—I hadn't spoken to her in years.

Still, we'd been close enough in college that I didn't hesitate in recommending her to Dana here. I didn't find out until months later that she hadn't come back to take the job. I tried to get in contact with her then, but she never returned my calls. Like I said, we hadn't been in touch for a long time, so I didn't think too much of it."

"I bet you thought she was too highfalutin to talk to a carney," Treasure Hunt said.

"Our lives had gone in a radically different directions," Sue admitted, "but I didn't hold it against her. Anyway, the more time passed, the more I started thinking something was wrong, especially when her phone got disconnected. I knew she hadn't come here, so I tried calling Bostock College, but all they'd say is that she didn't work there anymore. I didn't have an address for her, so I checked online to see if I could find her, but though I found a lot of Annabelle Mitchells, I never found the right one. Now you think you may have found Annabelle's body?"

"It's possible. The police in Pennycross have a body they haven't been able to identify."

"The police," Treasure Hunt said with a snort. "I wouldn't even talk to them about this, if I were you. We told Sue all about you, Georgia, how you've done this kind of thing before. I think you should handle it."

"I appreciate your confidence," I said, "but maybe the police ought to be told."

"I'd rather not go to them," Sue said, and would have said more, but Dana held up her hand.

"Sue's got her reasons," she said firmly.

"That's fine," I said. "I could tell them myself, but since they'd want to know where I got the information, that would be just as bad. An anonymous tip should do the job."

"Yeah, like they can't trace that," Treasure Hunt said.

"I'll use a pay phone or a library computer," I said, seeing no reason to mention that Sid had talked me into buying a prepaid cell phone a while back for just such occasions. He preferred to call it a burner because that sounded more street.

"Good plan," Dana said, rising from her seat. "Hate to chase you off, but I need Sue to do touchup painting on our dark ride while she's here, and it has to be dry before we open tonight."

"No problem. Ms. Weedon, can I get in touch if I have any more questions about Annabelle?"

Sue looked at Dana, who nodded, which she took as a sign of approval. "Sure. Let me give you my number." She fumbled in her overall pocket and handed me a business card for *Sue's Show Painting*, which I slipped into the sugar skull bag.

"Thanks for your help, Ms. Weedon. And you, too, Dana."

"What about me?" Treasure Hunt asked.

Dana snorted. "Why would she thank you? You didn't do anything."

"I stayed out of your way. That ought to count for something."

"Thank you, Treasure Hunt," I said.

Dana just rolled her eyes.

I was so happy I wouldn't have minded thanking him if he had gotten in Dana's way. Though I neither ran nor danced back to the car, I was humming to myself happily. Sid and I finally had a name to work with.

Chapter Fifteen

As soon as the car door was shut and locked, I unzipped the bag to make it easier to talk to Sid.

"We have a name!" I crowed.

"We have a name! Now to see if the name matches our body."

That concluded the conversation portion of the drive home. Thanks to Sid having had his hand and cell phone in the bag with him, he could go online immediately and start digging up what he could on Annabelle Mitchell.

"It's her!" he announced just as we reached Pennycross town limits.

"Are you sure?"

"Oh yeah. Annabelle Mitchell, a resident of West Litchfield who worked at Bostock College, was reported missing the first week of December, ten years ago."

Within minutes of our arrival back at the house, Sid was back in his attic, tapping away at his computer while I looked over his shoulder blade. "This has got to be her," he said, showing me a news story from the *West Litchfield Register*.

> **"Police are seeking the public's help in locating a missing woman. Annabelle Mitchell, 36, is described as a white female with brown hair, standing five feet, five inches tall and weighing 140 pounds. Mitchell was last seen leaving her apartment in West Litchfield wearing a dark green parka and blue jeans, police say. She is an employee of Bostock College. Anyone with information is urged to contact the West Litchfield police."**

All of that matched both Charles's poetic description and Yo's more prosaic facts, and of course the timing and the employer cinched it. There was even a photo. It looked like a badly reproduced copy of a driver's license or work ID picture, but it was infinitely more than we'd had before.

"Hello, Rose," I said. I didn't really see either the lover or the frightened runaway Charles had described. She was just a normal-looking woman with slightly stooped shoulders.

I reread the news story. "The report is kind of skimpy."

"Not really," Sid said. "I've looked at a lot of these missing person announcements these past few days, and it's pretty standard. The only time they go into more detail is if it's a child or somebody with impaired faculties. Or if the family makes a fuss, of course."

I nodded, thinking about how much fuss I'd make if anybody in my family went missing. "She lived in West Litchfield, not Pennycross." West Litchfield was the next town over and wasn't considered as desirable a place to live, so housing prices were lower.

Sid said, "Now that we've got this, we can—"

"Before we do anything else, we need to show this to Charles and make absolutely sure that Annabelle Mitchell is his Rose."

"You're right," Sid said. "Do you want privacy for this?"

"Definitely not." If I was going to break Charles's heart, I wanted company. I got out my phone to text him.

GEORGIA: *Are you available?*

Charles responded by calling me. I knew he had to be anxious, but of course he attended to the amenities first. "Good afternoon, Georgia. I hope you're doing well."

"I'm fine, thank you, and I'll be more polite next time, but right now I may have some information. Does the name Annabelle Mitchell mean anything to you?"

"Not that I can recall."

"It might be Rose's real name. Annabelle Mitchell disappeared from West Litchfield around the time Rose showed up here, and her description matches what you told me about Rose and what Yo said about the remains."

"And Miss Mitchell never reappeared?"

"I'm still looking into that, but it doesn't seem so." I hesitated for a second. "Charles, I've got a picture of Annabelle to send you. Can tell me if she was Rose?"

"I'll be happy to take a look," he said mildly.

"Hold on." Sid texted me the link, which I then copied to forward to Charles. "I just sent it."

"I see it." There was a long silence.

"Charles?"

"I beg your pardon for the delay. I wanted to be completely certain. It's Rose."

I wasn't sure if this was good news or bad news for Charles, which meant I didn't know what to say.

"How did you find her?" he asked.

"I'm sorry, but I can't tell you. My source wants to stay confidential."

"I certainly wouldn't want you to violate that. Do you think this will help you find out what happened to Rose? Or rather, to Annabelle."

"I'm sure it will."

"Have you told the police?"

"Not yet. I wanted you to know first."

"That's quite thoughtful of you. Then you'll be calling them this evening?"

"Well, an anonymous tipster will be."

"Could you tell me, in the course of your investigation, have you found out anything more about Annabelle?"

"A little, and I might find out more." Or Sid might, given that he was busy doing something on his laptop. "Would you like me to send you what I've got so far?"

"Tomorrow will be soon enough. Not that I'm assuming you'll

continue to work tonight, I hasten to add. You've already done so much."

"I'll have more for you tomorrow," I said firmly.

"Thank you, Georgia."

"I know this is a stupid question, Charles, but are you okay?"

"I'm not entirely sure how I feel."

"Do you want to go to dinner or something?"

"You're very kind, but I think I would prefer to be alone tonight."

"Call if you need me."

"Thank you again," he said, and hung up.

Sid, who'd typed quietly while I was on the phone, said, "Are *you* okay?"

"I guess. I was so excited about finally having a name, and now I feel terrible. Maybe I should have broken it to him more gently."

"It's not like Charles wasn't already pretty sure that was Rose we found."

"There's a big difference between pretty sure and completely sure. Anyway, now he knows. So what are you doing?"

"Tracking down the digital footprint of Annabelle Mitchell."

"Does that mean you want to stay on the case rather than leave it to the police?"

"After what Treasure Hunt said this afternoon? Of course I do. We're way ahead of the cops and getting further ahead every minute."

"Only because we know who the dead woman is and they don't. Where's your burner phone? I should go ahead and call it in."

"Yeah, about that…"

"Did you use up the minutes? Or did you misplace it during your cleaning frenzy?"

"No, I've got plenty of minutes, and I know exactly where it is, but I was thinking. Georgia, do we have to tell the cops?"

"Of course we do."

"Why?"

"Because they need to know so they can investigate."

"Is it even a priority for them?"

"Sid, you know Louis isn't going to forget about a murder."

"Yeah, okay, but I don't see why we should give him our lead. We're the ones who figured out the carney connection."

"Which we wouldn't have been able to do if Charles hadn't told me the dates to look at. Had I let him go to the cops, they'd have gotten to Fenton's ahead of us."

"Maybe, maybe not. I mean, do you think Dana or Treasure Hunt would have told them anything?"

"Isn't that all the more reason to share the information?" I said.

"Okay, say we tell them and now that they have pictures of Annabelle Mitchell to flash around the neighborhood and a more definite date. What if somebody remembers seeing Charles in the vicinity of the Nichols house that month? What if there's trace evidence on Annabelle's clothing, something they can compare with Charles's DNA? That wouldn't make much of a Christmas present for him."

"I never thought about that." Hadn't Louis mentioned something about getting the clothes Annabelle had been wearing analyzed?

"Or how about this? What if somebody saw Annabelle going to the carnival and starts asking questions there? Getting Brownie's parents arrested won't do much for your reconciliation with him."

"I'm not letting a murderer get away to help my love life."

"I'm not asking you to. I'm just suggesting that we continue our investigation as long as we keep making progress and only pass on information to the police as a last resort."

"And this is purely to help our friends?"

"Not purely, but partially."

I thought about it. "Okay, we'll try it your way. But if we get stuck, you pull out the burner phone and we call the cops. Deal?"

"Deal!" He had me in mid-pinky swear before I could change my mind. Pinky swears are not taken lightly in the Thackery household.

Chapter Sixteen

Even though my parents had chased off all their graduate students before dinner, a move I suspect was in response to Andrew's multiple foot-in-mouth offenses from the week before, Sid decided to forgo joining us. Either he wanted to jump onto the case, or he had more shopping to do, or most likely, a little of both. Dinner table conversation avoided both dissertations and the morality of crossing a picket line, and the meatloaf was enjoyed by all.

After eating, cleaning, laundry, and catching up on some of the work I'd shoved aside to go to see the Fentons, I went back up to the attic to check on Sid's progress. "Did you find anything?"

"I found out why I never spotted a missing person report for Annabelle."

"We didn't have a name or the town she lived in until today."

"It shouldn't have mattered. I've gone through a bunch of sites that list missing persons for the whole state. Annabelle wasn't included on any of them. She wasn't even listed on the West Litchfield police department's site."

"She did disappear ten years ago."

"I found listings for people missing way longer than that. I don't think the police were looking very hard for her."

"So you didn't find anything?"

"Did I say that?"

"Sorry." Sid tends to drag things out, but I've found it's usually faster to let him tell stories his own way than to push.

"Next I went to see what I could find out about Annabelle elsewhere. Google gave me nothing but that one story about her disappearance and stories about other women named Annabelle Mitchell. So I went on to social media."

"Did you find the digital footprint of a gigantic hound?"

"More like the footprint of a teeny-weeny guinea pig. Annabelle's Facebook page looks like somebody showed her how to set it up about a year before she went missing, but then she never did anything with it. The only thing useful was her profile picture, which is much better than the one we had before, so I printed it out."

He handed it to me. It was the same woman, but she was smiling, and I saw a glimmer of what Charles had seen in her.

"So much for social media."

"Did I say that?" Sid asked again.

"Santa Claus doesn't want you to tease your friends, especially this close to Christmas."

"Santa doesn't like people rushing him either, which is why you have to wait until Christmas to open your presents." Before I could rebut, he said, "While Annabelle herself was not an active Facebooker, I did find a Facebook group dedicated to her."

"A what?"

He turned the screen so I could see. The heading on the window said, "Missing Annabelle Mitchell," and there were some snapshots of her, plus the profile photo Sid had printed out. "It was created about a month after Rose showed up in Pennycross, and though there were a fair number of posts at first, it's mostly gone dormant. It has a hundred members, but only three of them have posted in the last month, and there haven't been any new members in a couple of years."

"Then they haven't made the connection with the body we found?"

"Not that I can see. Why?"

"I've read about people with missing family members who spend years checking out every single dead body that matches the description of their loved ones in hopes of finding out what happened. That's a nightmare scenario if I've ever heard one."

"Agreed. Anyway, even though this group is mostly inactive now, there's a little more information about Annabelle, though I had to sift through a lot of posts to get it."

"This sounds like a good time to tell you how wonderful you are."

"If you must."

I struck an adoring pose, complete with clasped hands and fluttering eyelashes. "Sid, you're wonderful."

"Thank you, thank you." He bowed in his seat before going on. "The weird thing is that most of the posts are people talking about other cases. It's like an online community formed around missing persons. There are a few tips dating back to when the page was first created, but mostly it's theories and sympathy, plus the occasional troll comment. Can you imagine trolling when somebody is trying to find a missing relative?"

"I wish I couldn't, but I can."

He made an expression that clearly showed his disgust, even though he didn't have the benefit of the usual facial components. "Now we get to the meat of the matter. The admin, who created this group, is a woman named Lauri Biegler and she still posts occasionally." He clicked around a little. "This is Lauri's Facebook page, where I found something potentially useful. She graduated from Bostock, which is presumably how she knew Annabelle."

"She must have known her pretty well to go to the trouble of setting up a missing person page for her."

"My thought exactly. I think we've found our next person to talk to."

We spent a while noodling over how best to approach Lauri Biegler. Speaking to her in person was out of the question—according to Biegler's profile, she lived in Ohio. We couldn't call her because we didn't have a phone number. That left two choices: either post something publicly on the group or send a private message. We didn't want to go public, and Sid said a private message was iffy because not everybody accepts messages from people they don't know.

Finally we decided on a public message telling her that we'd sent a private message, and a private message asking her to get in touch.

"Should I use my account?" I asked. "Or do you want to use yours?"

"Georgia, what the patella are you thinking? What if this Lauri Biegler turns out to be Annabelle's killer?"

"Excuse me?"

"If somebody I wanted to kill had run off, I might very well start a Facebook group in order to crowdsource the search for her. And once I'd found the person, killed her, and buried her, I'd keep the page going for camouflage. Plus I'd monitor it in case somebody found the body or if any witnesses came forward so I could go after them, too."

"You know, you have a disturbing way of looking at things."

"Thank you."

"But since Lauri Biegler lives in Ohio, don't you think we'd be safe?"

"She *says* she lives in Ohio. My Facebook profile says I have a cat and eyeballs. Everybody lies on the internet."

I still thought Sid was erring on the side of paranoia. "If neither you nor I can post a message, how are we going to get in touch with the woman?"

"I have several accounts under fake names. Well, technically they're all fake names, but one is for my real personality while the others were created for just such an eventuality."

I had to admit that he was thorough, though I wondered what other plans he'd made for "just such an eventuality."

Sid, using an account for an eyeball-equipped cat owner named Art Taylor, signed in and posted the following:

> *I may have some information about Annabelle Mitchell, but I'd rather not post publicly. Would you be willing to*

> *communicate via private messages or by phone? I've sent my phone number by private message.*

For the private message, he sent the number for his burner phone.

I said, "You realize that the downside of this approach is that we're going to have to wait for her to respond to us."

"Don't worry, Georgia," Sid said stoutly. "I will sit by the computer with the phone in my hand, day and night, until we hear from her. I won't even—"

The phone rang.

We'd already decided that Sid would do the talking, something he rarely got to do in our cases, so he answered and put the phone on speaker so I could listen in.

"Hello?"

"Yes, I was given this number to call. To whom am I speaking?"

"Art Taylor," Sid lied. "And you are?"

"My name is Lauri Biegler. I moderate the Find Annabelle Mitchell Facebook page. You said you have information about her?"

"I may have. I'm trying to see what I can find out about a woman who seems to match the woman on your page."

"Do you know where she is?" Biegler asked excitedly. "Do you know what happened to her?"

"First let me confirm that I've got the right woman. You say Annabelle Mitchell worked at Bostock College, correct?"

"Right."

"Were you one of her students?"

"One of her students? Maybe we're not talking about the same woman after all. The Annabelle Mitchell I knew was a custodian, not an instructor."

Sid looked confused, and I was, too, until I remembered what Yo had said about Annabelle's remains showing signs of manual labor and time spent on her feet. That matched a custodian a lot better than it did a college professor.

"Actually, I wasn't sure what Ms. Mitchell's position was, only that she was employed at Bostock, so it could be the same woman."

"What do you know about her?"

This was tricky. We wanted to find out what we could about Annabelle, but we didn't want to either imply that we were the police or say anything that would encourage Biegler to talk to the police.

Sid said, "First let me say that I'm looking into the case on an unofficial basis. I'm not a cop."

She gave a little snort. "I figured that. The cops never did care about Annabelle, not even when she first went missing. That's why I kept the Facebook page going. I live out of state, and I'm still more concerned about her than the cops or the college ever were."

She sounded angry, which might make it easier for us. Sid went on. "Okay then. I just wanted you to know that I don't have any official standing. I'm more of a concerned citizen."

Even that was stretching a point because Sid wasn't technically a citizen. The man he'd been, back when he was still traditionally alive, was American, but Sid's legal status was ambiguous at best.

Biegler said, "Oh, like in *The Skeleton Crew*."

Sid and I looked at one another.

"Beg pardon," he said.

"That book, *The Skeleton Crew*, about amateur sleuths solving cold cases?"

I had no idea what she was talking about, but Sid said, "Right, like that."

"So what have you found out?"

Sid looked solemn, and his tone reflected that. "I'm sorry, I know this isn't what you want to hear, but a body has been found that we think is Annabelle Mitchell."

"Oh," she said in a small voice. "I guess I knew she was dead. I mean, why else would she disappear the way she did?"

"Can you tell me about her?" Sid said gently. "There's not a lot of information on your Facebook page." When she didn't answer right away, he said, "Maybe it would be better if we spoke another night."

"No, I'd like to talk about her. I've been trying to get people to listen for years." I heard her blow her nose. "I met Annabelle during my freshman year. She was the custodian for my dorm. At first, I didn't notice her much. Kids can be self-centered, and as long as the place was clean, I never thought about who did the cleaning. I found out later that even though I didn't pay any attention to her, she was paying attention to me.

"About a month into the semester, I got the worst case of homesickness you can imagine. I hadn't made many friends on campus, and I was missing my girlfriend and my family and my dog so bad it hurt. I got so depressed that I didn't leave my room for three days straight other than to go to the bathroom. I didn't eat or bathe or even get dressed. I figured nobody cared about me anyway, so why bother?"

"That sounds awful," Sid said. Given his situation, he'd never been away from home without me, so I think Lauri's experiences horrified him that much more.

"One afternoon, there was a knock on my door. I yelled for whoever it was to go away, but when she kept knocking, I finally opened the door, and there was Annabelle with a pizza, a salad, and a bottle of soda. In fact, it was a pepperoni and pineapple pizza, a salad with creamy Italian dressing, and Diet Dr Pepper. All my favorites.

"She said, 'I thought you could use something to eat,' and I just started bawling. She hugged me, even though I must have smelled terrible, and stayed with me until I stopped crying and ate half the pizza and most of the salad. We talked and talked and talked. Well, I talked. Annabelle just listened. Afterward I felt so much better. It wasn't until she'd pulled some chocolate chip cookies out of a bag and apologized for not knowing what kind I liked that I even thought to ask how she'd known what to bring me.

"It turned out that she'd seen what trash I dumped in the can outside my door, and when she realized I hadn't left the room for so long, she decided to bring me food. Here I didn't even know her name, but she knew what kind of pizza I liked. Can you imagine?"

"She sounds special," Sid said, his voice choked up. He's a sentimental guy, and I had no doubt that he'd have had tears in his eyes if he'd had either eyes or a mechanism for creating tears.

"Anyway, I started finding my footing on campus after that, and even though I still got homesick, I was never that miserable again. Plus Annabelle checked on me regularly. I found out I wasn't the first student she'd helped, not by a long shot. Cupcakes for birthdays, tissues and chocolate for breakups, chicken soup for colds. She was the best. Until one day in my junior year, she disappeared."

"This was around Thanksgiving?" Sid asked.

"I guess, but I don't know exactly when. I'd been back from Thanksgiving break for about a week when I noticed a different custodian on our floor and asked where Annabelle was. The new custodian didn't want to talk about it, and neither did the head of the department, so it took me a while to find out that nobody knew where she was. That's when I went to the police to fill out a missing person report. Annabelle didn't have any family, so there was nobody else to do it."

"And the police didn't have any luck finding her?"

"I don't think they even tried," she said indignantly. "First the cops in Pennycross said I had to go to West Litchfield because that's where she lived. Then some West Litchfield cops came to the dorm and asked a bunch of us questions about Annabelle, and then they spoke to her boss and coworkers. But they never came back again, and as far as I know, neither police department did anything else. I got the local paper to print a story about it, hoping it would generate some leads, but as far as I know, that didn't do anything either. That's when I decided to create the Facebook group."

"I went through the posts—" Sid started to say.

"I'm sorry you wasted your time," Biegler said. "Nothing useful ever came out of it. At first it was 'thoughts and prayers' posts and a couple of psychics who wanted me to pay them to investigate. After a while, it was just people posting links to their missing person pages. I don't know why I kept it up, but every time I started to take it down, I'd think that maybe, maybe..." She blew her nose again. "I guess it was a good thing I stuck with it since it's how you found me."

Sid looked at me as if to ask what he should say next, and I shrugged, letting him know I didn't have any ideas. He said, "Ms. Biegler, here's the situation. The body I mentioned earlier was found in Pennycross. There was no ID found, but I have reason to believe it was Annabelle Mitchell."

"Has she been dead all this time?"

"It looks as if she died no more than a month after you last saw her."

"How did she die?"

"I'm not sure the police have issued a report yet," Sid said. I knew he just couldn't bring himself to tell Lauri that Annabelle had been strangled. "The police also don't know who she is."

"How did you find out?"

"I can't tell you," Sid said. "Two people have given me confidential information, and I'm trying to keep them out of this. But you might appreciate knowing that she met somebody during that last month, somebody she cared for deeply and who cared for her, too."

"Really? You're not just trying to make me feel better?"

"Really. Now I'm going to ask you a favor. I haven't spoken to the police, and don't want to quite yet. Are you comfortable with that?"

"You bet I am! They never cared about Annabelle. I found out what would be necessary to ID her body if they had to, and I told the police they should grab her hairbrush or her toothbrush or her um...dirty underwear to save so they could have something to compare DNA with in case they found, you know, a body. But they just blew me off."

"Maybe they were planning to use dental or medical records."

"For that, they'd have to get permission from next of kin, and Annabelle told me she didn't have any family."

Biegler had really done her research. I was impressed. I was also wondering how we'd be able to link the body to Annabelle Mitchell without bringing either Charles or Sue Weedon into it. Even if I sent the police my anonymous tip, how could they establish it was Annabelle we'd found?

Biegler said, "What are you going to do next?"

"It's a long shot, but I'm going to try to figure out what happened to Annabelle."

"You mean who killed her?"

"That's the plan."

"Art, you are the first person to give a single hoot about what happened to Annabelle in all these years. Even the other people she took care of at Bostock have forgotten about her. So you go ahead and keep those secrets for those other people. I won't tell a soul, other than my wife."

"Thank you, Lauri. I'll let you know when we know more. And don't take down the Facebook page yet. Just in case."

"I won't."

Sid hung up.

"Why did you want her to keep the page up?" I asked.

"I'm not sure—it just seems like the killer might be following it out of guilt or caution. Taking it down might alert them that something is up."

"Then you don't think Lauri killed Annabelle?"

"Do you?"

"Anything's theoretically possible, but no, I don't think so."

"Me either. Unfortunately, that leaves us without any suspects."

"We just found out Annabelle's real name this afternoon," I pointed out.

"True." Sid steepled his hands. "Given what we've heard today, what do we know?"

"We know Charles has great taste in women. Annabelle must have been a sweetheart. Also observant, to realize that Lauri was hurting and what would cheer her up. She sounds like a good worker, too."

"But the college didn't make much of a fuss about her disappearing. Never having been in the work force, I don't know how it's usually done, but it seems as if they should have taken notice."

"You're right, that is odd," I said. "I mean, I don't know that anyplace I've worked would freak out about an adjunct disappearing, but according to what Lauri said, Annabelle had worked at Bostock for at least a couple of years."

"That's something to check into," Sid said. He caught me yawning, then looked at the clock. "Coccyx, Georgia, it's late. You go to bed and let me putter around and see what I can find."

I would have argued the point with him, but I couldn't get a sentence out before I started yawning again, so I left him clattering away on his computer. I didn't envy Sid much of his lifestyle, but sometimes I wished I could get back some of the time I spent asleep.

Chapter Seventeen

Bostock had scheduled a meeting for all adjunct faculty at lunchtime on Tuesday, and thanks to my missing one shuttle and having to wait for another, I just barely made it on time. I would have been stuck in the nosebleed section at the back of the tiered lecture hall had Charles not been saving me a spot. When I made it to the third row and slid into my seat, I was surprised to find that Brownie was there, too, sitting on the other side of me from Charles. After an awkward pause, at least on my part, we collided for an even more awkward kiss on the cheek.

I gratefully turned to Charles. "Thanks for saving me a seat. How are you doing?"

He smiled faintly. "I'm fine, thank you."

I didn't believe him, but a packed lecture hall wasn't the place for a personal conversation.

"As for you, Dr. Mannix, I don't want you to think that I'm not glad to see you, but what are you doing at Bostock?"

"I was supposed to meet Charles for lunch, but he got his schedule confused, so when I showed up and he said he had to come to this meeting, I talked him into bringing me along."

"Really?" I said, when what I was thinking was more along the lines of *What the patella?* For Charles to forget a lunch engagement was shocking, and I was glad I'd already planned to check on him.

Brownie kept going as if Charles forgot lunch dates all the time. "I'm looking forward to this. I never could resist a contentious faculty meeting, and it's even better when it doesn't affect me."

"Are you that sure this one is going to be contentious?"

"Are you kidding? I just wish I'd brought a popper to park outside. I could have made a killing selling popcorn and candy apples for people to eat during the show."

"Maybe you do belong at a business school."

"It's true, I am a strong believer in the power of entrepreneurship. If I worked here, I could bring in my parents to lecture."

"I would pay to see that."

"With my parents? Everybody involved would have to pay to see it. They don't do freebies."

A moment later, six people came in through the door at the front of the hall. Or rather, two groups of three. The trios were careful to stand on opposite sides of the podium.

"That's unexpected," Charles said.

"What?" I asked.

"The woman in the pinstripe suit is Provost Kozlov, and the woman and man next to her are the Director of Human Resources and Director of Recruiting respectively. They're the ones who called this meeting. The other three women, the ones who are pointedly not looking at the provost's party, are the professors who've been leading the union efforts."

"I guess I'm not the only gate crasher," Brownie said.

"So it seems."

After consultation with her associates, Provost Kozlov stepped to the podium and tapped on the microphone to make sure it was on. "I think we should get started now, if people can take their seats."

The rumble of conversation in the hall died down.

"I wanted to make you aware of some issues concerning Bostock. As some of you may have heard, we are in the midst of renegotiating an agreement with our tenured and contract faculty members, and while talks are still proceeding, the process is not going as quickly as we'd hoped."

The most irate looking member of the trio of union proponents openly scoffed.

Provost Kozlov pretended she hadn't heard her and went on. "I've just been informed that since the various arms of support staff are not involved in the negotiations, they do not intend to take part in a strike, should one occur." I could tell that she was trying not to smirk at the union people, but she couldn't quite manage it, especially when they showed their own angry surprise so openly. "Our assumption is that adjunct faculty, who are also not involved in this issue, will meet with their classes as usual."

There were a lot of murmured comments from the adjuncts in the hall, but they weren't loud enough for me to determine the direction in which most people were tilting. Brownie leaned over to whisper, "#NotAllFaculty."

Professor Lefebre, a professor in the English department who had an office near my cubicle, said, "If I might speak to that point, Provost Kozlov?"

Provost Kozlov stepped aside, and Professor Lefebre took her place. She started by smiling warmly at the people seated in the hall. "Colleagues, I'm afraid I disagree with Provost Kozlov. Then again, what is academia without disagreement?" She smiled again, and I think she was going for collegial that time. "I believe that an issue that affects one professor at Bostock affects us all, and as fellow academics, we all welcome the chance to show support for one another. In that spirit, I would ask that all faculty members, even those not directly affected by the contract under negotiation, respect our efforts to improve working conditions."

More murmurs, and Brownie added, "#LibertyEquality Fraternity."

"Shush," I said, "or it'll be off with your head."

He just grinned.

Provost Kozlov retook the podium. "While I can certainly understand adjunct faculty members being in sympathy with the aims of the union, I feel I must remind you all that when accepting employment at Bostock, you signed contracts that define your obligations and the penalties for not meeting those obligations."

The resulting murmurs were definitely angrier. I wasn't happy about the intimidation technique myself, and when Brownie said, "#ThreatsRUs," I didn't try to quiet him.

Professor Lefebre reached for the microphone, but the provost maintained her hold. "In fact, if our Bostock adjunct faculty members wish to step into classrooms while the usual professors are on strike, so as to maintain continuity for our student body, our Human Resources department would be happy to talk to you." The head of HR waved at us cheerily. "The pay rate will be higher than usual to make up for the extra workload and short notice, and speaking as one who celebrates December holidays, bonus cash at this time of year is always welcome."

"#WeLoveScabs," was Brownie's contribution, and I heard snickers from the people who were close enough to hear him.

Professor Lefebre gave up on the microphone and projected her voice like the experienced speaker she was. "Colleagues, though I certainly agree that compensation for academics is rarely what it should be, I would be remiss if I didn't remind you that while this contract will not benefit you at the present time, it could well benefit you in the future, should you be chosen for a tenure track position."

"#DontBeAScab," Brownie said.

Lefebre went on. "Remember that even if you stay part of the adjunct faculty, we will remain your colleagues, not just here, but throughout your academic career, no matter where that career takes you."

"#WeNeverForget. #WeHaveConnections."

The volume of the voices in the hall was well on its way to becoming a roar, and the two parties at the front of the hall started talking at one another with furious gestures.

I just sat there, getting angrier and angrier. I don't take kindly to threats, and getting them from both sides made me want to throw something. Madison had asked me what I thought about the situation, and I hadn't been able to tell her, but now I knew.

I raised my hand, and when that went unnoticed, I stood up and waited. Charles and Brownie started hushing the people around us until finally Provost Kozlov noticed me. "Yes, Ms...." She looked at her companions, but it was clear that neither of them knew my name.

"It's Doctor," I said. "Doctor Georgia Thackery, and I've been working at Bostock for over three months. I realize you can't learn the names of all the adjuncts here, but your lack of recognition reinforces the point I'm about to make."

The union members nodded emphatically.

"What about you union people?" I asked. "Do any of you know what I teach?"

Their faces went blank, and finally Lefebre shook her head.

"Then you're helping make my point, too. I'm in English. Your department, Dr. Lefebre. In fact, my desk is on the same corridor as your office. I'm surprised that you've never seen me working there, since adjunct cubicles don't have doors or even real walls."

She looked more annoyed than embarrassed.

"This brings me to my point. Nobody in administration sees me as a valued employee, and none of the tenured faculty see me as a fellow academic. I'm just an adjunct. Temporary. Forgettable. Replaceable." I paused to let my words sink in. "I want to tell you a story. A married couple I know were in the middle of a nasty divorce. They had a bedroom set in the guest bedroom that neither of them really cared about, but when it was time to divide up their property, suddenly that bedroom set was the most important thing in the world to them because it was another bargaining chip in their dispute. Once the divorce was finalized, the winner stuck that bedroom set back in the guest bedroom and never thought about it until it became useful once more. I think that's how you people see me, how you see all of us adjuncts.

"I'm here to tell you that I'm not furniture, and I'm not going to let myself be used as a bargaining chip. I can't speak for my fellow adjuncts—neither the union nor the administration have let us band together in any meaningful way—but I will speak for myself. Provost Kozlov, as much as I would love a chance for a future with Bostock, I won't do it at the expense of my academic colleagues. I will continue to work the hours for which I'm contracted, but I will not step one foot into another professor's classroom to make it easier on you. Professor Lefebre, while I respect what you're doing for the tenured faculty, it's unfair of you to ask me to walk a picket line and miss paychecks to help you get benefits I've spent my entire career dreaming of. In short," I said, looking from one group to the other, "I will do my job. Settling this contract is your job."

I sat, partially because I was finished saying what I had to say, but mostly because my knees were about to give out. All members of the warring factions were staring at me, but if they'd had any rebuttal to offer, it would have been drowned out by the applause from the rest of the adjuncts.

Charles was beaming at me as proudly as if he'd written my script himself, and Brownie was laughing in delight. At least I hoped it was in delight. Provost Kozlov and Professor Lefebre stepped away to confer, then came back and eventually quieted the crowd. Provost Kozlov took the podium again.

"I think we can all agree that Doctor Thackery's remarks have given us food for thought, and I assure you that whatever decision you make regarding the strike, it will have no affect on your future employment here." She stepped back and Professor Lefebre took her place.

"I echo Provost Kozlov's feelings. The union recognizes that adjunct faculty members are in an uncomfortable position and that they must feel free to make the decisions that are right for them. We will respect those decisions."

Provost Kozlov took the podium back one more time, but only to adjourn the meeting.

I think that's when I finally took a breath. I hadn't really thought I'd be fired on the spot, but years of being employed at the whims of one college or another hadn't exactly reassured me about the sanctity of my career.

"Well said, Georgia," Charles said.

"#Don'tTreadOnMe," Brownie added.

Other adjuncts—some of whom I'd met but others I'd never even seen before—came to compliment me and to offer handshakes and pats on the back. Not that everybody loved my outburst, of course. While Provost Kozlov's party had beat a hasty retreat once she ended the meeting, the union trio was still talking up front, and Lefebre kept shooting unfriendly glances in my direction. I also heard disgruntled comments from fellow adjuncts on both sides of the divide who'd wanted all of us swayed to their opinion.

I could live with all of that.

Chapter Eighteen

We three were among the last in the lecture hall, and when we were nearly alone, Brownie said, "That exceeded my wildest expectations. Georgia, your speech is going to go down in adjunct history."

"Thank you," I said, "but I don't think so."

"Hey, who's the historian here? Charles, back me up."

"It was remarkable, and I think it likely that word will spread," he said.

"Anybody up for a celebratory lunch?" Brownie asked. "I'm buying."

Charles consulted his pocket watch. "As much as I wish I could accept your gracious invitation, unfortunately I have a class to teach in a few minutes. Again Brownie, please accept my most sincere apologies. I cannot imagine what came over me to cause me to neglect cancelling our lunch."

"Don't worry about it, Charles. We'll reschedule."

"You're very gracious."

I said, "Speaking of scheduling, Charles, do you have time to discuss our special project later today?" I was being circumspect because though Brownie had guessed that Charles was involved in Sid's and my investigation, I wasn't sure Charles would be happy to find that out. As for the *special project* stuff, a murder investigation certainly qualified as a special project.

"Will you be around campus this afternoon?" he asked. "Say in an hour and a half?"

"I can do that. Where would you like to meet?"

"Perhaps at the Stockyard for coffee?"

I was about to accept when Brownie said, "Georgia, have you had lunch?"

"I haven't, actually."

"Then how about a two-adjunct lunch, and you can talk to Charles afterward? I'm still buying."

"That sounds like an offer that's too good to refuse." If Provost Kozlov did find an excuse to fire me, it might be my last restaurant meal for a while.

The Stockyard, the campus burger joint, was in a nearby building, one that was close enough that it wasn't worth waiting for the shuttle, even with snow flurries falling. Still, it was cold and windy enough that Brownie and I didn't try to talk as we walked as quickly as possible to the place.

The pine fixtures and branding irons on the walls were presumably supposed to evoke a Texas mood but did nothing to hide the years' worth of initials carved into the tabletops. Since it was a little late for lunch, we got through the line quickly with our bacon cheeseburgers and fries, and even found a corner table where we weren't likely to be overheard.

"That was quite a meeting," Brownie said. "It was way better than the one at McQuaid."

"What was that one about?"

"Same topic. The triad of union organizers stopped by the adjunct building yesterday afternoon to bring us coffee, donuts, and solidarity."

"Seriously?"

"They said that they're ninety-five percent sure that they aren't going to be able to come to terms with admin, so they're making plans for a strike. They'd heard Bostock is looking to hire... Well, they called it *alternate adjunct assistants* rather than *scabs*, but the subtext was definitely scabby. Plus they played the don't-cross-us-or-we'll-blackball-you card."

"Yikes. How did you guys respond?"

"Pick a reaction, any reaction, and somebody was loudly

expressing it. Yo Jacobs is ready to grab all the bonus teaching hours she can get, Bob Hewitt was furious about being threatened, Sara Weiss is afraid to rock the boat because somebody somewhere said something that makes her think she might get tenure someday, and so on."

"It was just Bostock people, right, not anybody from McQuaid?"

"Actually, they brought a few McQuaid professors to add weight to the threat." When I winced, he quickly added, "But not your parents. In fact, there wasn't anybody from the English department."

That was a relief. Overall, McQuaid professors were more aware of the adjunct lifestyle than most, and my parents were a big part of the reason why. They never missed a chance to tell their colleagues about the problems faced by those on the other side of the tenure track. "You didn't mention your reaction."

"I'm still thinking it over," he said. "And on to a more pleasant subject...Okay, maybe not a more pleasant subject but at least a different one. I hear you met Sue yesterday afternoon."

"I did. I take it that you know her."

"Yes and no. I generally meet everybody in the show, but people come and go a lot. I remember Sue from when she was with us years ago, but her boyfriend was kind of a jerk, so I mostly steered clear. Later on, when she kicked him to the curb and then went freelance, she'd be around the show a few weeks every year, but we didn't often cross paths. I always liked her, though. What do you think of her?"

"An interesting lady with an interesting story."

"I want you to know that you actually heard it before I did. Mom and Dad didn't tell me about Annabelle Mitchell until last night at dinner."

"Really?"

"Carnies have elevated discretionary instincts and have elevated both turning a blind eye and keeping secrets into art forms. It's a reasonable adaptation to living in tight quarters, but it does cause its own problems." He took a bite of his burger. "Did you tell Charles what she said? I was wondering if that's why he forgot our lunch date."

"I did, and you're probably right. He was already pretty sure that Rose was dead, but having it confirmed really shook him up. You know, I've never known him to date anybody. Rose must have been the love of his life."

"It's tough to meet the woman you want to make a future with and then have her slip away," Brownie said.

I nodded automatically, then realized what he'd said. Part of me wanted to probe that potentially emotionally fraught remark, but part of me was scared to know what he'd say if I did. So I took a deep breath, metaphorically pulled up my big girl panties…and chickened out. "I did find out some other news for him," I said, and told Brownie about Lauri Biegler's encounters with Annabelle and her frustration with the police's inaction.

"It sounds like something hinky was going on with the West Litchfield police," Brownie said.

"I know, and I'm going to try to find out more. I also want to talk to the janitorial staff and see if anybody here still remembers Annabelle."

"From ten years ago?"

"Have you got a better idea?"

He considered it as he dipped a French fry into ketchup. "Not really, but I'll give it some thought. This sleuthing stuff is fascinating."

"It's not the most normal hobby, I admit."

"That's okay. Normal doesn't really appeal to me." He looked at his watch. "I better be going, but Georgia…"

I waited for a few seconds as he paused. "Yes?"

"Would you like to go out to dinner? With me, I mean?"

He sounded as nervous as the first boy who'd asked me out when I was in high school, though Brownie was much better looking.

"I would like that very much."

He smiled. "Good. I've really missed you."

"I've missed you, too." I was pretty sure he wanted to kiss me, and I was pretty sure I wanted to kiss him back, and since I was no longer in high school, I leaned forward enough to make my interest clear. He met me in the middle. It was a very nice kiss. So was the next one.

When we finally pulled back, we saw Charles was standing next to us.

Charles knew a little of Brownie's and my romantic trials and tribulations but was far too well-bred to comment other than to lift one eyebrow the slightest amount. "How was lunch?" he asked.

"Delicious," Brownie said.

Brownie smiled at me, I smiled back, and Charles smiled at both of us. In fact, several students, the serving staff, and a random security guard seemed to be smiling at us, too, but perhaps I was just being self-conscious.

Once Brownie was gone, Charles offered to get me a refill on my soda, which I was happy to accept because it gave me a chance to wipe the silly grin off of my face before I talked to him about a woman he'd loved and lost. Not that he would ever begrudge my happiness, but it just didn't seem appropriate.

When Charles returned, I took a good long swallow of my drink and started in on what Sid and I had learned about Annabelle. Sid had printed copies of all the photos we had, and Charles kept looking at them as I spoke.

"She really sounds like a wonderful person," I said when I came to the end.

"She was, Georgia. You would have liked her very much. May I keep these?"

"Of course."

"Thank you." He jogged the pictures together and carefully placed them in his breast pocket. "I've checked the online news sites several times today, but I didn't see any mention of Annabelle's body being identified. Do the police require more information to confirm your tip? Or is this one of those instances where they hold back information to aid in the investigation?

"About that…I never called them, Charles. If it's all the same to you, I think I'm going to keep Annabelle's name quiet for the time being. I'm a little worried that they'll find something that leads back to you. There could be forensic evidence or maybe somebody saw you in the neighborhood all those years ago and might have their memory jogged if the murder is tied to a specific date. Besides, even though I trust the Pennycross police, especially Louis Raymond, it sure looks like the cops in West Litchfield fell down on the job. I think I've got at least as much a chance of solving this as they do, and it'll be easier if I don't have to work around them."

"That seems eminently reasonable, but I don't know how I can repay your efforts on my behalf, and on Rose's. Or rather, on Annabelle's."

"That's what friends are for. And I wouldn't have been able to get as far as I have if it weren't for the details you told me in your letter. That must have been difficult to write."

"Revisiting that golden time was hardly a sacrifice. Is there anything else I can do to help?"

"Now that we know Annabelle was a custodian here, I'd like to talk to some of the other custodians and see if anybody knew her. Do you know anybody in that department?"

"I'm not sure that I do, but I will see if I can find any connections."

After that, he insisted on walking me to the shuttle bus stop. Charles is usually a bit too reserved for me to consider showing physical signs of affection, but when I saw the shuttle arriving, I said, "Charles, would you like a hug?"

"Yes, Georgia, I believe that I would."

For somebody who doesn't hug often, he had a very firm embrace.

Chapter Nineteen

Rather than go back to my cubicle so late in the day, I went home to work for the rest of the afternoon. My parents had been invited to a Christmas party that night, and as Mom dragged him out the door, Phil quoted a lengthy list of meals I could defrost for dinner. They all sounded good, but before I could open the freezer, Madison said, "Can we order pizza? G-Dad is a terrific cook, but I'm grease-deprived!"

I wasn't, thanks to that bacon cheeseburger, but I couldn't disappoint my daughter. I called for a delivery of a large pepperoni and a Greek salad. After making sure there were no grad students working or sleeping in odd corners of the house, we pulled the blinds and locked all the doors so Sid could come join us.

To complete our debauch, we eschewed the dining room table and ate in the living room while watching *The Year Without a Santa Claus* and *Santa Claus is Comin' to Town*. I felt like the world's oldest teenager.

After we demolished the pizza, leaving nothing for foraging grad students, we left the TV playing in the background while Madison pulled out a book she was reading for school and I caught Sid up on the events at Bostock.

"That college keeps cropping up in this case," Sid said. "Don't you think it's an odd coincidence that we find the body of a woman who worked at Bostock, while you're working at Bostock, just at the time when Bostock is having labor issues?"

"Not really. I've been in and around academia for mumble-mumble years now—"

"Georgia, I know how old you are."

"So do I. I just don't feel like stopping to add up all the years right now." Before he could add them up for me, I went on. "As I was saying, I've been in and around academia for a long time and have never had dealings with a college that didn't have problems. Bizarre bequests, budget shortfalls, lawsuits, and who knows what. I bet we'd have found some complication no matter where Annabelle worked. As for me being there myself, Pennycross has two colleges. I've worked at both."

"Then you don't think all this happening at this time of year is kind of a Christmas miracle?"

"Sid, have you been watching Hallmark Channel holiday movies while I'm at work?"

"I may have seen one or two," he said, not meeting my eyes. "Speaking of Bostock, tell me more about the place."

"You saw it when you came to work with me."

"We went from parking deck, to shuttle bus, to classroom, to shuttle bus, to parking deck. This does not make for a well-rounded view of a campus. I wasn't even by the window in the shuttle."

"If there'd been a window seat available, I'd have taken it."

"But there wasn't, and I don't have a good mental picture."

"Okay, here's what I know. It's a four-year college, so they've got a core curriculum, but their focus is on business. It's not nearly as old as McQuaid, and some of the teachers have a chip on their shoulders about it. Others feel superior because they provide practical information as opposed to academic knowledge."

"And?"

"And what? I've only been there a few months. As a place to work it's about average. Was there something special you wanted to know?"

"Not really, I just want to know more about Annabelle's environment. I can do a lot of research online, but there's no substitute for being there in person."

"Knowing how thoroughly you research, you probably know

as much about the campus as I do. They don't give campus tours to adjuncts, Sid. Those are for wealthy alumni and prospective students."

"Prospective students?" he said speculatively.

As one, we turned to look at Madison, who had been receiving brochures, catalogs, emails, and letters from colleges ever since she took the PSAT.

"Oh, Madison?" I said.

"Hmm?"

"How would you like to tour a college?"

"What college?"

"Bostock."

"Didn't I just hear you say that it's mostly a business school?"

I nodded.

"I'll pass. You know I'm a liberal arts kind of gal." She went back to her book.

I tried again. "Madison, how would you like to help me and Sid with a case?"

She closed the book. "You know, you really should have led with that."

Chapter Twenty

Like most colleges, Bostock provided year-round guided tours of the campus as part of their never-ending recruiting efforts. December wasn't exactly a prime time, so when I went online to see if any tour slots were available, I was able to sign us up for one the very next day. That meant that on Wednesday, I left work, picked Madison up at the high school, stopped by the house, and headed back to Bostock.

I'd only booked seats for two, but then again, they weren't going to know Sid was accompanying us. Or at least part of him was—his skull ready to observe everything from the confines of the sugar skull bag, and his hand was holding his phone in case he wanted to text me.

For once I could avoid the parking deck and the shuttle because guests got to park at the visitor's center. When we went inside, Madison and I were met by a familiar-looking man in his midthirties with blond, fiercely trimmed hair and a sport coat over his Bostock sweatshirt.

"Hi, I'm Edward Humphries, and I'm in charge of recruiting here at Bostock. You must be the Thackerys." He looked at me curiously as he handed us name tag stickers and brightly printed info packets. "Have we met, Ms. Thackery?"

Now I remembered where I'd seen him. He'd been part of the provost's contingent at the adjunct meeting. Since I didn't know his views on my speech, I decided not to draw his attention to it, and instead said, "I'm an adjunct here, so you may have seen me on campus. I've been telling my daughter all about the school, and she just had to come visit. I'd have shown her around myself, but I didn't want my enthusiasm to sway her too much." I patted Madison's shoulder. "Kids need to make their own decisions."

"Absolutely—I wish all of our parents felt that way. Now is it Madison, or do you prefer Maddie or Mad?"

"Madison is fine. You'll know when I'm mad."

He chuckled. "What are you interested in studying, Madison?"

"I'm still undecided," she said, "but I definitely want something in business. I mean, why would I go to college if I couldn't get a job afterward? Am I right?"

We all chuckled that time, and I reflected that Madison's numerous roles in school plays were paying off in a way I had never expected.

"Well, you'll find plenty of great programs here in all the business disciplines." He checked his watch. "Shall we get started?"

"Are we getting a private tour?" I asked.

"As matter of fact, you are. We don't get many prospective students right before Christmas, especially not at this time of day. That's also why you're getting me as a guide instead of one of our students."

"Now I feel guilty about dragging you away from your desk."

"Not to worry. It's always a pleasure to talk to a prospective student about the Bostock Difference."

Apparently, the *Bostock Difference* was their recruiting slogan—it was all over the info packet he'd given us and printed on the scarf he wrapped around his neck before we left the building.

One Bostock difference I'd noticed since coming to work there was that the campus was much larger than most of the schools where I'd taught. The buildings were spread out over gently rolling hills, which is why the shuttle bus system was so important. It was scenic, but since it was thirty degrees that day, I was relieved when we walked outside and saw a shuttle waiting for us at the curb.

"Business is all about efficiency," Humphries said, "and that means getting where you need to go in a hurry. Joe here is going to drive us around campus."

Joe and I had a nodding acquaintance, meaning that we'd never exchanged anything more than nods. We did so once again as the three of us climbed on board. When Humphries cleared his throat pointedly, Joe pasted on a smile and said, "Welcome! I hope you're ready to hear all about the Bostock Difference."

With just two of us, it seemed silly to sit in the same seat, so Madison and I sat on opposite sides of the aisle. That left me room to put the sugar skull bag next to the window. The bag was moving slightly, so I could tell Sid was already wiggling around to look at everything.

Though Sid always said he was perfectly content with his life with us, even if it was mostly spent in the house, he got the biggest kick out of things that were mundane to the rest of us. Not only was he excited about seeing Bostock, but he was even enjoying riding a shuttle bus.

I admit I didn't pay much attention to the spiel Humphries rattled off as we drove away from the visitor's center and past a selection of classroom buildings, most of which he described as having state-of-the-art facilities and design. I didn't know about that, since the equipment in my classrooms was fairly standard, but it was a handsome campus, heavy on brick and with enough trees to decorate without obscuring. We stopped frequently so we could walk through a couple of classroom buildings, view an obviously staged dorm room, stick our heads inside the library, and visit various other points of interest. We ended up at the student center, where Humphries gave us hot chocolate and cookies in a private room and promised to tell us about the biggest Bostock Difference of all.

"It's been said that the only way to learn about business is to do business," he said, "and that's what happens here. By the middle of sophomore year, each student will be ready to go to work with a vetted business plan for a product or service that meets a need here on campus. There are businesses that do student laundry, run errands, and deliver groceries. We have a co-op store for selling just about anything a student needs or wants, two restaurants, and even a bar." He pointed to Madison's info packet. "Our recruiting materials? Designed and written by students. Those cookies you're eating? Baked by students. The shuttle bus we were just in? Driven, owned, and maintained by students. They provide on-campus transportation and drive students to Pennycross for shopping, movies, and special events. It's called Bus-Stock Shuttles."

He paused as if hoping for another chuckle in appreciation of the clever title.

"How could students afford to pay for buses?" I asked.

"Bostock provides business loans, which have to be repaid by graduation, which means students are very careful about setting goals and working out how to meet them. They can choose to create a sole proprietorship, a partnership, or a corporation. They can even acquire an existing business from a graduating senior. Several companies are on their third set of owners, and a couple are even older."

He paused for us to express our admiration and Madison played her part with vim and vigor before asking, "Do student businesses ever fail?"

"Of course, but that doesn't mean a failing grade. After all, as you'll learn in Business 101, the vast majority of startups of any kind go bankrupt. Analyzing why a business fails and then building on that to create something new is an invaluable learning experience. Of course, there are rewards for those whose business are particularly successful. Not only higher grades, but business owners keep any money earned above and beyond expenses, which can help offset college tuition costs. Assuming that they tell their parents about it, of course." He gave us another one of those chuckles, which I was beginning to think were produced in a lab on campus.

After that, he offered to answer questions, and having been around colleges her whole life, Madison knew the kinds of things she was expected to ask. What was the social life like? What kind of organizations were there to join? How was the cafeteria food?

My role as a parent was to check into financial aid and security. The security part was the part I was actually interested in, and I was disappointed that it wasn't provided by students. I was ageist enough to think I might be able to fool student security guards. I'd have asked about the janitorial staff but didn't think that would have been covered in Humphries's training about the Bostock Difference.

While Humphries was telling Madison about the array of outside experts Bostock invited to explain the workings of the real business world, I snuck a look at my phone to see if Sid had sent any additional questions to ask, but he hadn't.

Once our hot chocolate and questions had been disposed of, I checked to see if it was okay for Madison and me to roam around on our own.

"Absolutely," Humphries said. "Whenever you're ready to go back to the visitor's center parking lot, just head for a shuttle stop. They come by every ten minutes in the afternoons, and any of the drivers will be happy to take you back to your car."

After exchanging handshakes and accepting Humphries's business cards in case we had any more questions for him, we were on our own.

As soon as we went outside, I pulled out my phone and held it as if it were on speaker, which gave us effective camouflage as long as nobody was close enough to realize Sid's voice was coming from the bag and not the phone. "Sid, did you get anything out of the tour?"

"Not much, other than the fact that Madison is getting to be an excellent actor," he responded.

"You're too kind," she said graciously. "Did you like that part about college only being worthwhile if I get a job afterward?"

"Education is valuable in and of itself," they said in unison, making me think that perhaps I'd said that too often.

"Look at me," Sid said. "I take lots of classes, and I'm never planning to get a job."

"Not that a job isn't a good thing," I pointed out.

"You mean you aren't expecting me to move into the attic with Sid and play video games 24/7?" Madison said in well-feigned amazement.

"Don't scare your poor old mother that way!"

She snickered. "I have to admit that as business colleges go, this one seems pretty good. It's just not for me."

"Whatever you choose will be fine." I'd been careful to keep from pointing her toward or away from either my alma mater or any of the many schools where I'd worked. Since she hadn't decided on a major, that had been easier than it might have been otherwise. "Anything particular you want to see, Sid?" I asked.

I felt him twisting around in his bag to get a better look around. "I don't think so. The students that knew Annabelle will have graduated by now, and we don't know if she cleaned anywhere regularly other than the dorms, so there's no reason to try to buttonhole any instructors. Unless you know any custodians we can talk to—"

"Nope, though Charles said he'd try to make a connection or two."

"Then we may as well... Wait, what's that?"

"Where?"

"The little building to your right."

He was directing me toward a small wooden building. It was isolated from the rest of the campus, with a steep incline on one side and a service road on the other, and from a distance, I'd taken it to be some sort of storage building. From this angle, it looked like an old church.

"I don't know. It wasn't on the tour, but I think there's a map in the info packet." I handed Sid off to Madison and found the map I remembered seeing. "It's labeled the McClelland Museum."

"What do you think? Ancient Egyptian ledger books, Roman abacuses, and colonial adding machines?" Madison said.

"Displays of deposit slips over the years and pictorial histories of innovative accountants?" Sid suggested.

"Or we could go look," I said, walking in that direction while they came up with even more ludicrous ideas.

The building really did look like a rustic chapel, which made it more than a little out of place on the mostly modern college campus. There was a sign on over the front door that said *John Albert McClelland Museum* and a less grandiose plaque said *Open 1 to 5 Weekdays Only*.

"They should be open for another hour," I said and tried the door. Unsurprisingly, it creaked loudly as it opened. "I'm hanging up now, Sid," I said, and tucked the phone away.

I felt pretty safe in assuming that the woman we saw as we came in the door was a student. She was the right age, was sitting at a book-and-paper-cluttered desk, and was typing furiously on a laptop. Without lifting her head, she said, "Students are free with ID. Adults $5. Please sign in. We close in an hour."

"What about people on the campus tour?" I asked, tapping at our visitor badges.

She looked at us briefly. "Bostock Difference tour visitors are free. Please sign in. We close in an hour." And back to typing.

I'd intended to ask what the collection was like before committing ourselves, but with a welcome like that, how could we resist going inside? I wrote Madison's and my names down in the thick guest book on the desk.

There was a wooden holder on the wall next to the set of heavy-looking double doors in front of us. It may have been intended for hymnals or missals, but now it held black-and-white brochures titled, "Highlights of the McClelland Collection." I took one as Madison heaved the door open, making another mighty creak, and we entered the exhibit room.

"Wow," she said as the door slammed behind us.

"Wow," I agreed.

I've got a fondness for eccentric museums like the Isabella

Stewart Gardner Museum in Boston, the New England Pirate Museum in Salem, and the Plumbing Museum in Watertown, but this one might just win the prize for eccentricity.

It was one large room with long glass-and-metal display cases breaking it up into aisles. Had I not seen the identifying cardboard tags in front of each item, I'd have thought it looked like an extra-large booth from the famous Brimfield flea market, only one that had been stocked by a dealer who hadn't made up her mind about what kind of merchandise to specialize in.

In my first glance, I saw ship models, two suits of armor, various kinds of pottery, a battered steamer trunk, animal skulls, what I thought was a chamber pot, embroidered gloves, and taxidermy birds under bell jars. And that was just the stuff in front.

"How did this happen?" Madison asked.

I opened the brochure. "According to this, affluent businessman John Albert McClelland began collecting 'exotic objects' as a child and stored and displayed them in an abandoned church on his estate grounds. When he died, he left a generous financial bequest to Bostock, his alma mater, on the condition that they move the building and his collection to the campus and maintain it."

Madison ran her hand over a dusty display case. "That maintaining part could use some work. Is all of this from that one guy?"

I read a little further. "Nope. His plan included providing space for curios and valuables gifted by other alumni." I looked around. "It's my guess that when Bostock grads end up with oddities they don't know what to do with, they give it to the school for a tax write-off."

Since nobody else was in the room, I figured it was safe to talk to Sid directly. "Sid, are you seeing this?"

"Seeing but having a harder time with the believing. Can I come out?"

I looked around for security cameras, but while I didn't see any, that didn't mean there weren't a dozen hidden by the masses of stuff. "Better not, but at least we can talk."

"Then hold the bag up higher. Is that ship model made of matchsticks?"

I lifted him and looked more closely myself. "I believe it is. The label says it's late eighteenth or early nineteenth century."

"Sure it is," Sid said.

"But it's from McClelland's own collection."

"McClelland was either amazingly gullible or had horrendous eyesight."

"Agreed."

Madison had moved on to a different aisle. "Mom, do you think I can take pictures?"

"I don't see any signs that say not to, and there's nothing in the brochure. Just don't use a flash."

"And airdrop the pictures to me," Sid said. "I'm going to want to glory in them later."

She pulled out her phone while I moved on to a pair of paintings of geisha hung on the wall. "I believe these are paint-by-number."

"How can you tell?" Sid said.

"I can see the lines, and everything that's yellow has faded so much I can see the numbers under those sections."

"You say McClelland was a *successful* businessman?" Sid said in amazement.

The bizarre part was how genuine antiques and artifacts were scattered in amongst the dreck. I knew a real skull when I saw it, and if it wasn't from a hippo, it was from an even more unusual animal. Some of the Native American baskets looked authentic, Madison assured me that the shelf displaying padlocks included several unusual specimens and classic Rabsons, and I'd seen enough blunderbusses in other museums to be reasonably sure that the one there was real. Of course, the Egyptian stool was only a replica of the one from King Tut's tomb, but it was made of ivory and bronze and dated back to the 1920s. The contradictory part was that standing next to an early or mid-nineteenth century medicine chest was a decorative suit of armor that was clearly modern—I'd seen one just like it on sale at the mall.

We had intended to just take a quick look, but the sheer scope of the collection kept us there until the attendant came to the door and said, "I've got to lock up."

"Sorry, we got involved," I said.

"Yeah, there's a lot to see," she said with absolutely no trace of enthusiasm. She guided us out, grabbing her already packed backpack on the way, and locked the door behind us with an old-fashioned iron key before heading toward the student center.

Madison waited until she was gone to look at the lock. "Some security! I could open that thing in a couple of minutes."

"Why so slow?" Sid said. "I could do it in a minute, easy."

"I could do that fast, too," Madison said. "I just take my time so as not to scratch up the locks, unlike some people."

"Hey, you try picking a lock without scratching when all you've got is bare bones."

"I'm sure either of you would do an excellent job of breaking and entering, but it's time to go." I started off for the nearest shuttle stop, ignoring Sid's comments that I was just jealous because I couldn't pick locks as well as he could.

Chapter Twenty-One

I'd decided that Madison deserved a treat after helping with our reconnaissance mission, so I'd already told Phil not to expect us for dinner. Instead we went to Frontera Café, my daughter's favorite Mexican restaurant. The place is always loud, and the booths had high partitions separating us from the neighboring diners, which meant I could put Sid on the table so he could participate in the conversation as long as he was careful. Mostly he played on his phone while Madison and I ordered and ate, but he appreciated the gesture.

Madison and I were halfway through our burritos when Sid, speaking much too loudly for discretion, said, "Oh my spine and femur!"

I looked around to make sure nobody had noticed. "Inside the bag voice, Sid."

"Sorry," he said at a lower volume. "I was looking at Madison's pictures, and I found one of all the locks."

"Yeah, I was going to show those to Aunt Deborah," Madison said.

"She may have already seen them. The label says they were donated by Mrs. Margo Nichols."

"Nichols? As in the Nichols house?" I asked.

"The one and the same. I bet you a vertebra that those are some of the locks Deborah helped open."

"Keep your spine to yourself—I agree with you."

"Is that important?" Madison asked.

"Probably another piece of our Christmas Miracle," Sid said in a tone that made it obvious he was capitalizing the words.

"I don't think it qualifies as miraculous—we already knew the house's contents had been left to Bostock. It would have been more surprising if the stuff hadn't been at the museum." Then I remembered something. "Didn't Deborah say that the executor hired cleaners? What if they brought in a cleaning crew from the college? Including Annabelle! That would be how she knew the house was empty and available for squatting."

"And why is *that* important?" Madison said.

"It may not be," I said. "It may mean nothing at all. You should know by now that lots of our most exciting epiphanies go nowhere, and this might be one of them."

"On the other hand," Sid intoned solemnly, "this could be the epiphany that breaks the case wide open."

I waited for more, but when he didn't go on, I said, "Coccyx, Sid, don't leave us hanging! What have you figured out?"

"Nothing. I was just saying this *could* lead us somewhere."

Madison and I simultaneously started shaking the sugar skull bag despite Sid's protests. It was the closest we could get to *thunking* his skull under the circumstances.

He started berating us as soon as we got into the car and unzipped the bag for easier conversing, but as Madison told him, he deserved it for teasing us.

"Anyway," she said, "I don't know how you two put up with so much effort for so little progress."

"This one is particularly frustrating," I admitted. "I don't think we've ever been this long without having a viable suspect or two. Or at least a motive."

"We'll get there," Sid said airily.

"Any ideas for next steps?" I asked.

"Now that we've seen Bostock and the museum, I'm thinking about the Nichols house."

"It's a shame I never snuck in when I was a kid," Madison said. "I might have seen something useful. But Aunt Deborah went inside."

"That's right," Sid said with a noisy finger bone snap. "She should be able to tell us if Annabelle was on the cleaning crew, too."

"What time is it?" I asked.

Madison said, "Just after seven."

"I'll call her now. Madison, can you dial your aunt for me and put her on speaker?"

She did so, and Deborah answered. "What do you need, Georgia?"

"I'm here, too, Aunt Deborah," Madison said.

She softened her voice considerably. "What's up, kiddo?"

"Me too," Sid said.

"Anybody else? Mom, Dad, the dog?"

"No, just us," I said.

"Fine, then what do any or all of you need? I'm at bowling."

"Sorry, I forgot it was bowling night." I should have recognized the flavor of noise in the background. "We've got some pictures we want to show you to see if you recognize the person in them."

"I'd ask why, but I probably don't want to know."

"I can email them to you right now," Sid said.

There was a pause. "Yeah, it can be hard to see stuff on the phone. Georgia, why don't you come down here to show me, have a drink or something?"

"Sure, I can do that. I'll drop Madison and Sid off at home and then head over. Be there in half an hour or so." After I hung up, I said, "Sid, when we get home can you print more of those pictures of Annabelle?"

"I've already got copies, but why doesn't she just look at them online?"

"I'm guessing that she wants to talk about something. Maybe she wants me to go in with me on a present for Mom and Phil. You want to come with?"

"No, thanks. Madison and I have a Runes of Legend session tonight."

"Homework?" I asked my daughter. "Dog?"

"One chapter to read, and I'll take Byron out for a walk before I touch my computer."

"Good enough. You two have fun storming the castle."

I stopped at the house just long enough to take a bathroom break, tell my parents where I was going, and get the pictures of Annabelle. Though it would have been easier to send the photos to Deborah electronically, I didn't really mind getting out again. It was a clear night, just cold enough to make one think holiday thoughts, and perfect for admiring the twinkling of Christmas lights as I drove down the four blocks that made up Pennycross's downtown. Even the bowling alley felt festive, with colored lights reflecting against the tinsel garland hung everywhere imaginable, including places that had to be getting in the way of the employees.

I saw Deborah sitting at lane eight in her purple-and-black Pennycross Paralyzer team shirt and waited for her to finish yelling at one of her teammate's last pins to fall before saying, "Hey."

"Don't sit down. As soon as I bowl this next string, we can go get something to drink."

"Nice to see you, too," I said, but honestly, I wasn't offended. Deborah isn't what one would call a touchy-feely person, but she's always there when I need her. Sometimes she mocks me thoroughly after she helps out, but I was used to that.

I nodded at the other Paralyzers, which included both Louis Raymond and Oscar O'Leary. Deborah and Louis had been on the same team for years, but Oscar had only joined after the three of them began their dating dosey doe. I looked at the score and saw that Louis was ahead for the game, which explained why he was smiling and Oscar wasn't.

Deborah sighted carefully before striding down the lane to release her ball. Then she calmly stood, awaiting the strike that resulted. She tried to keep her poker face intact as she walked past her teammates and returned their high fives, but I saw a smirk slip out.

"Georgia and I are going to get something to drink," she announced, and I followed her to the snack bar.

My sister got a beer, but since I intended to drive home before too long, I stuck to Diet Coke.

"I've got a few minutes before I have to bowl again," she said. "Have a seat." There were half a dozen orange plastic laminate benches and tables by the snack bar, and Deborah picked the one that gave her the best view of her team's progress.

"You don't have anybody in that bag, do you?" she said, eyeing my backpack.

"No, Sid was busy. Besides, he gets claustrophobic in this bag."

"How does a skull get...No, I don't need to know. What did you need to show me?"

"I've got a couple of pictures of a woman, and I want to see if you recognize her." I handed her the three photos Sid had printed.

She studied them one by one. "She looks familiar."

"You're sure?"

"What kind of joke could I make with 'she looks familiar?' Wait, don't answer that. I'm sure you've got a bone pun already queued up. But yes, she looks familiar."

"Do you remember where you know her from?"

Deborah looked for a minute longer, then shook her head. "I'm not sure. Who is she?"

"Sid and I are pretty sure that this is the woman whose body we found at the site of the Nichols house."

"Louis said they haven't identified her yet."

"As Sid said the other night, we have sources the police don't."

She sighed loudly. "Please tell me you're not withholding evidence from the police and especially not from my boyfriend."

"We don't have any evidence, just hearsay and speculation."

"Hearsay and speculation that you're pretty sure are true."

"Yeah, something like that." Deborah knew I was holding back, but to her credit, she didn't push. "Anyway, we've been trying to find a way to link this woman to where her body was found."

"The Nichols house."

"Right, at least where the Nichols house used to be."

"I mean that's where I know this woman from. She was part of the cleaning crew at the Nichols house."

"I knew it!"

"If you knew it already, then why did you ask me?"

"Okay, I didn't know for sure, but I was hoping we were right. What can you tell me about her?"

"I met her over ten years ago, spent some time with her over the course of one week, and never saw her again."

"Deborah, how long did it take you to pick your first lock?"

"Twenty minutes, thirty-seven seconds."

"What kind of lock was it?"

"Mul-T-Lock."

I looked at her, eyebrows raised, until she got my point.

"Fine. I have a good memory." She took a long swallow of beer and stared at it while she thought. "Okay, I think I told you Mrs. Nichols left the contents of the house to Bostock."

"Right."

"So the school sent out a bunch of students and custodians to help with the sorting and the cleaning. Not that they did that much cleaning once they realized the house was going to be demolished. Still, a lot of the stuff we brought out of the house needed to be cleaned. As in dusted, dirt scraped off, and in some cases, disinfected."

"And you're sure this woman was there?"

"No, Georgia, I made it up just to mess with you."

"Sorry."

"Anyway, this woman was one of the cleaners, not a student. I'm trying to remember her name. Amy, Annie, something like that."

"Annabelle?"

"That sounds right. I noticed her because when she'd bring a locked box for me to open, she'd wipe it off first. Most of the others would just dump it on me, no matter what crud it was covered in. I talked to her at lunch, too."

"What about?"

"Locks, hoarding, antiques, the stuff we'd found. Then when I saw the way the students were treating her, we compared notes about people who think they're better than you are because of your job."

I paused. "Do I act like that?"

"Jeez, Georgia," she said, rolling her eyes. "Do you think I'd have let you live this long if you didn't show me respect? Not to mention the fact that you let your daughter work with me, which says everything that needs to be said."

For Deborah, that was almost sweet.

She went on. "Some of the students were okay, but some of them were real snots, if you know what I mean. One day Annabelle was showing me a decorated glass cup she said was made in Venice, explaining how glassmakers back then were required by law to stay on a nearby island. Not that I asked, but it was interesting. Then one of the snots came by and asked how she knew what it was. He didn't say *because you're just a janitor* out loud, but that's what he was thinking. Then he tried to take it from her. Not asking, mind you, just grabbing. Except he kind of tripped over my foot." She grinned. "You know that annoying babysitter we had, the one who used cutesy talk?"

I made a face. "All too well."

"I imitated her to tell brat boy that he better not try to carry it because he might drop it and break it." She snickered. "If looks could kill, you'd be an only child."

"Good for you."

"Anyway, about the only other thing I remember about Annabelle is that she was a hard worker."

That was solid praise for her. "Thanks, Deborah. I should probably let you get back to your game."

She looked over to check the progress of the game. "Wait here a minute. I won't be gone long."

She went back to her lane, made another strike, accepted the customary accolades, and returned.

"Georgia, there's something I want to talk to you about." She looked at my backpack again. "You sure Sid doesn't have something in there to listen in with?"

"Don't worry, he's back at the house gaming. All of him." I thought maybe she wanted to talk about a present for him, but I wasn't even close.

She said, "I heard that Brownie Fenton is back in the picture."

I hadn't expected that. "I've run into him a couple of times. How did you know?"

"Oscar knows one of the security guys over at Bostock, who said he saw the two of you making out at that hamburger place on campus."

"We were not making out. It was two kisses, no tongue. They were practically Sid-like."

She shuddered. "Don't try to distract me. Are you seeing him again or not?"

"He said something about dinner, but we haven't set a date."

"Do you want to see him again?"

"Quite a lot."

"Then why did you break up with him before?"

"We didn't break up. Not exactly. We had a disagreement, and we needed some time to cool off."

"What did you fight about? Pardon me, what did you *disagree* about?"

I cocked my head to look at her. "Deborah, I can count on the fingers of one hand the number of times you've asked about my romantic relationships. Why the sudden interest?"

"I just think Brownie is a good match for you. I didn't care about the other guys you dated." Before I could respond to that, she said, "You two fought about Sid, didn't you?"

"Since Brownie doesn't know about Sid, that's not exactly possible."

"Yeah, but you fought because he invited you somewhere, and you wouldn't go because of Sid."

"If you know what the problem was, why did you ask?"

"I just want to make sure *you* know what the problem is."

"Sid isn't a problem."

"Sure he is." She held up one hand to forestall my retort. "Everything about a person can be a problem. Your daughter would be a problem if Brownie wasn't willing to be a stepfather. Your job would be a problem if he didn't respect academics. Byron would be a problem if he was allergic to dogs. Anything in your life can be a problem if you or he make it one."

"And I suppose you have a suggestion on how I can make Sid not be a problem?"

She shook her head. "I only open a locked box—you've got to look to see what's inside yourself."

"That's an interesting metaphor."

"You don't spend your life around English nerds without learning your way around a metaphor. So what are you going to do about Brownie? He won't wait around forever, you know."

"You're a fine one to talk," I said. "You've got two guys waiting for you."

"That's different. I don't know if I want a serious relationship, let alone marriage, and until I decide, there's no reason to pick either of them. You, on the other hand, want to be married."

"I do?"

"Georgia, you got engaged in grad school, knowing how hard it would be to start a life together in the middle of all that, and even though he turned out to be the wrong guy, you've never stopped dating in hopes of finding the right one."

"You're right," I admitted. "I look at what Mom and Phil have and I want that for myself. I just don't know if Brownie is the right guy."

"For what it's worth, I like him." She drank down the rest of her beer. "Good talk. See you later." Then she went back to her game.

I didn't notice the Christmas decorations on the way back through the bowling alley or as I drove back home. I was thinking. My sister really had opened a metaphorical locked box for me, and now I had to look for a real-life answer.

Chapter Twenty-Two

On Thursday, I had plans to eat lunch with Mom and Phil at McQuaid before Mom and I went Christmas shopping. With Sid's help, I'd found out what games would be a good match for the new Switch I was giving Madison, and Mom wanted me to go with her to make sure she bought the right ones.

Either I was running a little early or they were running a little late because neither parent was at the Campus Deli when I got there. I saw Oscar sitting at a table by himself, and went to say hello and poke at him.

"Hello, Oscar. I would shake your hand, but somebody might think we were arm wrestling or Kung Fu fighting or something. You know how things get exaggerated."

He choked down a bite of his ham sandwich. "Look, Georgia, I didn't mean to say that you and Brownie were doing anything untoward. I know a guy who works security there, and he was just patrolling—which is his job—when he saw you two eating together, and he mentioned it to me. That's all I told Deborah."

"Then how did Deborah get from our eating at the same table to 'making out?'"

"My friend might have mentioned kissing."

"Uh huh."

"It wasn't a secret or anything, was it?"

"We were in a public place where I'm known, and apparently so is Brownie. Of course it wasn't a secret. I just never cease to be amazed by how quickly gossip travels between campuses."

He shrugged sheepishly.

After that I let him off the hook, and we chatted about the weather and the busyness of the season until I had an idea which called for a subtle conversational segue. Unfortunately, I was out of subtle conversational segues, so I went with my usual direct approach. "Hey, Oscar, can I ask for a favor?"

"Sure."

"Well, I've been looking into the case of that body our dog found."

"I hoped you might be. The police around here can use a little extra brainpower, if you ask me."

"They are stretched pretty thin," I said, as if Pennycross had suddenly become a hive of mob activity. "I've got a name that might match the body, a woman who went missing in West Litchfield. The thing that has me confused is that as far as I can tell, the police there didn't really look for her very hard, and I don't know why. I don't have an in with the police there, but since she worked for Bostock, I thought the security people there might have some information, but I don't know who to ask and thought you might. I mean, you always seem to have your finger on the pulse of things here, and I'm hoping your counterparts over there are equally as efficient." Poor Oscar puffed up his chest, which made me feel a little guilty, but he really did run a pretty tight ship at McQuaid.

"I could do that. Do you want an introduction, or would you rather I speak to my buddy?"

"I think it would be better coming from you, but could you keep it on the QT? Maybe you can come up with some excuse for asking."

"No problem," he said. "I'll tell him I've had a few students disappear and ask how they handle similar cases, then work my way over to your lead. What's the name of the missing woman?"

"Annabelle Mitchell. She would have disappeared roughly ten years ago, in late November or early December."

He pulled out his phone and typed himself a memo. "Consider it done."

"Thanks, Oscar."

"Hey, we're practically family." Then realizing that he might be going a little too far, he added, "I mean we're McQuaid family, what with you having worked here and your parents still being here."

"Absolutely. You won't say anything to Louis, will you?"

He grinned widely. "Mum's the word."

My parents arrived a minute later, and Oscar flashed me a conspiratorial wink as I went to join them. He was clearly hoping that he'd be able to help me pull something over on Louis.

The rest of the day was all about the holidays as my mother and I knocked a lot of items off our Christmas shopping lists. First was the game store, where I got Madison's Switch, and Mom got *Super Smash Brothers Ultimate* and *The Legend of Zelda: Breath of the Wild.* Then we hit Wray's to pick up action figures and assorted geeky stocking stuffers for both Madison and Sid. Next to the mall to get a snazzy new cooking knife for Phil. I was going virtual for most of Sid's Christmas gifts—a hefty Steam gift card for online gaming and a subscription for the Disney streaming service—and I already had Deborah covered. Of course, I couldn't very well shop for Mom with her there, but I took note of a couple of things she admired to check out later. Though I knew I'd be picking up more odds and ends along the way, that took care of most of my list. All that was left was something for Charles.

We were ready to head home when Brownie called my cell phone to invite me to dinner Saturday night, and I happily accepted. Afterward, Mom announced that she had one last stop to make. She told me I could wait with the bags to rest my feet and came back a few minutes with an expression of faux innocence that wouldn't have fooled me as a child, let alone as an adult.

I'd called the house to say not to delay dinner for Mom and me, and though they were finishing up by the time we got home, Phil, Madison, and Sid stayed at the table to keep us company while we ate. More importantly, they'd left us plenty of Phil's famous Enamel chili, which was so spicy it could melt the enamel off of one's teeth.

Mom couldn't wait to tell everybody that I had a weekend date with Brownie planned, which led to raised eyebrows and speculative expressions all around. Well, except with Sid—he only managed the speculative expression.

"Lunch, making out on campus, and now this," Madison said.

"How did you know about lunch and something that was not making out?" Then I answered my own question. "Deborah."

Madison nodded. "I called her to see if she wants me to work this weekend so I can make some cash for shopping. Speaking of which, what are you getting Brownie for Christmas?"

"Coccyx, I hadn't thought about that. What does one get an on-again/off-again boyfriend?"

"So he's back to being a boyfriend?" Madison asked.

"I guess. I don't know. But he is a friend, so I need to get him something. Any ideas?"

"I would suggest something small," Phil said. "Not in cost, per se, but in physical size, given that he resides in a trailer."

"It's a lot more spacious in his trailer than you might think," I said.

"Is it?" Mom said with a smile.

I turned bright red. Not that my parents didn't know I'd spent the night with men in the past—I had a daughter, which was pretty solid evidence—but it wasn't something I wanted to talk about.

After that, I beat a hasty retreat to my room, saying, "I've got wrapping to do." Sid joined me, and was glad to hear that I'd reached out to Oscar.

"I haven't had any luck today," he said.

"I wouldn't say that. You don't know what we got you for Christmas."

Sid kept trying to wheedle a hint out of me while he helped me wrap presents, which kept us occupied for the rest of the evening.

Chapter Twenty-Three

Enlisting Oscar turned out to be a good move. He called while I was teaching a class the next day and left a message that he already had information for me. When I called back, he offered to meet me that afternoon at Kimota's, the closest thing Pennycross has to a hip coffee shop. It's located next door to Thackery Locks, Deborah's locksmith shop, but I'm sure that was just a coincidence.

Since I was coming straight from work, I didn't have Sid with me, and I hoped he wouldn't fuss too much.

Oscar was saving a place at one of the tables, ignoring several glares from coffee drinkers who wanted a place to work on their laptops. "Have a seat," he said, waving me over. "What can I get you?"

"I should buy since you're doing me a favor."

"I wouldn't hear of it. Besides, I want to ask you about something."

"Then hot chocolate would be great."

"Whipped cream?"

"By all means."

Now it was my turn to guard his seat until he returned with a coffee for himself, my hot chocolate, and a couple of muffins.

"These were the last two chocolate chip, so I thought I better grab them while I could."

"I respect you too much to disagree with you," I said, helping myself.

Once we were situated, Oscar began. "So I called my friend Julio yesterday afternoon. He's the second-in-command in Bostock security, and the one who observed your, um, conversation with Brownie. I told him I was info gathering for an update to our procedures manual, particularly how to handle students going missing. Their procedures are solid, by the way. They go to the cops immediately when a student is unaccounted for, with no messing around trying to keep it quiet to avoid bad publicity. They might move a little faster if the student lives on campus, but it's pretty much the same for off-campus students."

"That sounds like a good plan."

"It is, which is why we have a similar one. Unlike McQuaid, however, Bostock doesn't really have a policy when it comes to faculty and other employees. They expect the family to do the reporting."

"Annabelle Mitchell didn't have any family as far as I know."

"That's what I figured, so I posed that as a what-if scenario. That's when Julio remembered hearing about a case with a custodian who went missing, which turned out to be your Annabelle Mitchell. He's only been at Bostock for eight years, but when I asked for details, he asked his supervisor Bernice if she remembered the case. They put the phone on speaker so I could hear them both."

He hesitated. "Georgia, this Mitchell woman wasn't a friend of yours, was she?"

"No, I never met her. Why?"

"Because according to Bernice, she wasn't somebody you'd want to be friends with. She was a thief."

"Excuse me?" I said, thinking I must have misheard him. "Are we talking about the same person?"

"You know Mitchell was a custodian, right?"

I nodded.

"She worked in one of the dorms, and some of the students reported things had been taken from their rooms but only when Mitchell was working: jewelry, electronics, cash. Mitchell was off that day, and when they opened up her locker, lo and behold, some of the stolen items were in there.

"Her boss and some of the security crew were waiting for

Mitchell the next morning, but somebody must have tipped her off because she never showed. She didn't answer the phone either. Bernice said they went to her apartment, but she'd skedaddled."

"How do they know she didn't just ignore the doorbell?"

"Yeah, they might have peeked in the window. Not the best thing to do, but under the circumstances I can't say I blame them."

"Didn't they call the cops?"

He made a face. "Admin told them not to because it would be bad publicity. Instead they returned the items they'd found, reimbursed the kids for the rest, and tried to sweep the whole incident under the rug. Which worked until a student started asking about why there was a new custodian at her dorm and found out Mitchell was gone. They think that student is the one who filed the missing person report in West Litchfield."

"You don't have a name for the student, do you?" I said, thinking it might look odd if I didn't ask.

He shook his head. "Bernice didn't mention it. Anyway, once the report was filed, the West Litchfield cops came to Bostock to find out when Mitchell was last seen and so forth. Bernice was there when her old boss—the former head of security—told them that if he had to guess, he'd say Mitchell left town on her own hook. Bernice asked if any of the other missing items were found in Mitchell's apartment, but the cops called later and said Mitchell had cleared the place out. Not the furniture, but all her clothes and all her personal stuff were gone. They figure she wasn't planning on coming back.

"West Litchfield was willing to put out a bulletin to get Mitchell back so she could be prosecuted, but the Bostock people said not to bother. Even if they found her, admin wouldn't let them press charges because they didn't want the story getting out." He took a final bite of his muffin. "That's why West Litchfield didn't pursue it any further. They couldn't arrest her without Bostock's cooperation, and a missing person isn't missing if she leaves willingly, which is what Mitchell had done."

"Did they tell that to the person who reported her missing?"

"I don't think so. The impression I got was that everybody involved was asked to keep it under their hats."

I took a long swallow of my hot chocolate, trying to reconcile what Oscar had said with what everybody else had told me about Annabelle, but I couldn't imagine Charles falling in love with a petty thief. Besides, hadn't he said that Annabelle had arrived in Pennycross with nothing more than a small bag? Could she have stashed the rest of her belongings somewhere? Where and when, if she was afraid of somebody? For that matter, why would she have taken the time to pack up everything she owned if she was on the run? Then there were Lauri Biegler's memories. Could Annabelle have bought treats for lonely students only to sneak into their rooms to steal their iPods?

Granted that people are walking contradictions, and nobody is all good or all bad, it still didn't compute.

I realized it had been a while since I spoke. "Sorry, Oscar, but you've thrown me for a loop. I'm not sure what I was expecting to hear, but this wasn't it. I don't suppose you know who reported Annabelle for theft?"

"It didn't occur to me to ask, honestly, and even if it had, that would have made it sound like I didn't believe them when they were pretty convinced it was true. The only reason Bernice told me as much as she did was because she was still mad that her old boss didn't do more to find Mitchell. If it had been up to her, they'd have made sure the woman didn't get away with all those thefts. But if you're right, and that body is her, maybe she didn't get away with anything."

"Thanks a lot for your help, Oscar. And for the snack. Wait, you said you had something you wanted to ask me about."

"Yeah, that. I've been having a terrible time trying to come up with the right present for Deborah, and I thought you might have some advice."

"She can be tricky to buy for."

"With most women, I'd go with jewelry or perfume, but Deborah isn't like most women." His admiration for my sister's differences was obvious from the look on his face. "She got a new bowling ball a few months back, so that's out, and I don't know where that leaves me."

"I wish I had a suggestion for you, but…Wait, I do have one idea, but you'd have to do some research to make it work." I told Oscar what I had in mind, and though he looked doubtful, he said he'd see what he could find.

Chapter Twenty-Four

Sid was peeved when I got home and told him I'd met with Oscar without him. I let him complain for a few minutes but finally said, "Look, Sid, do I get upset when you find stuff online without me around?"

"That's different!"

"Why? The fact is, there are things you can do online that I can't, or at least I couldn't without taking a lot longer. And there are things I can do in person that you can't do without extra preparation. Teamwork doesn't mean we have to live in each other's back pockets."

"As if I had pockets," he scoffed, but then said, "Okay, you're right. I'm just frustrated."

"I'm not sure hearing Oscar's story is going to help you." I told him about Annabelle supposedly being a thief. "Coccyx, Sid, this case just keeps getting worse and worse."

"Are you kidding? This is great news!"

"In what way?"

"Because we know why the cops closed their missing person case on Annabelle, and the fact that they weren't looking anymore explains why I couldn't find anything on the web. It also tells us that the Pennycross police aren't likely to figure out Annabelle's identity anytime soon."

"True, but I'm not sure I'd call that great news."

"Think it through. Now we have two possibilities to consider." He pulled off a bony finger and lay it on the desk. "One, Annabelle was a thief."

"I don't think Charles would fall in love with a woman with sticky fingers."

"From what I hear, love is both blind and complicated."

"True."

"So hypothetically, say that Annabelle was a thief. That could be why she was killed. One of her victims tracked her down and killed her for revenge. Or maybe she stole something incriminating—drugs or stolen gold bars or—"

"Stolen gold bars? In a college dorm room?"

"Okay, bad example, but it could have been something that could get somebody into trouble, and she was killed to cover that up."

"I guess."

He popped off another finger. "Second possibility: Annabelle wasn't a thief at all, and somebody was framing her. Whoever was framing her is probably the person she was running from and quite likely the one who killed her." He put both his fingers back into place. "We finally have motives to work with!"

"Possible motives, and we'd still need a motive for someone to want to frame her, preferably one that doesn't include gold bars."

Sid opened his jaw and glared at me.

"Sid, what are you doing?"

"Sticking my imaginary tongue out at you."

"Ah. Maybe you can find an app for that."

"I could use a raspberry blowing app, too, now that you mention it. In the meantime, I want to talk to Lauri Biegler again and see if she knows who reported Annabelle for stealing. That should give us a suspect list!" Sid has a particular fondness for suspect lists because they lead to spreadsheets and dossiers.

After trading Facebook messages with Lauri, Sid arranged to talk to her on the phone later that evening, and she called Sid's burner phone promptly at eight. Sid answered and put it on speaker while I sat quietly.

"Have you found out anything about Annabelle?" she asked.

Sid said, "I have some new information, but I want to see if you can either verify or refute it."

"Okay." She sounded confused.

"According to a source in the security office at Bostock, Ms. Mitchell was accused of stealing items from student dorm rooms."

"What? That is total bull! Annabelle would never do anything like that."

"Are you sure? I understand there were multiple instances of students reporting missing items after Ms. Mitchell cleaned their rooms."

"I don't care if the whole student body reported it, I still wouldn't believe it."

"And you never heard any rumors about that from any of the other students?"

"Not from anybody I believed."

"But from somebody you don't know?"

Lauri made an exasperated sound. "Okay, not long after I created the Facebook page, somebody posted that I shouldn't bother looking for Annabelle because she was a crook who'd lifted all kinds of stuff from people's rooms. He claimed she took his iPod and stole money out of his wallet. But I didn't believe him."

"Why not?"

"Because I'd never heard of him. I mean, I didn't know everybody in my dorm, but none of my friends knew who he was either. So I deleted the comment from the page, and he never posted again. I'd forgotten all about it until you brought this craziness up, and I swear, that is the only time I ever heard anything about Annabelle stealing."

"Good," Sid said with a satisfied expression I could see, even if she couldn't. "As a matter of fact, I think you're right about her."

"Then why did you mention it?" she asked indignantly.

"Because it could speak to why Ms. Mitchell left Bostock so suddenly. Being accused of theft might have frightened her, or she might have known who the real thief was."

"Right, that makes sense," she said, mollified.

"That leads me to my next question. Can you give me the names of the other people from your dorm?"

"Seriously? There were over two hundred people living in

North House," she said. "Like I said, I knew some of them, but I definitely don't remember them all."

"I don't suppose there was a student directory."

"Not that I know of."

"Are you in touch with any of the ones you do remember?"

"Yeah, sure. I'm close to a couple and Facebook friends with a few more."

"Then if you've got time, I'd like you to crowdsource and come up with a list of people who were at your dorm. Maybe we can figure out who accused Ms. Mitchell of stealing."

"It won't be any of my friends," she said. "They all liked Annabelle, too. But there were some jackwagons who treated her like dirt because she was 'the help,' or made fun of her, or just ignored her."

"Send me the names of anybody you can track down, especially the jackwagons, and I'll take it from there."

As soon as they hung up, Sid messed around with his computer and started it playing the Twisted Sister version of "Deck the Halls." Then he jumped up and spun around a couple of times. "Dance party time!"

"For what?"

"For progress. Motives! A suspect list in the making!"

"Sid, I am not going to dance for a potential suspect list!"

"Sure you are!" He grabbed me by the hands and pulled me to my feet.

I crossed my arms in front of my chest. "I'm not dancing."

"If you don't dance, I will twerk. In fact, I will do the "Single Ladies" dance and *then* twerk."

It was a good dance party. Sid has a surprising number of rocking Christmas songs.

As I explained to him later, I wasn't entirely against the idea of a celebration dance, but I wanted to be sure there was something worth celebrating. He countered that if we got bad news later on, at least we'd have had a good time first. I had to admit that he had a point.

Chapter Twenty-Five

The next day was Saturday, meaning my date with Brownie was set for that night. It was hardly our first date, so there was no reason to watch the clock all day, get so distracted while grading papers that I barely got any done, or to allow three hours to shower and get dressed. Which isn't to say that I didn't do all of those things.

I'd picked out a nice-but-not-fancy outfit, but when I got back to my room after the shower, there was a wrapped package on my bed. The tag said *Don't Open Before Christmas*, but the *Don't* had been emphatically crossed off, and I opened it to find a sapphire blue blouse I'd eyed longingly at the mall the other day. Now I knew why Mom had snuck off. After her efforts, of course I had to wear it along with black velvet slacks and my good black boots that were both stylish and moderately winter appropriate.

Madison had spent the day working with Deborah but got back home while I was doing my hair and makeup, and I found myself using a lot more beauty aids than I'd intended. Though my daughter spends ninety percent of her time in jeans and T-shirts, years of theater and cosplay have taught her more about makeup than I'll ever know.

Despite the extra primping, I was ready well ahead of schedule and went downstairs to show off the new blouse and Madison's artistry. Phil said, "Very nice, very nice," which is his go-to compliment for any occasion, and Sid produced a wolf whistle despite being lip-free. As for Mom, she looked exceedingly pleased with herself.

When I thanked her for the blouse, she said, "I never have

understood why they market holiday clothes as gifts when you really want them before Christmas. Consider this my act of revolution against the man."

"You're such a rebel, Mom."

She raised her fist and said, "Rage against the machine, Georgia!"

I only had to wait a few minutes for the doorbell to ring, which was a relief. I'd been afraid to sit down for fear of picking up some of Byron's fur on my clothes.

Sid dove for the armoire where he could hide and listen, and Madison let Brownie in while I got my coat and my purse. There was an exchange of handshakes, cheek kisses, fist bumps, and head rubs between Brownie and Phil, Mom, Madison, and Byron, respectively.

"It's lovely to see you again, Brownie," Mom said.

"I'm glad to see you, too," Brownie said. "I hope it won't be such a long time between visits from here on out."

Everybody turned to look at me, but I just smiled. So did Brownie, and while the blouse from Mom was part of the reason, I also thought he was feeling optimistic about our relationship.

I was feeling pretty good about it myself until Phil said, "If you're free tomorrow, perhaps you'd like to join us. We'll be putting up our Christmas tree."

I tried not to react, but all I could think of was how much Sid loved decorating the tree, and I was almost certain I heard a pained gasp from the armoire. Fortunately, Brownie said, "I'd love to, but unfortunately the only way I could get off tonight was to promise my parents I'd work the zoo lights tomorrow night."

"Another time then," Phil said.

I nudged Brownie out the door before any other invitations could be offered. Obviously my family approved of my seeing Brownie, which was lovely, but they were pushing just a bit.

We went to Irvine's, a nearby restaurant that has a habit of redoing the menu every year or so. Its current incarnation was rustic

French, and we both ordered the special of cheese and smoked ham in puff pastry. Service was slower than usual because the place was filled with a combination of exhausted shoppers and people celebrating early, but I didn't mind because we weren't in any hurry.

When we were waiting for our food, Brownie said, "Have you heard the latest from Bostock?"

I shook my head. "I left campus early."

"As of Tuesday morning, the union is officially going on strike."

"Picket lines and everything?"

"That's the plan."

"Good luck to them, I guess. For their sake, I hope it doesn't snow."

"Speaking of Bostock, I finally had lunch with Charles yesterday. He seems to be doing okay, though it's hard to tell with him."

"He's a private kind of guy," I said. "It was nice of you to make the trip to Bostock again. The shuttle bussing alone was a major sacrifice."

"Actually, I had an appointment out there."

"Did you? Wait, you didn't take a job, did you?"

"Not exactly."

"What does that mean?" I asked.

"It means I want to keep it a surprise for now."

"Surprises can be good."

"Well, if this one works out, starting Tuesday morning I'll be in the vicinity if you need any assistance with your investigation."

"You'll be what now?"

"I've told you that I find this sleuthing stuff fascinating, and I thought having an ally close by might come in handy. Not that you can't work the case on your own, of course, and I don't have your experience, but I might be useful." He paused. "Are you mad?"

"As an independent woman and staunch feminist, I should be, but honestly I think it's kind of sweet."

He exhaled in what I took to be a sign of relief. "I promise not to get in your way, but if there's anything I can do, I'm at your service. Part of the time, anyway. I've still got classes at McQuaid to teach, plus the carnival. But other than that, I'm ready to help."

"You know, you don't have to do this. It's not a prerequisite for dating me."

"I know, I just thought..." He fiddled with his fork for a minute. "I just thought that we were getting along really well for a while, and then suddenly you drew back from me." He reached over and laid his hand on mine. "I want to get back to where we were, maybe even beyond that."

Our eyes met like couples' do in the Hallmark movies Sid wouldn't own up to watching, and for a moment, I was tempted to tell Brownie everything about my skeletal best friend. Then I started trying to imagine the resulting reaction and the moment passed. So all I did was smile without speaking, and hope that I'd imagined that flash of disappointment I saw on Brownie's face.

Our food arrived, an interruption that I appreciated, even if Brownie didn't.

To keep away from topics I wasn't ready to talk about, I spent the next few minutes eating and making appreciative noises. When I thought he might speak up again, I said, "I did get some new information on the case. It turns out the police in West Litchfield didn't bother looking for Annabelle because they thought she was stealing from Bostock." I explained what Oscar had told me and how it had been thoroughly denied by Lauri Biegler, concluding with, "I may be being hopelessly naive, but my gut says Annabelle wasn't a thief, and that it would have been easy to frame her. So far, the Annabelle-was-framed and Annabelle-was-a-thief scenarios are the only possible murder motives I've come up with. I was thinking my next step will be to try talking to some of the custodians, if any of them were there when Annabelle was. Charles said he'd check for connections, but he hasn't been in touch yet. I don't suppose your secret plan could help with that?"

"If that's a serious question, then the answer is no. If it's a cunning ploy to try to find out what I've got in mind, I'm not saying a thing until I'm sure I've got all the pieces in place."

He resisted my blandishments, even though I used the exact tone Madison used to use on me to get a new toy. Then again, it rarely worked for her either.

We decided to split an apple tart for dessert, and conversation shifted to a grant proposal Brownie was working on for a study of sideshow gaffs like Fiji mermaids, shrunken heads, pickled punks, two-headed turtles, and giant rats which were actually capybara. "If that doesn't work, I might do something more specific about Homer Tate, who was called the King of Gaffs because of the so-called artifacts he created."

"If you like fake artifacts, you should check out the McClelland Museum at Bostock." I told him about it, adding, "It's actually kind of linked to the case."

"It is? How so?"

"Annabelle was part of the crew that cleaned out the Nichols house after Mrs. Nichols died, and the contents of the house were left to the museum."

"Then I'll have to pay a visit."

By then the tart had arrived and been eaten, and after Brownie paid the check, we went back out to his car.

"What would you like to do now?" Brownie asked after he'd started the engine and more importantly, given the bitter cold, turned on the heat. "Movie? Bar? Bookstore?"

"It's hard to talk during a movie or at a bar."

"Bookstore it is!" When we'd been seeing each other more frequently, we'd often ended up at the Barnes & Noble to browse through the books and then drink coffee at the cafe while we discussed and/or argued about those books. On most occasions, we could easily spend a couple of hours there, but it was so crowded with Christmas shoppers jostling us that we'd only been there half an hour when Brownie noticed my growing annoyance and said, "Maybe we should get coffee elsewhere."

"We could go back to my house, but it's not exactly private." I really appreciated my parents letting Madison and me live with them and allowing us to pay much less than I had for our previous apartments, but at least with an apartment, I only had to wait for Madison to sleep over with a friend to be able to have quiet moments alone with a guest.

Brownie said, "We could go to my place."

I looked at my watch. "It's a long drive to the zoo, and as much as I enjoy the hurly-burly of a carnival lot, maybe not tonight."

"As it happens, I'm not staying at the lot. The commute was getting to me, so I'm housesitting for a friend of mine here in Pennycross. He's gone away for the holidays."

"No parents, kids, pets, or carnival rides playing Taylor Swift songs?"

"Nope. Just quiet, an excellent coffee maker, and a nice selection of DVDs and streaming services."

As it turned out, I was unable to vouch for the coffee or the videos, but I could say with authority that the guest bedroom wasn't nearly as cramped as Brownie's carnival trailer.

Chapter Twenty-Six

I'd been sorely tempted to stay with Brownie overnight but instead slunk back home at two in the morning, hoping that everybody was long since asleep. Byron did come downstairs as I came in the front door and reset the alarm, but once he saw it was me, he trotted back to Madison's room. I was more than ready for my bed, but I saw the light was on in the attic. Sid doesn't sleep, of course, so his light is usually on, but seeing it reminded me of my father's faux pas earlier in the evening.

I knocked on the attic door, and when Sid buzzed me in, I headed up the stairs to address the reindeer in the room.

I said, "Sid, I'm really sorry about Phil inviting Brownie for the tree trimming. He should have known better."

"No, it's okay. Mind you, Madison was about ready to bean Dr. T with a candy cane after you guys left, but his apology was pretty terrific."

"What did he say?"

"He said that I'm such an integral part of the family that sometimes he forgets that others aren't aware of me." He beamed. "That's right, I'm integral."

"Of course you are."

"So, how was your date?"

"Very nice."

He looked pointedly at his wrist, despite not having a watch. "I don't eat out often, but it seems to me that it must have been awfully slow service at the restaurant."

"The restaurant was fine. We just went to the bookstore afterward."

"Wow, they really stay open late during Christmas season. I had no idea."

I started to dodge the issue again but decided to go with a full-frontal assault instead. "I could tell you what Brownie and I did after we left the bookstore if you like. In detail. In fact, I took a few photos. Let me get my phone."

"Fa la la la la! I can't hear you! I refuse to hear you! Or look at any pictures!" he said, slamming his hands over his ears and bending in a particularly impossible way to cover his eye sockets with his feet.

"Don't ask questions you don't want the answer to," I said, thinking that I should have tried that approach years ago. I would have avoided a whole lot of ribbing.

When Sid finally put his hands and feet back where they belonged, I said, "There are a couple of things you might actually want to know. Bostock is definitely going on strike, and Brownie has some sort of scheme so he can be around to help with the case."

"Really? I'd have thought he had plenty to deal with between McQuaid, Fenton's, and 'bookstore visits.'"

"He says he wants to nose around on our behalf."

"You mean your behalf." For once, Sid had no expression on his skull.

"Are you okay with that? You know I didn't ask him to help."

"It could be useful," he said, which wasn't really an answer.

"Any progress here?"

"Nope, not a thing." He turned back to his computer. "I've just been gaming. I'll see you tomorrow."

"Are you sure?" But he was already tapping away. "Goodnight, Sid."

He didn't answer, and before I went back down, I saw that his bones seemed looser than they should have been. I was too tired for it to keep me awake, but I was concerned.

The first part of Sunday was filled with the errands and chores I'd neglected while getting ready for Saturday night's date: grocery shopping, laundry, and grading papers. I'd decided to give Sid some space but was relieved that he seemed fine when he came down that afternoon. Together we brought the Christmas decorations up from the basement, and when Deborah and Madison got off work, they came to the house for our dinner of grilled cheese sandwiches and tomato bisque before Phil and Deborah took their annual trip to the tree lot.

Long ago we'd realized that Deborah had a knack for picking the freshest trees, and it became a ritual for her and Phil to do the honors while the rest of us hung garland and mistletoe and put up the other holiday decorations.

When they got back, it turned out Phil had taken an extra step in apologizing to Sid for nearly making him miss the tree trimming. After they'd brought in our tree and wrestled it into the stand, Phil brought in a second, much smaller tree, which he carried up to Sid's attic. So after we'd decorated the family tree, we all trooped upstairs to the attic and helped Sid adorn his own tree. Madison must have been in on the plan because she'd bought a batch of Christmas ornaments with Marvel superheroes and *Nightmare Before Christmas* characters. As Sid declared when we were done, it was just like a Hallmark Christmas movie if they ever made one starring the Addams Family.

We spent the rest of the evening watching *A Miracle on 34th Street*, *Frosty the Snowman,* and *A Charlie Brown Christmas*, and talking Phil out of trying a fruitcake recipe he'd found. My father is a really good cook, but the rest of us weren't convinced that even he could make a fruitcake we'd want to eat.

Murder was the last thing on my mind that night, and didn't even take up much of my mental bandwidth the next day at Bostock, which turned out to be a long one. I had several meetings with students, including one with a freshman who'd apparently just realized that he wasn't going to pass my class without taking extreme measures. He showed up with three papers he'd neglected to turn in earlier in the semester and then tried to talk me into giving him full credit because of excuses that were far more creative than his papers were. I wouldn't budge, which took him an inordinate amount of time to accept.

So while I was thinking murderous thoughts on my drive home that evening, they had nothing to do with Annabelle. That changed when I got to the house and found a text from Sid on my phone.

SID: *We have a problem.*

Chapter Twenty-Seven

I'm sure Sid expected me to immediately run up to his attic, but other obligations prevented me from doing so. First off, as soon as I came in the front door Madison grabbed me because she was having an issue with her friend Samantha and wanted guidance on how to handle it. By the time I'd helped her, Phil had dinner ready for the family and the seemingly ever-present Andrew. Once we'd eaten, I had to help clean up.

When I finally got upstairs, Sid was tapping his foot loudly. "It's about time!"

"Good evening to you, too. What's wrong?"

"Lauri came through with some names of people from her dorm a little after midnight last night, and while some people were snoring away—"

"I don't snore. Do I?"

"You both snore and drool. Sleep is a disgusting habit."

"Coccyx, you're a Scrooge tonight. Who stole your sugarplum?"

He sighed heavily. "I'm just exceedingly annoyed at Lauri, who would be getting coal in her stocking if I had anything to say about it."

"But you said she sent you a list of names."

"She did, and I spent most of the day doing research, but this afternoon I realized how she got that list. She posted a request on the Bostock alumni Facebook page. That wasn't too bad, if not as discreet as I would have liked, but when somebody asked why she wanted to know, she said she was looking for information about Annabelle Mitchell. She didn't say it in a private message, Georgia. She posted it publicly."

"Oh my spine and femur!"

"I know! For all we know, the killer saw the post. Now he or she knows we're on the case."

"They know somebody is on the case, anyway. Thanks to your thinking ahead, Lauri doesn't know about me, and you didn't give her your real name. 'Art Taylor' can't possibly be tracked back to us." Not that knowing Sid's real name would be a huge danger, since he wasn't exactly listed in the phonebook, but there weren't enough Thackerys in the area to make tracking us down impossible.

"I guess," Sid said, "but I hate having so much of the investigation out of our control. Not just Lauri but…other things, too."

I thought I knew which other thing was bothering him. "Are you unhappy about Brownie sticking an oar in? I swear, I never asked him to."

"I know you didn't, but—"

I gave him a minute to figure out what he wanted to say.

Unfortunately, either he didn't know what he wanted to say or wasn't ready to say it because he waved it aside. "Anyway, Lauri gave me a couple dozen names to start with, and since she made it so public, I'm keeping an eye on the Bostock alumni Facebook page as people add more."

"Isn't the page private?"

"It is, so just call me Liz Kent, Bostock Class of 1967. I rambled to the moderators about how my grandkids just talked me into joining Facebook, and I found this page hoping to reconnect with old classmates because I've never been able to make it to a reunion because of living overseas, and so on and so forth. I think they approved my access request so I'd quit telling them the story of my life. The upshot is that I have authorization to lurk, and since my persona is so old, chances are against any members of the real Class of 1967 challenging me."

"Very clever. Have any of the alumni said anything about Annabelle? Like maybe having accused her of theft?"

"Not yet, but at least we've got suspects. I told you we deserved that dance party."

"I guess," I said.

"You don't sound excited."

"I'm mostly confused. All we have is a list of names of people who were in Lauri's dorm."

"Right. The people who accused Annabelle of theft must be among them."

"I get that, but I don't know how that makes them suspects."

"You still believe Annabelle is innocent, don't you?"

"Of course."

"Why would anybody have accused Annabelle of theft if they weren't framing her?"

"So somebody steals a few items from dorm rooms, successfully frames a custodian for it, and then hunts her down to kill her?"

He frowned somehow. "That does sound stupid when you put it that way."

"Come to think of it, Sid, how do we know the accuser is the framer?"

"You've lost me."

"We've been assuming the students who accused Annabelle of stealing were lying. What if things really did go missing from their rooms, and they honestly thought it was Annabelle?"

"You're right. It could have happened that way." He drummed his finger bones on the desk. "How about this? I create a new profile and post that Annabelle has passed away and that I'm the executor of her estate. I say that after she left Bostock, she struck it rich, but always felt guilty about stealing from students, so on her death bed, she tasked me with finding her victims so I could give them reparations. If nobody steps up to say they were a victim, we'll know there were never any thefts."

"Or that the victims aren't on Facebook or in that alumni group. Or if they are, that they don't believe you. Like you keep telling me, everybody lies on the internet."

"It does kind of sound like a Nigerian prince scheme, doesn't it?"

"Plus people might claim to be victims just to see if they can make a quick buck."

"People can be very dishonest."

I looked at him, waiting for him to recognize the irony in his statement, but when he didn't, I went on. "I don't want to be a downer, Sid, but I don't know what to do next."

He looked back at his computer. "We're missing something, aren't we?"

"We are, and I have no idea what."

"Me, neither," he said, his bones loosening.

I patted him on the scapula. "This is our process, Sid, as weird as it is. We come up with ideas, we shoot 'em down, and we come up with more."

"Which we also shoot down."

"Repeat as necessary until we find one that's bulletproof."

He sighed, but then sat up straight and tightened his bones. "I'm on it. I'm going to Google the names Lauri sent and put together a spreadsheet. There's nothing like a spreadsheet to get the brain pumping. Am I right?"

Most of the time, spreadsheets put me to sleep, but I said, "You be you, Sid."

I offered to help, but he let me off the hook to go grade papers, and he was still at it when I went to bed.

Chapter Twenty-Eight

I left for work early Tuesday in case the strike was going to make it harder for me to get to class on time. That turned out to be a good thing because traffic started backing up a quarter of a mile away from the campus. When I finally inched closer, I saw the strikers were out in force, with people holding signs on both sides of the main entrance road. Though they weren't actually blocking access, people were slowing down to look.

I didn't like crossing a picket line, but I'd made my decision rather publicly, so I was stuck with it.

I was about to turn in when I saw something in the church parking lot across the street, and went that way instead.

There were two food trucks set up directly facing Bostock's entrance and a quartet of porta-potties. Or rather, two grub joints and a row of donnikers, which is what Treasure Hunt would have called them. The carney slang was relevant because I recognized the equipment as being from Fenton's Family Festival. Both trucks were doing land-office business.

I parked a few spaces away and went to tap at the back door of the busier truck.

An unfamiliar man in a purple Fenton's Family Festival polo shirt answered. "What?"

"Is College Boy around?"

"Yeah, sure." He went back inside, and a minute later Brownie came to the door. When he saw it was me, he stepped outside and gave me a quick kiss.

"Brownie, what's going on?"

"Your talk last week inspired me."

"Funny, I don't remember saying anything about bringing food trucks to Bostock."

"Not explicitly, but you did talk about us adjuncts being true to our own consciences. Well my conscience wanted to support the strikers, but it also wanted to be close by in case you need me for your investigation. So I met with the union people to point out that if they were going to have people marching in the cold, they'd need food and bathroom facilities or they'd be losing a third of their picket line at any given time to make Dunkin' Donuts runs. As an alternative, I suggested that I help arrange for coffee and food, plus use of porta-potties. They're subsidizing my setup, so coffee and food are free for any faculty member with a union card, and after I insisted, to any adjunct as well. Assuming any of them want to come all the way out here to get it, of course, but I figured it was at least a symbolic gesture on the union's part."

"You are brilliant, and given the amount of coffee you're handing out at the moment, you're going to make a hefty profit."

"Nope. I'm operating at cost, plus pay for my workers and a donation to the church for letting us use their lot. I'm not even charging for my time."

"Wow. You're brilliant *and* generous. What did your parents think about this plan?"

"Dad used so much carney slang that even I lost track of his meaning, but I don't think he entirely approved. On the other hand, he didn't try to talk me out of it. Mom just said I better make sure the trucks are back at the zoo and ready for business by opening time this evening. I'll count that as a win."

I accepted coffee and a muffin, courtesy of the union, and headed onto campus for class. It was a good day. Papers came in on time, classroom discussions were lively, none of my students asked for extensions, and I didn't see a single helicopter parent. When I stopped back by Brownie's food trucks on my way home, I even got a free lunch, again thanks to the union, and Brownie took a few minutes to keep me company.

There was no progress on the case, but all in all, I was feeling pleased with life until I got home and climbed to the attic.

Sid was staring at his screen, tapping his finger bones on his jawbone.

"How goes the spreadsheet?"

"Never mind the spreadsheet, Georgia. I want you to look at something and see if I'm nuts."

"Okay."

"You know I was feeling discouraged last night, right?"

"It happens to the best of us."

"Working on the spreadsheet didn't help. I mean, I got data on forty former students, but it just seemed like a waste of time. I kept thinking that we had to be missing something that would narrow the suspect pool. Since we got our best info from Charles and Sue Weedon, I went back through my notes on them and dug some more."

"Did you find anything?"

"Nothing from Charles, other than the fact that his PhD dissertation is surprisingly readable, but then I checked out the web site for Sue's show painting business. Confirm something for me, would you? Didn't she say she hadn't been in contact with Annabelle for a long time?"

I nodded. "She said that the two of them had mostly lost touch after college, though obviously Annabelle knew that Sue had been working with a carnival."

"That's what I thought. Now look at this." He got up so I could sit at his desk to see his laptop screen better, leaving his right hand on the desk to manipulate the mouse while he stood behind me. "This is her web site."

"Right." The header said *Sue's Show Painting: Specializing in Ride Decoration and Restoration*. The site was crammed with photos of Sue painting rides and carousel animals. I was particularly impressed by a black horse wearing gold battle armor that was labeled as being a stander from a 1917 Muller carousel. She also sold matted photos of some of her most spectacular work and some original watercolors of carnivals. "She does good work."

"Agreed, though irrelevant. I learned today that when you restore a carousel, you don't just repaint the animals and chariots. You redo the scenic panels, which are those big panels in the center of the carousel that hide the motor and other machinery, and the rounding boards, which are on the canopy. The paintings can be of anything, but a lot of them are landscapes of forests or castles or English manor houses." He used a pull-down menu to switch to a page of examples. "These are scenic panels from carousels Sue has painted."

"Okay."

"Now look at this one." He clicked on a photo to enlarge it.

It was a picture of a white house with a dark green front door and shutters, and a pair of bay windows, with a forest scene behind it. The light made it seem almost magical, but without people, it also felt a little melancholy.

"Very pretty," I said.

"Now look at this."

He brought up another window with a photo of a white house with a dark green front door and shutters and a pair of bay windows. It wasn't in front of a forest, though, and the car parked in front showed it was modern.

I looked from one to the other. "Is that the same house?"

"You tell me."

I leaned forward to compare the details. "Same color door, and the windows are in the same place. Look, there's even the same cast iron mud scraper on the stoop. It's got to be the same house."

"That's what I thought."

"Why is that important? Was Sue working from a photo of this house?"

"She could have been," Sid said, "but that still begs the question. Why was Sue so interested in the Nichols house?"

Chapter Twenty-Nine

"Wait, that's the Nichols house?" I asked. I must have seen it at some point since I'd lived in Pennycross for most of my life, but I didn't have strong enough memories to recognize it.

"That's it. This photo was in the *Pennycross Gazette* when the whole hoarding thing came out."

"That makes no sense. When did Sue paint that panel?"

"According to the caption, six years ago."

"If she hadn't seen Annabelle since college, then she would never have seen this house."

"That's right."

"So she was lying to us."

"That's right."

"Coccyx."

"That's right."

I ran my fingers through my hair. "Now I don't know what to believe."

"I believe we've got a viable suspect for Annabelle's murder."

"But why would Sue have spoken to me if she was the killer?"

"The Fentons. They connected her with Annabelle, and if she hadn't come up with some explanation, they'd have been suspicious."

"Yeah, okay, but why would Sue have killed Annabelle?"

"It could have been anything. Charles said Annabelle had cash. Maybe it was a lot of cash, and Sue wanted it. Or how about our hidden MacGuffin theory? Maybe Sue wanted the MacGuffin, and either Annabelle wouldn't sell it to her or wanted too much money." He shrugged noisily. "I confirmed that they went to the same college, but we don't even know that they were really friends. We only have Sue's word for it."

"Would Annabelle have put an enemy down as a job reference?"

"That's a fair question." He drummed his fingers noisily on the desk. "Okay, say they had a falling out back in college, which is why they lost touch, and maybe Annabelle had gotten over it, but Sue hadn't."

"After all these years?"

"Don't you still have a grudge against your college roommate? What was her name?"

"You mean Jean? You bet I hold a grudge! She stole from me, and when she wore my best earrings without asking, she lost one and threw out the other to make me think I'd misplaced them myself." I took a breath. "But I wouldn't kill her for that."

"Maybe Annabelle did something really bad to Sue."

"But Charles and Lauri said she was so nice."

"And other people said she stole from them." He held up a hand to stop me from continuing my rebuttal. "I'm just speculating. All we know for sure is that Sue Weedon lied to us. We just don't know why or how much of what she said was false."

We went back and forth about whether or not we should call Dana and Treasure Hunt, but finally decided against it. Either they didn't know Sue was lying, so we wouldn't get anywhere with them, or they did, which meant they'd been lying to me, too. Moreover, if the Fentons had lied, then they'd had a reason, and I didn't like where that thought led. Getting back together with Brownie had already been touch–and–go. Accusing his parents of being involved in a murder would not lead to wine and roses.

That meant I needed to talk to Sue, and since it didn't seem like the kind of conversation we should have by phone, that left going to see her in person. Needless to say, Sid insisted that I was not to be alone with her, and I was entirely in agreement with that.

Sid had the business card she'd given us, and after he did a little Googling for more information, I called her cell phone number.

"Sue Weedon, Sue's Show Painting."

"Ms. Weedon, this is Georgia Thackery, the Fenton family's friend." At least I hoped I'd still consider them friends after this revelation. "We talked about Annabelle Mitchell the other day."

"I remember. What can I do for you?"

"I've got some more questions about Annabelle, and I wondered if you had time to talk." When she hesitated, I added, "You did say I could call if I needed to."

"Sure, of course. I'm just kind of busy right now."

"I'm not surprised. Is the restaurant really going to be ready to open by New Year's?"

"That's the plan," she said with a laugh. "We've got workmen swarming this place like discount day at the fair."

"Then I'll let you get back to it. Can I can call later tonight?"

"Tomorrow would be better."

"Sure thing. I'll talk to you then." I hung up and looked at Sid. "Up for a drive to Windsor Locks?"

"Ready when you are."

We had no intention of waiting for Sue to consult the Fentons and come up with a reasonable-sounding story before I confronted her. She likely didn't remember she hadn't told us the name of the place when I spoke to her before, but she had mentioned working at a restaurant. So Sid had done an internet search for "carousel restaurant Windsor Locks" and found a local news article about the Carousel Restaurant being refurbished. I'd only called ahead of time to confirm the information and to make sure she was still there.

It was a short drive over the Massachusetts-Connecticut border to Windsor Locks, and I found the restaurant easily thanks to the neon carousel horse on the sign and the banner that said, "Undergoing Renovation—Reserve Now for New Year's Eve." The parking lot was about a third full with pickup trucks and delivery vans, and as Sue had said, there were plenty of workmen wandering around. They took no notice of me as I picked my way around stacks of pipes, wooden beams, and other building supplies, but there was a man with a clipboard and a harried expression at the front door.

"Can I help you?"

"I'm looking for Sue Weedon."

He turned around to yell, "WEEDON! Visitor!" before hurrying away.

Sue was kneeling in front of a carved zebra installed in a niche with a table and bench encircling it, and when she saw me, her eyes widened like those of a deer caught in a car's headlights.

I walked over without waiting for any more of a greeting than that.

"Well, this is a surprise," she said.

"I was in the neighborhood," I lied. "I figured you'd need to take a break at some point, so I brought these." I held up a to-go tray with two cups of Dunkin' Donuts coffee and a box of donut holes.

"That's nice of you, but I've got to get this done tonight and—"

"No problem. I can wait until you're finished."

With an air of resignation, she said, "On second thought, I could use a breather. I've got a workshop out back where it's a little quieter."

I didn't need the shove from Sid-in-the-bag to remind me why that was a terrible idea. "I'd rather stay out here, if you don't mind, so I can admire your work."

"Okay." She pulled a tarp off of the bench and we sat, with me giving her a little more space than I might have otherwise.

She took one of the cups, blew on the coffee to cool it, and took a swallow. "You said you have some questions?"

I'd decided not to dance around it, so I pulled out a printout of the photo of the scenic panel depicting the Nichols house and handed it to her. "This is your work, right?"

"It might be."

"It's on your web site."

"Right, of course. Yes, it's mine."

"Can you tell me how you happened to paint the house next to where Annabelle's body was buried? Please don't try to convince me it was a coincidence."

She sagged a little and put the coffee cup down. "It looks like I owe Treasure Hunt fifty dollars. He bet me that you'd figure it out somehow."

"Then Dana and Treasure Hunt did know you were lying to me?" I said, feeling profoundly disappointed. That meant they'd lied to me, too, at least by omission.

"No. Well, yes, but only because I asked them to. Look, what I told you before was partially true. The two of us really were as close as sisters during college."

"But after all that, you quit talking?"

She nodded sadly. "We had a falling out over the guy I was dating, who talked me into dropping out of college to go out on the road with him. Annabelle told me he was a loser, and she was right."

I nodded, remembering Brownie saying that he'd avoided Sue's boyfriend.

"The lie was when I said I never talked to her again. The truth is, I spoke to her the day before she died."

Since there were plenty of people around, I managed to resist edging further away from her. "How did that happen?"

"I guess you found out she was a custodian at Bostock College."

"Which you could have told me in the first place and saved me some time."

"I figured that if I told you too many details, you'd realize that she and I had been in touch."

Sue had a point, but I didn't know that I wanted to agree with her about anything when I was still suspicious of her motives. I settled for a nod.

"Besides I thought that you might not work as hard to solve the mystery of a dead custodian as you would for a college professor or an administrator, what with you being a professor yourself."

"Wow. That's insulting."

"I know, but I hadn't met you when I decided that. Treasure Hunt told me I was being a chump because you like sticking your nose into mysteries, and you don't care what kind of mystery it is."

That sounded like his brand of backhanded compliment, but I had to admit, "He's not wrong."

She smiled, just for a second. "This is the real story. Ten years ago, Annabelle called me out of the blue, saying she was in trouble and didn't know who else to ask for help. She'd found out about some thefts at Bostock."

"You mean the stuff stolen from the dorm rooms?"

She cocked her head. "You heard about those?"

I nodded, feeling a bit smug.

"Actually, that part came later. I'm talking about stuff being stolen from the museum."

I went from smug to confused in seconds. "You mean the museum on campus? The one with all the odds and ends?"

"It shouldn't have been odds and ends. At least, that's what Annabelle thought."

"I don't understand."

"She said nobody paid much attention to the museum's collection. It was a mess, and a lot of the stuff in it was worthless. She figured that if somebody realized that items that were labeled as antiques or historical artifacts were actually nothing of the kind, they just thought it was another eccentric alum or a former student playing games with tax deductions. You know, claiming they'd donated something worth a thousand dollars when it was only worth ten. Illegal, of course, but not worth causing trouble over.

"Only she was at that hoarder house when it was cleared out and knew some of the things from there were really valuable because she'd been an art history major in college. After everything from the house was supposedly added to the museum's collection, she went to see them again.

"That's when she realized that some of the objects weren't what she'd seen at the house. Instead they'd been replaced with junk. She said she'd seen some Japanese ink block prints, but that's not was hanging in the museum."

"Were they replaced by paint-by-number pictures?" I said, remembering the ones I'd seen.

She nodded. "Some of the other items had just disappeared, with no mention of them in the museum's records at all. Annabelle realized something was going on, but she wasn't sure who to tell. She started documenting the pieces she knew had been stolen while she tried to figure out where to go next, but somebody must have realized what she was up to. The next thing she knew, a coworker called to warn her that students were claiming that she stole from their dorm rooms, and some of the missing stuff had been found in her locker. The only reason she hadn't already been arrested is because she had the day off when it happened. Annabelle panicked. You see, she'd made some mistakes when she was younger and had done some things she regretted."

"So I heard."

Sue looked surprised again, but went on. "She got caught for shoplifting a couple of times and drinking while underage, but the worst incident wasn't even her fault. A so-called friend took her for a joy ride, not telling her the car was stolen, and since Annabelle was driving when the police found them, they thought she was the thief."

"You were the friend, weren't you?"

"Close enough—it was my jerk boyfriend. Annabelle only took the fall for my sake. Even though she got a suspended sentence because it was a first offense, she had a record, and she was afraid that she'd be put in jail or, at the very least, lose her job. Still, I don't think she'd have run if somebody hadn't tried to kill her."

"Someone did what?" I felt Sid vibrate with excitement from inside the bag, and I nearly did the same. That hadn't showed up in any of Sid's spreadsheets.

"After her friend called, Annabelle decided to talk to a lawyer.

She called a guy who'd been a student at Bostock, and he said to come to his office right away. She didn't have a car, so she started walking, and was on her way there when a car came up from behind, hopped the curb, and drove right at her. She realized it at the last minute and was able to throw herself into somebody's yard. She started to pull herself together and saw that the car had turned, and she thought the driver wanted to check on her. Then she realized he was coming toward her again. She ran and got a tree between her and the car, and the guy raced away."

"Was she hurt?"

"No, but she didn't know what to do. Call the cops? They'd arrest her. Call her friend from work or the lawyer? Maybe they were in on it."

"No wonder she panicked," I said.

"She got back to her place and packed a couple of things, but she didn't know where to go or who to trust. That's when she remembered that house in Pennycross."

"The Nichols house."

"Right. She knew it was empty, so she figured she could squat there for a while until she decided what to do next. She took the bus to Pennycross and walked the rest of the way. Then she got to the house, found a room to sleep in, and woke up in the middle of the night with a man standing over her."

"A man?" I said, as if I didn't know who'd been there with Annabelle. "Was he part of what was going on?"

"No, he was another squatter. Annabelle didn't tell me much about him, only that they shared the place for a while and then things got more...romantic."

"Wow," I said, hoping that was neutral enough.

"She said he was wonderful, and being there with him was like a dream, but when they found out the house was due to be demolished, she knew she was going to have to run again. She still didn't know who the thief was or who'd tried to kill her. She hadn't even been able to find out who accused her of theft.

"That's when she called me. I was working at a carnival in Florida, so I couldn't get to Massachusetts, but I found out that Fenton's was in Pennycross. I trusted Dana and Treasure Hunt and told Annabelle to go to them. Then I called them, and they promised they'd help her hide out. They would have gone to get her, but she couldn't just leave without saying goodbye to her fellow. She asked them to wait until after the carnival shut down that night. They were supposed to pick her up outside the house, but she never showed. They waited for her for a good while, but a cop car cruised by a couple of times and they got nervous. Carnies and cops don't always mix, you know. So they went back to the lot, hoping she'd show up. She never did."

"You're still not telling me everything. When did you see the Nichols house?"

"About a week later, I finally made it to Massachusetts. It took me a while to talk my boss into giving me the time off, and then I got stuck in a snowstorm along the way, and—basically, everything that could go wrong did. I arrived in Pennycross right before the demolition team showed, and I watched them working all day long, thinking that if Annabelle was in there, they'd find her. I guess that's why the place was so vivid in my mind when I was painting that panel."

"Did you know she was dead?"

She looked down at her coffee cup. "I must have, though I didn't want to admit it. The Fentons thought the same thing. But we didn't know who had done it or where the body was. I wanted to go to the cops, but Dana and Treasure Hunt talked me out of it."

"I know, carnies and cops."

"It wasn't just that. Annabelle said the cops were after her for thefts she hadn't committed, so who's to say they weren't involved in stealing from the museum or her death?"

It sounded paranoid to me, but since Sid's death took place before I met him, I'd never experienced the murder of my best friend. "So why all the 'I haven't heard from Annabelle since college' rigmarole?"

She looked embarrassed. "I don't trust easy. I was afraid you were looking for Annabelle for some other reason."

"And I just happened to have found a body that fits Annabelle's description?"

"I know it doesn't sound reasonable, but I *really* don't trust easy."

"Then why tell me anything at all? If you hadn't shown up at Fenton's, I doubt I'd ever have found you."

She sighed. "Once I heard that my friend's body had been found after all this time, I had to know what happened to her. I failed Annabelle all those years ago, and I can't ever make it right, but at least she'll be laid to rest properly. I wasn't going to go to the cops—I'm a carney, too—but the Fentons seemed to think that you could find out for me. They trust you."

"Yeah, they sure trusted me," I said, not bothering to hide the bitterness.

"I mean it, Georgia. Dana said all along that you were okay for a towner, which she doesn't say about many people, and like I said, Treasure Hunt bet me you'd figure out on your own that there were things I hadn't told you."

"What about Brownie?"

"He liked it even less than his parents did, and he's not real happy with me right now. I'm sorry, Georgia. I should have given you a chance. If you wanted to call it quits, I wouldn't blame you."

What I really wanted was to consult Sid, but Sue was watching me, looking like nothing so much as Byron when he knows he's in trouble for chewing something up.

Finally I said, "I guess I can see why you acted the way you did, but if I'm going to figure this out, I need to know what you know. Did Annabelle have any idea of who might have stolen the stuff from the museum or from the dorms? Did she know who tried to kill her?"

"She said she didn't have a clue."

"You're sure?"

"I'm sure, but if I can think of anything that could help, I swear I'll tell you. If you're going to keep investigating, that is."

I felt a resounding knock from inside the sugar skull bag, which was Sid's and my code for *Yes!*

"Yeah, I'm going to keep going. Treasure Hunt has me pegged."

"It would mean a lot to me to know what really happened. Is there anything else you want to ask?"

She'd given me so much new information that my head was already spinning, but I said, "Did Annabelle mention the name of the friend who warned her about the cops?"

"Let me think." She took a swallow of her rapidly-cooling coffee. "Samuel, Sean…Sebastian, that's it. Not sure about the last name. Do you think he was involved?"

"Even if he wasn't involved, I'd like to know how he found out Annabelle had been framed and if he knows who accused her of the dorm thefts." I made a show of typing the name onto my phone, which gave me a chance to see if Sid had texted with anything he wanted me to check on. He hadn't, so I said, "I'd better let you get back to work."

We both stood, and Sue said, "I'm sorry I didn't trust you before."

"If a stranger showed up and started asking me questions about a horrible time in my life, I'd probably be suspicious too."

"That's good of you to say. I really appreciate what you're doing on my friend's behalf. She deserved so much better than what she got."

"I'm going to do my best to bring her killer to justice." It sounded very pretentious, even to me, but Sue was right. Annabelle had deserved better. Nobody deserved to be murdered, buried, and nearly forgotten.

Chapter Thirty

Once we were in my car, Sid was free to talk again, and that's what he did. "Hurray! At last we have a good murder motive. Well, not good, but you know what I mean. Annabelle's death had nothing to do with the stuff stolen from the dorms—that was just a distraction. The real reason was to keep her from telling anybody about the stuff stolen from the museum. Coccyx, I wish I had both of my hands here so I could rub them together with glee."

"So you don't suspect Sue after all?"

"No, not really. I don't know that I'd want you meeting her alone at midnight in a deserted house, but I think she told us the truth this time."

"As much as anybody does, anyway," I said.

"Don't you believe her?"

"I do. I just have a hunch that there might be something more to what happened between her and Annabelle than she's saying. That doesn't mean it's relevant, of course."

"I'll see if I can dig up anything on that when I get a chance, but my Number One priority is finding out who was at the Nichols house during the cleanup."

"The people other than Deborah?"

"That's right! Deborah was there. Let's invite her to dinner and talk to her afterward."

"I have to check with Phil, first. This late in the day, he might already have the meal planned out."

As it turned out, Phil was putting together a vat of beef stew and was happy to throw in more ingredients to accommodate Deborah. Knowing him, he'd already had plenty, but he's big on freezing leftovers. He also agreed to call her and ask her to join us.

When we got off the phone with Phil, it rang again. I looked down at the caller ID but let it ring.

"You want me to get that?" Sid said.

"Nope."

His hand emerged from the bag to pick up the phone and hold it where he could see it. "It's Brownie."

"I saw."

I should have realized that Sue would immediately get in touch with Dana and Treasure Hunt, who would in turn call Brownie.

"Are you mad at him?" Sid asked.

"I'm still deciding."

"Which means that you are."

"It means I am, but I'm not sure it's justified. I know it wasn't his story to tell, and that he was following his parents' lead, and maybe I shouldn't blame him, but I do. That's why I'm not answering."

The phone stopped ringing, and Sid looked at the phone again. "He didn't leave a message."

"Okay." I wasn't sure if that was a good thing for my state of mind or a bad one.

"Do you want to talk about it? I don't have any experience with romance, but I can listen."

"I appreciate the offer, but not right now."

His hand snuck out again and patted my leg comfortingly. At least it was comforting for me, though it probably wouldn't have been for anyone outside my family.

By the time we got to Pennycross and I checked in with Madison to see how her day had gone, it was time to set the table for dinner. Deborah arrived in the middle of that, so there was no time to speak to her until after we ate.

I didn't know if Phil had warned her that he'd been nudged to invite her or she just recognized the gleam in Sid's eye sockets, but she didn't seem surprised when we asked if we could speak to her once dinner was over and the cleanup was taken care of.

I said, "Deborah, would you care to demonstrate your memory again?"

"Are you two still obsessing about the Nichols house?"

I nodded. "We think Annabelle's death was connected to some thefts at the McClelland Museum at Bostock, and we think those thefts—"

"Stop. I don't want to hear anything else that starts with 'we think.' Just tell me what you want from me now, and when you've wrapped everything up, you can tell me the rest."

"Okay," Sid said, and he opened his laptop to a fresh spreadsheet window. "We need to know everybody who was there when you were clearing out the house."

"Everybody? It was a crowd of people, most of whom were useless."

"Everybody you can remember. We already know about you and Annabelle, of course." He waited with his finger bones on the keyboard.

She sighed deeply. "All right, I'll try. It was the guy who runs Hoarder Helper that hired me. Umar..." She reached for her phone to check the contacts list. "Umar Kalu. He had two guys that worked with him: Reo and Gun, but I never got their last names. I tell you, that company has the job down to a science. As bad as the house was, Umar said it was worlds better than most of them he'd been involved in because the hoarder was already dead and didn't argue with them every time they tried to throw out a stack of ten-year-old newspapers.

"When I got to the house, they'd already brought a dumpster for the outright garbage and three storage pods—one for the stuff to donate to charity, one for the stuff to take to the museum, and one for the stuff they were going to send to the family. Even though the contents of the house were left to the college, the woman from Bostock wasn't being a jerk about it. Whenever they found family photos or baby shoes or things like that, they'd box it up for the heirs."

"Then there was a Bostock person on site?" I asked.

"Yeah, some guy from the department of people giving stuff to the college—"

"The Office of Development?" Different colleges used different terminology, but *Office of Development* was the most common title for the people who managed gifts and bequests.

"That sounds right. He never introduced himself and didn't stay long. He left his admin in charge—Ingrid Fischer. She was in charge of sorting everything."

I asked, "Were any of the family members there?"

She shook her head. "Nobody was even close to local, so they were represented by the executor Holden Quincy, who was a lawyer here in town. He was only there the first day, when they had that argument over whether the china cabinet was part of the house's contents, and then on the last day to sign off on paperwork."

Sid had been typing all of this in as fast as she spoke. "Who else?"

"There were two other custodians with Annabelle, but if they told me their names, I don't remember them. I think they were a couple. He was a really big man and she was a tiny woman, but she could lift nearly as much as he could."

I said, "You mentioned some snotty kids before."

"They weren't all snotty, but it was a high percentage."

"Names?" Sid asked.

"Are you kidding? First off, it was ten years ago. Second, they didn't introduce themselves. Third, it was ten freaking years ago!"

"Sorry," Sid said.

"All I remember is that there were six of them wearing matching T-shirts."

"They dressed alike?" I asked.

"Green one day, red the next, blue, and one day a hideous orange. All of them with the same stupid logo: 'CSI: Clean Scene

Instigation.' I guess they were uniforms, but I never heard of any such company."

"I bet it was a student business," Sid said. "Bostock students have to create companies as part of their course work, and this crew must have been working together."

"That's not a totally stupid idea," Deborah admitted. "If those kids had done more working and less poking around looking at things, it might have impressed me more."

"Was there anybody else?" I asked.

She thought for a minute. "Some neighbors wanted to stick their noses in, but we chased them off, and a reporter took some pictures. Food delivery people—Umar made sure we got something to eat. That's all I can think of. Does my remembering any of that do anybody any good?"

"You bet," Sid said. "This is great stuff!" He actually gave her a quick hug before skipping up the stairs. "Thanks Deborah!"

"What's he so excited about?"

"Suspects, spreadsheets, and search engines."

"You know, I used to think being an ambulatory bag of bones was the weirdest thing about that guy. Now I'm not sure that even makes it into the top five."

I couldn't argue with her, so I just said, "Thanks for the help," and followed Sid upstairs.

"Suspect list, suspect list!" he was crowing as he spun himself around in his desk chair.

"We already had a suspect list."

"But now we've got a better suspect list, one that might actually get us somewhere."

"Shall I get my laptop so I can help with the research?"

"You bet!"

An hour and a half later, we'd made considerable progress in eliminating people. Since it wasn't just a case of items stolen from the Nichols house, but of substitutions made at the McClelland Museum, we could cross off people who had no reasonable access to the Bostock campus. As far as we could tell from our background searches, that took out all the Hoarder Helper crew and the cheapskate lawyer; and we didn't think the head of the Office of Development, the nosy neighbors, the reporter, or the food delivery guy would have had a decent opportunity.

Sid summed it up. "That leaves Ingrid Fischer the administrative assistant, the other two custodians, and the six-student cleaning crew. Did I miss anybody?"

"I don't think so. I just wish we had more names."

Sid waved it away. "I can track down the custodians on an employee list or something—the descriptions should make it easier."

"What about the students? It's not like we have a list of Bostock's student companies."

Sid grinned widely.

"We do have a list?"

"When I was investigating the names Lauri gave me, I discovered the Golden Pages."

"The what now?"

"It's an online directory for Bostock student companies. Though Yellow Pages isn't a registered copyright in the US, they preferred to dodge the issue. Anyway, the Golden Pages is one of those companies that gets bought up by a new group when the owners graduate, and each year they produce a new edition. All the companies are listed, but just by name. If they want anything else, they have to buy ad space and hire somebody at the Golden Pages to design an ad. It's one of the most consistently profitable companies at Bostock, and bless their chest cavities, they maintain archives."

Sid turned back to his laptop and started typing. "We lucked out! Clean Scene Instigation bought a full-page ad!"

"Does it list all the employees?"

Sid grinned even more widely. "Nope. Just the company email address and phone number."

"And yet you're smiling."

"We don't need names. The ad includes a group photograph."

Sure enough, there was a photo of five kids wearing T-shirts that were even uglier than I imagined, posed as if they were cleaning up a gory crime scene starring the sixth kid as a murder victim. Despite their questionable taste in company name, T-shirt design, and ad campaigns, at least they'd taken a crystal-clear photograph.

"Now I can compare these faces to the people from Lauri's list, and if they're not there, I can go through yearbook photos for those years to see if I can find them."

I rubbed my eyes but said, "Do you want me to take Lauri's list or the yearbooks?"

"I think you need to go to bed."

"But—"

"Santa knows when you're awake, Georgia, and you've got work in the morning. Besides, I live for this kind of job! More or less."

I let him talk me into heading for bed. As I plugged in my phone to charge it overnight, I saw Brownie had called twice more, but again, hadn't left a message. I still didn't know how I felt about that.

Chapter Thirty-One

When I drove to Bostock the next morning, I saw Brownie's food trucks and porta-potties were back in business, but I didn't stop or even glance in that direction more than seven or eight times.

Classes went well, but when I got back to my desk afterward, I spotted my favorite helicopter parents hovering near my cubicle. Since they'd seen me, too, it was too late to go back the way I'd come, so I took a deep breath before nodding at them.

Mrs. Gleason said, "Hello, I don't know if you remember us, but we're the Gleasons. Reggie Gleason's parents?"

"Yes, I remember. What can I do for you?"

"It's about the strike. Aren't you on strike?"

"No, that's a tenured faculty issue. I'm an adjunct so I'm not affected by it." That wasn't entirely true, but I saw no reason to cloud the issue.

"Well, all those angry people outside campus waving those signs are making Reggie very anxious."

"I'm sorry, I didn't know Reggie had problems with anxiety."

"What? No, I don't mean that." She hesitated, and I think she considered giving Reggie an imaginary issue but decided against it. "I just mean it's making him nervous, and it's harder for him to concentrate on his work. We wanted to know what accommodations you'll be making, under the circumstances."

"You do realize that the strike only started yesterday, don't you?"

"They were picketing today, too," she said, as if doubling the timeline made an enormous difference. "The parents' group on

Facebook says that a lot of professors are giving their students extra time."

"I wasn't aware of that. The administration has instructed those of us still in the classroom to stick to our previously announced due dates in order to keep the semester on track. If Reggie is having problems getting his work done, he's welcome to come talk to me himself."

"Coming to talk to you makes him nervous, too."

"Then email or a phone call will work," I said, though having seen Reggie, I was pretty sure Reggie's only worry was finding out when the next beer bash was. "Of course, as I explained on the first day of class, late papers are penalized a letter grade."

She looked alarmed. "I don't think he knows that."

"It's in the syllabus, which Reggie signed off on at the beginning of the semester."

Mrs. Gleason seemed to be trying to come up with another excuse when my salvation arrived in the form of Charles coming down the hall at a brisk walk.

"Dr. Thackery," he said sternly, "I dislike rushing you, but you're already past time for our meeting."

I made a show of looking at my watch. "Dr. Peyton, I'm so sorry. These parents had a question, and I lost track of time."

He frowned at me. "Parents? I hope you are not in violation of FERPA regulations regarding dissemination of information to parties other than students. I'm sure I don't need to remind you of the penalties incurred by all parties for such action."

"She didn't tell us anything," Mrs. Gleason said, either in my defense or her own.

"I'm relieved to hear that. Now if you will excuse us, Dr. Thackery and I have a pressing engagement." He actually tapped his foot as I said my goodbyes to the Gleasons and packed up my things. Then he rushed me down the hall while the Gleasons watched with their eyes wide.

I'd have felt sorry for them if I hadn't heard Mrs. Gleason say,

"If she gets fired, do you suppose Reggie can get an extension on his deadline?"

We didn't speak until we were well out of the couple's range. "Charles, you are a lifesaver."

"I didn't think you'd mind an escape route."

"From those two? Never." Since he hadn't quit moving, I said, "I think we can stop now."

"Actually I was not entirely dissembling. We do have a meeting. I have located the one custodian still at Bostock who knew Annabelle."

"Good job!" I hadn't even come up with an approach to use to find somebody.

"I'll caution you that Mrs. Silva is not the most affable of women, but she agreed to speak to us if were there when she takes her lunch break." He pulled out his pocket watch. "We have precisely seventeen minutes to meet her, so I'm afraid we must make haste."

"Lead the way," I said, saving the rest of my breath for our trek. There was no shuttle bus in sight, of course, so we had to cross a good chunk of the campus on foot to reach the student center. Charles led the way around to the back of the building and knocked on the door marked *Employees Only*.

A tiny woman with light brown skin, gray hair tucked tightly into a bun, and a severe expression on her face opened the door. I remembered Deborah's description of a small custodian who'd cleaned at the Nichols house and guessed that Mrs. Silva was that woman.

"Coming this late, I thought you'd changed your mind," she said with a sniff.

I glanced at my watch. We were, in fact, one minute early, but given Charles's earlier warning, I thought it best not to point that out.

The woman led the way to what looked like a break room with a row of vending machines, a refrigerator, and counters holding a microwave and a coffee maker. A quartet of plastic laminated tables and chairs filled the space in the middle.

Mrs. Silva said, "I only get an hour for lunch, so I will eat while we talk." Then she gave us a pointed look. "You are welcome to use the vending machines, but the coffee is paid for by those of us who use this room."

"Understood," Charles said. "Would you care for something to drink, Georgia?"

"Thank you, a Diet Coke would be great."

While he was buying our drinks, Mrs. Silva used the microwave to warm up a bowl of rice, peas, tomato sauce, and olives. Then she brought the bowl and a mug of coffee over to one of the tables and nodded for us to join her.

"That smells wonderful," I said.

"It's only arroz con gandules," she said dismissively. "So, Professor Peyton tells me you want to know about Annabelle Mitchell."

"Yes, we're trying—"

"I don't need to know," she said imperiously. "I only want to clear my conscience."

I nodded and took a swallow from my drink.

"Annabelle Mitchell came to work at Bostock with my husband Sebastian and me. It did not take me long to realize that she was a fool."

I saw that Charles was gripping his soda can rather more tightly than usual.

"She was here to clean, nothing more, but she decided to be a friend to the students, to give them things they did not need. I know how much money she made, and she should not have been wasting it. I told my husband that she was a fool."

"Did he agree with you?" I asked.

"My husband was a big man, with a big heart, and about some things, he had a small brain. Me, I'm a little woman, and my heart is no bigger than it needs to be, but my brain is large. So when my husband disagreed, I said nothing more. As long as Annabelle did her job, it made no difference to me that she squandered her money in foolish ways." She paused, then added, "She did her job well, that I must admit. Thorough and dependable. So not a complete fool."

There was now a visible dent in Charles's soda can.

"We worked together two, maybe three years. Then one day Sebastian comes to find me, and he is upset. He says that our manager is saying that Annabelle is in trouble, that she has stolen from students."

"Did you believe it?"

Mrs. Silva shrugged. "I never saw her steal, and when students leave expensive phones and computers alone all the time, it would have been easy to do. Or maybe that's why she made friends with students, to find ways to steal from them. So I didn't know what was true, but Sebastian was sure she was innocent, even when they found stolen things in her locker. He said anybody could have put them there, and I agreed she would have been stupid to leave things like that in her locker. She was foolish, but that is not the same as stupid."

She looked at us as if to make sure we understood the difference, so I nodded. Charles was still gripping his soda.

After another bite of rice, she went on. "Annabelle had the day off, and when Sebastian heard that the police were going to be waiting for her the next morning, he wanted to call her so she would know. I told him to stay out of it, that if anybody found out, he could be fired." She made a face. "But he had a big heart."

"Then he did call her?"

She nodded. "That is when I decided she was a thief. Why would an innocent person run from police the way she did?"

"I can think of a lot of reasons."

"I know the police and the courts get things wrong, but I also know guilty people run, which makes innocent people who run look guilty. Annabelle was either guilty or even more of a fool."

I slid the can away from Charles before he completely crushed it.

"I told this to Sebastian, and this time he agreed," Mrs. Silva said. "A year later, he died." Before I could express my condolences, she said, "That was nothing to do with Annabelle. I'm only telling you because of something that happened before he died. A student found out that her boyfriend was cheating on her, and after she broke up with him she told the provost that it was her ex-boyfriend who stole those things and put them in Annabelle's locker."

"What happened to him?"

"Nothing. He's rich and white. His father sent him to another college and Bostock got expensive new computers, and maybe the father paid the girl off, too. Nothing more was said. I only know because the girl cried on Sebastian's shoulder, and it was he who told her to go to the provost. I said it would make no difference, but he said it would. I was right, and he was wrong." She shrugged. "Of course, he was right about Annabelle when I was wrong. He wanted to find her so she could come back to her job because she may have been a—"

"Do not call her a fool again," Charles said through gritted teeth.

Mrs. Silva regarded him and relented. "Whatever else she may have been, she was not guilty of those thefts. Only my husband didn't know how to find her, and not long after that he had a heart attack and died. He would have wanted Annabelle to know what happened, so if you know where she is, please tell her."

I looked at Charles, and from the expression on his face it was obvious that he wasn't willing to share any information with Mrs. Silva. I asked, "Do you remember the name of the student who was the real thief? Or the students who accused Annabelle of stealing?"

Despite my having several inches on her, she managed to look down her nose at me. "I don't make friends with the students. No good ever comes of it."

I doubted that Lauri Biegler would agree with her, but I saw no reason to argue. I didn't think it would be worthwhile to ask more questions, either, and when I looked at Charles again, I decided it was past time to get him out of there. I stood and said, "Thank you for talking to us."

Charles rose, too, but didn't say a word before walking out of the room. I was going, too, but noticed that Mrs. Silva was glaring at the soda cans we'd left on the table. I picked them up and tossed them in the recycle bin before going after Charles. I found him outside with his coat unbuttoned, staring at nothing.

"Charles?"

He didn't reply.

"Charles?"

Silence.

I waited another five minutes, getting colder and colder, when finally I quoted, "'The greatest fools are ofttimes more clever than the men who laugh at them.'"

He gave the hint of a smile. "Shakespeare?"

"George R.R. Martin, but it's still a good line."

"It is indeed." He took a deep breath and finally seemed to realize how frigid it was because he buttoned his coat and pulled his gloves out of his pockets. "I'm so sorry, Georgia. Here I am making you stay out in this weather."

"It's okay. I wanted to slug that woman, too."

"I hope that the information we gleaned will help you."

"I think it will. I just need to let it percolate a little." In other words, I needed to talk it over with Sid. "I'm starved. Want to get some lunch?"

"That would be lovely, but would you mind if we left campus? I find myself wanting to be almost anywhere else."

"That sounds like an excellent idea."

We found a shuttle back to the parking deck and retrieved our cars to make the drive into town. The food trucks were still there, and this time I resisted the impulse to look and see if Brownie was around.

We met up at Jasper's, a diner that has terrific vegetable soup, which was what I needed to warm myself up. Since Charles didn't bring up Annabelle, I followed his lead and we talked a little about the strike, a little about history, and a lot about the weather. He left afterward to teach an afternoon class, and I went back home.

I was feeling time pressure on this case in a way I hadn't before. Digging up memories was too hard on Charles to let it go on much longer.

Chapter Thirty-Two

Though Sid really did enjoy the kind of tedious task he'd dived into the night before, as soon as I saw him I knew he was tired of it all. It wasn't just the looseness of his bones, though that was a red flag. It was the fact that he was slumped over his couch, rather than at his computer, and that he wasn't tapping his bony foot to the song that was playing. I'd never known him to resist the musical allure of "I Want a Hippopotamus for Christmas," though he sometimes substitutes his own lyrics.

"What's wrong?"

"I'm stuck, Georgia," he said mournfully. "You know those neighborhood canvassing montage scenes they put in cop shows?"

"The what now?"

"You know, when they have to canvass the neighborhood, and they want to show cops pounding the pavement for hours to make it seem more realistic, only hours of pavement pounding wouldn't fit into an episode and it would be wicked boring? So they do ten-second snippets of the cops talking to an old guy, a mother with kids, a mail carrier, and a kid on a skateboard before finally getting around to the nosy neighbor who saw everything. Then there's a nice long scene of them talking to that neighbor."

"That does sound familiar, now that you mention it."

"That's what my day was like. I Googled the heck out of all the people from the Nichols house cleanup project. The cheap lawyer who runs bad TV ads on late-night local TV, the hardworking chairman of development having to drum up college donations and deal with odd bequests, his harder-working administrative assistant with two kids and a mortgage, the hoarder helpers who heroically work in the most disgusting situations imaginable, and so on."

"What about the nosy neighbor?"

"That's the problem. I never found a nosy neighbor." He sighed heavily.

"You haven't been able to eliminate anybody else?"

"I tried, and I thought for sure I had one to mark off the list. Jetta Silva—one of the custodians—didn't have a driver's license, and since the first attempt on Annabelle was with a car, I thought that let her out. Unfortunately, she was married to Sebastian Silva—another custodian—so I had to allow for the possibility that the happy couple were co-killers. Sebastian died several years ago, but Jetta still works at Bostock."

"She certainly does, and she is a piece of work." I told him about my interview with Mrs. Silva.

Sid said, "What if she was jealous? She could've framed and then killed Annabelle because she and Sebastian were having an affair."

"If I even suggested such a thing to Charles, he would never speak to me again."

"Okay, maybe Sebastian wanted to have an affair with Annabelle, and Mrs. Silva went for the preemptive strike. A crime of passion!"

I was going to point out that Mrs. Silva gave no impression of having enough passion to drive her to murder, but two things stopped me. One, I could be wrong. Two, Sid's bones had snapped together, and he was humming with the music. I didn't have the heart to take away his best suspect. Instead I said, "We'll keep both Silvas on the list, but tonight is all about music."

"I could go for a dance party." He jumped up and started rattling around more or less in time with "All I Want for Christmas Is You."

"Maybe later. I was talking about Madison's concert."

"Is that tonight?" He perked up even more. "I'd lost track

because of the case. Is it time to leave? We need to go early to get good seats."

He packed his away team of skull and hand into the sugar skull bag, and his headless, one-armed skeleton handed it to me. "I'm ready!"

Though Madison had been in chorus for years and that usually meant a holiday concert, last year's had been snowed out, meaning that this one was going to be Sid's first time in attendance. He was outrageously excited about it.

I said, "I've got to warn you, you might not be able to see well from the bag. I can't really hold it up because it'll block the view for other people."

"That's okay," Sid said. "I'll be able to listen, and somebody's going to video it, right?"

"Phil has his phone all charged up."

"Then let's go!"

With Sid rushing us, we were at school extra early. I took Madison backstage to join the rest of the performers and left Mom in charge of finding seats in the auditorium. She has a way of weaving through crowds politely, yet swiftly, and snagged front-row seats for me, Phil, Deborah, and herself. Deborah's job was to defend those seats against any interlopers.

I'd always said that I wouldn't be one of those parents who was insanely intent on sitting up front for every performance, but that was before I had a daughter with a penchant for performing. Being in the first row this time meant that not only was Phil going to be able to get great footage but Sid would get a terrific view after all. I could feel the bag vibrating in excitement while we waited for the concert to begin.

Since it's a public school, the focus was *holiday*, not *Christmas*, so the kids spread nondenominational cheer with "Sleigh Ride," "Jingle Bells," and "Winter Wonderland." For the grand finale, they segued from "Let it Snow," to the Disney song, "Let it Go," and when Sid realized Madison had a solo verse, he started jumping up in down in the bag so hard I nearly dropped him. The applause was satisfyingly loud, and nobody noticed the cheers from the bag in my lap.

After the inevitable reception with cookies, watery punch, and students complimenting other's performances, we piled into my minivan and drove home. I'd pulled into the driveway and stopped the car before I saw Brownie sitting on the wicker loveseat on the front porch chatting with Andrew, Phil's most ubiquitous grad student.

"Coccyx," I said.

Chapter Thirty-Three

"Is something wrong?" said Phil, who was riding shotgun.

"Brownie's here," I said.

I hadn't told anybody I was mad at Brownie, but either Sid had or I'd been too obvious in ignoring the phone messages he'd left because nobody seemed surprised by my reaction.

"Ah," Phil said. "I see he has company. Perhaps I'll go see what Andrew wants." He ushered the rest of the family into the house, gathering Andrew along the way, while I continued to sit in the car and Brownie waited.

Sid said, "If you want me to, I will jump out of this bag, roll over to him, and bite him. Hard. Just say the word."

"Interesting suggestion, but no thanks. At least, not yet."

I stewed a while longer but finally got out of the car.

Brownie stood up as I walked toward the porch. "Hey."

"Hey."

"I hear you talked to Sue again."

"I hear you lied to me." He opened his mouth, but before he could speak, I said, "Lying by omission still counts as lying."

"I don't disagree. Can I come in to explain?"

I considered it. On one hand, I was still angry with him. On the other, it was cold that night, and with the wind blowing, it felt even colder than the thermometer claimed. What really decided it was that I wanted to have that conversation without Sid listening in. "Okay, let's try that."

Madison and Deborah were in the living room, Phil and Andrew were in the dining room, and I could hear Mom clattering around in the kitchen. Since I wasn't going to take Brownie to my bedroom, that limited my options. "Phil, can I borrow the office for a little while?"

"Certainly," he said. "Hello, Brownie."

"Hello, Dr. Thackery," he said with a polite nod as we took off our winter gear and left them on the coatrack. I left Sid's bag on the table in the hall since I wasn't planning on having him bite anyone.

My parents' office was a good-sized room, but with two desks with accompanying chairs, stuffed bookcases, and a loveseat, that didn't leave a lot of room to move around. Brownie sat on the loveseat, but I wasn't sure I wanted to be that close to him, so I rolled over Mom's chair instead. Then I waited. I wasn't going to make it easy on him.

He cleared his throat nervously. "I didn't want to lie to you, Georgia, not even by omission, but by the time I found out how my parents and Sue had decided to spin things, they were all set on it. I mean, have you ever tried to change my mother's mind once it's made up?" He laughed weakly.

I said nothing.

"I told Sue she should tell you everything, but she has trust issues."

"Being lied to does tend to give one trust issues," I said. "I'm having some of my own right now."

"I know. It's just that carnies have this whole insider/outsider thing and—" He stopped and sat up straight. "No, forget that. Forget everything I've said so far. The fact is I screwed up. I knew it was the wrong way to go, and I should have told you everything my parents told me, but I let myself get talked into it. I'm sorry, Georgia, I really am."

A part of me was still mad, but that part was shrinking rapidly. Brownie sure did know how to apologize. Besides, it was hard to fault a man for being close enough to his parents to follow their lead. Then there was my own guilt. I hadn't lied to Brownie about

Sid—it wasn't as if he asked if I had an ambulatory skeleton living in my attic—but it was still a big secret to keep from him.

I was taking so long to answer that Brownie tried again. "If there is any way I can make it up to you, I will. I'll help you investigate Annabelle's murder, or not, if you don't trust me to. I want to make this right."

The mad part was pretty much gone by that point, but I didn't think I should entirely let him off the hook. "Tell me this. Do you know anything else about Sue or Annabelle that nobody's told me?"

"I don't think so, but I will be happy to tell you everything I do know."

"Over dinner?"

"Tonight?" he said hopefully.

"If you don't have other plans."

"May I treat you, as part of the apology?"

"Food has always been an important part of apologies, but I warn you, I'm very hungry. Dessert may be required."

"That's a small price to pay."

We didn't kiss, though I suspect we both wanted to, because there was a knock on the door before my father opened it.

"Brownie, would you care to join us for dinner?"

"No, thank you," Brownie said. "As a matter of fact, I'll be taking Georgia out to eat."

"Another time, then."

"I'd like that."

Before he retreated, Phil gave me a look with both eyebrows raised, which is generally a sign of his approval.

I said, "Just let me tell Madison I'm going out."

"Would you like to bring her along?" Brownie asked. "Also as my treat?"

"Coccyx, you really do know how to apologize."

"That, and I like spending time with Madison."

"Me, too, but not this time."

He grinned.

I went upstairs, stopping to grab the sugar skull bag.

"Do you want to go to the attic?" I said to Sid as we climbed.

Instead of a proper response, all I heard was exaggerated smooching sounds. I have no idea how Sid does that without lips, but then again, I don't know how he does most of what he does.

"Wow, that is so mature," I said.

More smooching sounds.

"Or I could leave you downstairs in the hall, in the bag, knowing that Andrew is around, and you'll be stuck in there for most of the night."

The smooches stopped. "Attic, please."

"All right." I stopped in Madison's room and explained my change in plans, which meant I had to hear two sets of smooching sounds. "Did you two coordinate this?"

Madison said, "Great minds think alike, Mom."

"Thinking? Is that what kids are calling it now? When you two are finished with the sound effects, would you take Sid to his attic? I need to switch pocketbooks before I go."

"You're going to change clothes, too, aren't you?" Madison said.

"Brownie has already seen me in this outfit."

"Which means he'll appreciate an upgrade that much more."

I looked in the mirror, and since I was wearing an Overfeld College sweatshirt and scruffy jeans, I said, "Fine."

Madison, being the helpful daughter that she is, made sure the jeans I picked were appropriately snug and that the red sweater I switched into was appropriately low-cut. She also covered Sid's eyes while I changed. Then the two of them conferred and decided I could limit my jewelry to shiny gold earrings as long as I put on lipstick that matched the sweater. Madison also transferred everything but the subset of Sid and his phone to a smaller purse for me.

Once they were satisfied, I kissed Madison's cheek and the top of Sid's skull, leaving as perfect a pair of lip prints as I could.

Madison started rubbing and Sid objected, "Hey, that stuff isn't easy to get off!"

My only response was to make kissing noises as I went down the stairs.

Maturity runs in the family.

Fortunately for my dignity, Brownie had not heard me smooching my way down the stairs. He was in the living room chatting with Andrew about life in dissertation purgatory.

Andrew had the good grace to look embarrassed when he saw me. "Good evening, Dr. Thackery."

"Andrew, how's it going with the Transcendentalists?" I realized immediately it was a mistake because his eyes lit up and he opened his mouth.

Brownie hurriedly said, "Sorry, Georgia, but we've got to book if we're going to make our reservation."

I tried to look disappointed while I threw on scarf, coat, and gloves as fast as I could. Brownie was moving nearly as quickly as I was, and we were out the door and halfway to his car in record time.

"We have reservations?" I said.

"Not at a restaurant, but I have grave reservations about the entertainment value in that guy's dissertation. I know Nathaniel Hawthorne was a great writer, Georgia, but I never could stomach him."

"Stop right there, Brownie Mannix." I grabbed him by his coat, pulled him over, and gave him a big kiss. Then I wiped the lipstick off with one thumb.

"Whoa. Is there any other great writer I should not like?"

"I'll let you know."

When Brownie announced that we were going to Marion's Steakhouse, I was glad I'd changed clothes. It wasn't an overly fancy place, but it was definitely a step above sweatshirt-related ensembles. Along the way, and after we got to our table and ordered, I gave Brownie a synopsis of what Sue had told me, ending just as our tossed salads were delivered.

"Does that match what you know?" I asked.

"It exceeds it. You got a lot more detail out of her than I got from my parents."

"I think she felt bad about lying to me."

"My parents aren't big into guilt."

"Speaking of guilt, is that why you brought food trucks to Bostock? Because you felt guilty about keeping the real story from me?"

"Maybe a little, but mostly I really want to help with the investigation. In fact, I did a little nosing around already." He paused while the waitress brought our steaks and baked potatoes. "I went on campus looking for you yesterday since you weren't returning my calls."

"I admit that was not a particularly adult reaction."

"No worse than when I quit calling you a few months ago. Anyway, you weren't at your desk, so I was heading back to the trucks when I spotted that museum you mentioned. Which of course I already knew was involved in the case. And I'm still really sorry—"

"Stop. You've apologized, I've accepted, and this is an excellent steak. We're good."

His smile before he went on was a thing of beauty. "I tell you, Georgia, that place is bizarre enough to be a sideshow attraction."

"At least now we know why it's such a hodgepodge."

"I bet the thief targeted the place because it was a hodgepodge, not the other way around. If I were a stealing man, there are plenty of things I could have walked off with. There's no security to speak of, just that one student at the door who never looked up from her laptop."

"There must be a curator in charge of the place," I said.

"That's what I thought, so when I got back to the food trucks, I chatted up some of the professors. According to them, the head of the history department is technically in charge, but in reality, he has as little to do with the place as possible. When donations come in, he gets the departmental secretary to type up the labels, going purely by the inventory they're given, without doing any additional research. Somebody eventually lugs the stuff to the museum and finds a spot to squeeze it in. No chronology, no explanation of an item's significance, and certainly no climate control. It's enough to make a historian cry!"

"What about the attendants? Don't the students who run the museum have a company with a cutesy name?"

"The museum is spared that particular indignity. McClelland's bequest included funds to pay for museum attendants. If it weren't for that, I doubt the place would be open to the public at all. The attendant I spoke to said the job was considered easy money."

"That would put the attendants high on the list of potential thieves, wouldn't it?"

"It would if any of them had spent a decade at Bostock. While the thefts might have started ten years ago, they're still going on."

"Seriously?" I said. This was news to me.

"I looked at the dates on the object labels, and one of the fakest of the fakes was a so-called suit of medieval armor donated earlier this year. Georgia, I could buy a suit of armor just like it at the mall."

"I thought the same thing when I saw it."

"I made a list of the most obvious phonies, the ones that are so bad they don't deserve to be called forgeries. Shall I email it to you?"

"That would be great. I can add it to the file."

"You keep files?"

"One has to keep track of data somehow," I said modestly. The modesty came naturally since Sid did the vast majority of the filing.

"I also asked the attendant if there was a more thorough listing of the contents of the museum, since that brochure was next to useless. She didn't know and neither did the research librarian."

"Did you ask the history department secretary?"

"And thus was my thunder stolen."

"Sorry. Department secretaries know where all the bodies are buried." I remembered how I'd gotten involved in this case in the first place. "Though usually not literally."

"Metaphorically, you're right on the money. The secretary appreciated the coffee and muffins I brought her enough that she dug up a database file for me. I'll send that along, too."

"Terrific." Sid would love it.

"She also told me that if I wanted to know more about the museum, I should talk to Professor Dallas Sieck. She's retired now, but when she was still working, she was as close to a real curator as the place had."

"Did you get contact information?"

"I did." I was expecting him to offer to email me that as well, but instead he said, "I thought we could go talk to her together."

I blinked. "Um, I'll have to check my schedule, but maybe tomorrow or the next day?" Though it seemed like a good opportunity, I had a feeling Sid wasn't going to like the idea, even if I promised to bring him along.

Despite my threat of requiring Brownie to provide a dessert to achieve full apology, I decided that the salad, steak, and potato were more than enough food. Nor did we indulge in a dessert of another kind, since we both had to be up early the next morning. Instead Brownie drove me straight home after we left the restaurant, and we enjoyed a short interlude for fond farewells.

Mom, Phil, Madison, and Sid were waiting for me in the living room. Even Byron was sitting expectantly.

"Did you have a nice time?" everyone but the dog said in perfect unison.

"How long did you guys practice that?"

"Fifteen minutes," they replied together, then we all broke up into laughter.

I took off my coat and winter accessories and joined Madison and Sid on the couch. "We had a very nice time."

"Did you two kiss and make up?" Sid asked.

"We made up," I said. "As for the rest...You know carnies and their secrets."

That stopped them cold.

We finished watching *The Year Without a Santa Claus* and then headed our separate ways: Mom and Phil to their office, Madison to bed, and Sid and me to the attic.

"I'm glad you finally got away from the computer," I said.

"I was too excited to be alone. After Sue's revelations, I did some more research into the McClelland Museum. And guess what I found out?" He was too eager to wait for the obligatory *What?* in response. "Somebody is *still* stealing from the museum!"

Chapter Thirty-Four

Sid looked at me in clear expectation of my enthusiasm and adulation, and I tried my best to provide some.

"Wow, really?" I said. "That's amazing! How did you find that out? Good going, Sid!"

He ignored reality long enough to narrow his eye sockets. "You're a terrible liar, Georgia. You already knew it, didn't you?"

"Yes, I knew," I admitted, "but I didn't lie about it."

"I stand corrected. You're a terrible actress. How did you figure it out?"

"I didn't. Brownie did."

"Oh." His expression turned even blanker than the expression on most skulls.

"He visited the museum and—"

"The museum he already knew was involved in Annabelle's story but didn't trust you enough to tell you?"

"He apologized for that."

I think he muttered, "Not to me," but I didn't call him on it. Instead I explained how Brownie had discovered that the museum thefts were a long-term scheme. "How did you find out?"

"I found a couple of scholarly papers that referenced items in the museum, and unless that historian was an utter buffoon, the artifacts cited were real as of five years ago. So I compared the photos from the papers to the ones Madison took, and obviously they weren't the same items, which means that somebody has continued to steal from the museum."

"It's good to have it confirmed, isn't it?"

He sniffed. "The papers were written by a Dr. Dallas Sieck, who used to be at Bostock, but she retired." He gave me another look. "How much of what I just told you did you already know?"

"Not all of it. Brownie found out that Dr. Sieck took a lot of interest in the museum, and that she was retired from Bostock, but he didn't find out about the papers. That's good work, Sid."

"Don't patronize me, Georgia."

That was as much as I could take. "Coccyx, Sid, what do you want from me? Do you want me to tell Brownie not to help, even though he's giving us access to information we wouldn't have otherwise? It's not like it's the first time we've had help. It's not even the first time with this case. Madison went with us to Bostock to provide cover, and Deborah told us about the Nichols house cleanup. Should I tell them I don't want their help either?"

"They're different. They're family. Brownie isn't."

"Neither are Charles, Dana, Treasure Hunt, or Sue, all of whom have helped us."

"They're not the same, either. Brownie is—" He stopped.

I waited for him to finish the sentence, but when he didn't, I said, "He's my friend, Sid, and I'm sorry he's not yours. Maybe you can take an online class with him like you did with Charles and get to know him."

"He never teaches online classes," Sid said in a low voice. "I checked."

"I didn't know that."

"Coccyx, Georgia, I should just get this off my rib cage. I'm jealous of Brownie."

I know it's impossible for somebody's heart to literally sink, but it sure felt like mine did. I put my hand on his bony one and said, "Sid, you know I love you, but not like that."

Sid leapt up from his chair. "Coccyx, Georgia, don't even go there! That's just gross. I'm going to have to pour hydrogen peroxide inside my skull to get that image out of there."

"Oh," I said, incredibly relieved. "I was afraid you meant that—"

"I know what you thought, but all the EWWWWWs in the world could not express my feelings on this matter."

"Now I'm feeling insulted."

"I'm freaked out and you're insulted! You see, no good could ever come of this topic. We should never speak of this again."

"Agreed."

He sat back down, but considerably further away from me. "As I was trying to explain, I'm jealous because Brownie can do things I can't, like going to restaurants and bookstores without being stuck in a bag."

"I thought you wanted me to make up with him."

"I did. I have no problems whatsoever with Brownie as a boyfriend."

"You just don't want him taking your place as my partner in crime-solving."

"Yeah, that."

"First off, he's not going to take your place. Nobody can work the computer the way you do, Sid. Even if Brownie had your abilities, he'd never be able to keep up with your speed, let alone your tenacity. He's got to work two jobs, wear clothes, eat at regular intervals, and deal with countless other biological issues you can safely ignore."

"Plus has to sleep hours and hours every day, which is disgusting."

I let that slide for the time being. "However, during one of his rare waking moments, Brownie can arrange for us to see the retired professor who wrote those papers. Are you up for it?"

"No, you two go."

"Are you sure?"

He nodded. "I'm sorry I was being a pain in the patella."

"Sid, you don't have to put yourself in timeout. If you want to come, come. You might catch something Brownie and I miss."

He stroked his jawbone. "That's true."

"Ahem."

"I mean you're experienced, but Brownie is a newbie. So okay, I'll come."

"All right then. Oh, were you able to delete anybody from the suspect pool?"

He cocked his skull. "I told you I hadn't. The cop show montage, no nosy neighbor. Remember?"

"Yeah, but that was before you knew that museum thefts weren't a one-time deal and are still going on. Now you can eliminate people who no longer have access."

His eye sockets got as big as an anime character's. "I am a total bonehead. I never thought of that." He jumped up and clattered to his desk. "I'm on it!"

I checked my watch. "Then I'm going to get some of that oh-so-repellent sack-time."

He waved in my general direction without looking away from his computer screen, and I went downstairs.

I felt as if Sid and I were on a better footing than we had been earlier, but I was still uneasy about his feelings toward Brownie. Neither Brownie nor I had said the L-word out loud, but after our dinner, I realized that I was about ninety percent in love with him. How would Sid react when I told him? Of course, Madison's approval was the most important, and I cared what my parents thought, too, but none of them relied on pure force of will to stay alive. If Sid ever decided he was being replaced by Brownie, he might fall apart forever.

Chapter Thirty-Five

I didn't have time the next morning to stop at the food trucks for coffee with Brownie, but I did tap my horn, and when he looked up and saw me, he actually blew a kiss. I was grinning like an idiot as I drove to the parking deck, found a place, and waited for the shuttle bus. Receiving a text from Brownie wishing me a good morning didn't hurt either.

I maintained my happy mood until the shuttle arrived a minute or two later and I climbed on board.

"Allons-y!" I chirped to David, the driver of the day.

I expected him to reply with *Geronimo!*, *Hello, sweetie!*, or some other catchphrase from *Doctor Who*, but he just nodded and said, "Hey, Dr. Thackery."

I took the seat closest to him and once we started up, I asked, "Is something wrong?"

"I'm just wondering about this strike stuff. My parents are worried that the union rally tomorrow might get ugly."

"What, bad grammar on the picket signs?"

"No, seriously. People are talking about a riot, but I don't think that could happen here. Do you?"

"No, of course not. Where is this coming from?"

"There's a parents' group on Facebook."

"Sounds as if somebody is pulling their leg."

"That's what I thought, but a couple of the other shuttle drivers have heard rumors, too."

"What about campus security? They must be on high alert."

"Yeah, but it's a big campus and they can't be everywhere. We drivers are going to meet to decide if we should suspend service tomorrow afternoon for safety reasons. It would be bad for business, and we hate to strand people, but—"

"You do what you have to do to stay safe," I said, though the idea of having to make my way around campus on foot didn't appeal. "Just give us as much warning as you can manage."

"Will do." We pulled up at my stop, and he opened the door. "You be careful, Dr. Thackery." Then he mustered up a grin to say, "I've got a bad feeling about this."

After that, my mood was soured, but I made it through classes. It did seem as if the students were unusually restless, but it could just as easily have been end-of-semester anxiety or something completely different. I didn't know that I should attribute it to rumors, but it worried me just the same.

Brownie had sent me a text inviting me to join him at the food trucks for lunch, and not only did I have the obvious reasons for accepting, but I wanted to get a good look at the picketers and see if I could gauge their state of mind.

At Brownie's suggestion I drove to the church lot and then moved to the backseat so we could have a private picnic in the heated car rather than shivering outside. A couple of minutes after I arrived, he delivered a tray.

"I share with you the delicacies of my people," he said, then placed it reverently in my lap.

I laughed when I saw that he'd brought me classic carnival treats: hot dogs, popcorn, and fried dough. "Perfect."

"I also have news. Professor Emeritus Dallas Sieck can meet with us this afternoon if you're available."

"As long as there's time for me to run by my house first." In other words, I needed to grab Sid.

"That's no problem. As soon as we get through the lunch rush, I'm going to shut down here and send the trucks back to the zoo. I'll swing by your place so we can go in one car."

As we finished up our lunch, I found myself staring out the

window at the picket line and would have apologized to Brownie if I hadn't seen he was doing the same.

"Have you been told anything about the strike getting nastier?" I asked.

"You've heard rumors, too?"

I nodded.

"Some of the professors were told that Bostock was going to bring in outside security to break up the picket line. Plus a few strikers have been going on campus for one thing or another, and they've heard that those security thugs are going to escort off anybody they find with extreme prejudice."

"Why would Bostock do that? The lawsuits alone would cost them huge bucks, not to mention the price of the bad publicity." I tried to imagine Humphries the Bostock tour guide doing his best to talk up the Bostock Difference after news of a riot went viral.

"I don't know," Brownie said, "but there's something in the air. If I were on the carnival lot, I'd make sure I had a baseball bat or some other weapon handy, just in case of a clem."

"I thought a clem was a dumb towner."

"It can also mean a fight between a carney and a towner, depending on context."

"Have you seen many clems?"

"Some. More often it's towner versus towner, and if it gets beyond that, a bunch of us holding bats usually calms things down. You just never know how things are going to go."

The idea of academics rioting seemed crazy, but as I watched the angry-looking picketers, I wished I knew how things were going to go.

Chapter Thirty-Six

After lunch I drove back home to gather up as much of Sid as could fit in the sugar skull bag. Brownie picked me up a little while later, and we drove to a yellow Cape Cod house on what local real estate agents called the desirable west side of Pennycross. Dr. Sieck answered right away. "Doctors Thackery and Mannix?"

When we nodded, she waved us inside.

The professor was several inches shorter than me and built like a little snow woman: a round figure and a round head with close-cropped white hair. Her eyes weren't quite as black as if they were made out of coal, but they were close enough.

"Head on into the study," she said, nodding at an open doorway. "I've got tea and cakes ready."

Brownie and I walked into the comfortably cluttered study with a desk, a plush sofa, a trio of recliners around a table, and one wall lined with built-in glass-fronted shelves.

I would have expected those shelves to be filled with books, and the bottom row was, but the contents of the rest of the shelves astounded me. I'd never seen so many McDonald's toys in my life. I thought I felt Sid taking a picture from inside his bag.

I recognized a handful from Madison's Happy Meal days, which is how I realized what the rest had to be, but those were just a small oasis in the middle of what seemed to be a chronologically arranged display.

"You can blame my collection on the McClelland Museum," Dr. Sieck said as she came back in with a wooden tray. "A box of these babies came in as a donation, and after we quit laughing at the letter that insisted a box of these chewed-on, beat-up pieces of plastic were valuable pop culture artifacts, I realized something."

"What was that?" Brownie said as he took the tray from her and placed it on the table.

"That they really were valuable pop culture artifacts. Not financially valuable, of course, but as an example of marketing acumen. You see, my primary research interest is historical business practices. I ended up writing quite a few papers about Happy Meal toys: how they spread to other fast food venues; how they became a standard of Disney movie campaigns only for Disney to later distance themselves from McDonald's because of nutrition concerns; how they played a role in Beanie Baby mania; how a McDonald's Collectors Club was created, which led to an annual convention. I've even done research into the ethics of marketing aimed at children. Somewhere along the way, I started collecting them myself."

She looked fondly at her toys then gestured for us to take seats. "But that's not why you two came, is it?" she said as she began pouring tea. "On the phone, Dr. Mannix said he had some questions about the McClelland."

Brownie looked at me, letting me take the lead, so I said, "We've both visited it, and we were impressed by the collection."

"Impressed or depressed?" She laughed. "Of course, a lot of it is absolute rubbish, and when somebody who collects Happy Meal toys says it's rubbish, you know it's rubbish. But there are some very interesting pieces buried amongst the junk. When I first came to Bostock and was the low professor on the totem pole, I was encouraged to volunteer to oversee the running of the museum. The idea was that when a newer new kid was hired, I'd pass it on, but I actually grew fond of that ridiculous accumulation of tax write-offs."

"I read a couple of your papers," Brownie said.

"At my age, flattery will get you nothing but a smile, Dr.

Mannix," she said with a smile. "Now tell me what's wrong with my paper."

"Nothing," Brownie said.

"Come, come, you didn't come see a retired professor to express admiration for an obscure paper about an obscure artifact."

"Brownie, this is your field." I said.

"Okay." He pulled a printout from his pocket. "I found this paper about a suit of armor."

She took it from him. "Medieval manufacturing, I remember. I spoke a lot about the museum's fifteenth century German suit. Some of the bits were missing, and of course there was rust, but it's not a bad specimen. What about it?"

He handed her a printed photograph. "This is the armor in the museum now."

She looked at the picture. "I don't understand. They replaced the fifteenth century German with this reject from a renaissance faire?"

"That's what I thought, but it's still labeled fifteenth century German." He pointed to where the label was clearly visible in the photo.

"What the hell?!" she said.

"You referred to a Grover sewing machine in another article, but this is the machine in the museum now."

"That's not an 1800's Grover!" she said. "It says Singer right there on the machine."

Brownie showed her more examples, and she got increasingly aggravated.

"Enough," she finally said. "What has happened to my museum?"

"That's what we're trying to find out," I said. Sid and I had decided to omit mentions of murder. Later I'd had the same discussion with Brownie. Keeping everybody on the same page was going to be tough. "Since it seems unlikely that these substitutions were made by mistake—"

"Yes, yes, I know you're talking about theft," she said angrily.

"Not just theft, but long-term theft and substitution. We're trying to find out who could have stolen the artifacts and switched them out with lesser items."

"Lesser items? What you meant to say is utter trash. Have you called the police? Who's running the history department these days? Did you talk to them?"

I said, "We didn't want to do anything official until we know more."

She regarded me shrewdly. "You think it's an inside job, don't you?"

"How could it not be?" I said.

"You've got a point. So what do you want from me?"

Brownie said, "I've got a recent inventory of what's supposed to be in the museum, and I took pictures of a lot of the actual items. We were wondering if you could help us identify which items have been stolen and maybe give us an idea of what they're worth."

She took a deep breath and squared her shoulders. "This is going to take some time and concentration. You two scoot and leave me to it."

"Are you sure you don't want help?"

"I'll go faster on my own. Just email me what you've got. And Dr. Mannix, do me a favor. Take this tray back out to the kitchen and bring me a beer from the refrigerator. For this job, tea just isn't going to cut it."

While he took care of that, I got Dr. Sieck's email address and then did some back and forth with Sid. He sent me the picture files from our visit to the museum, and I forwarded them on to Dr. Sieck. When Brownie got back with the beer, he sent what he had and left the printouts as well. Then a text from Sid reminded me of something.

"There's one other item that should have been added to the collection about ten years ago, a decorated glass cup from

Venice. I don't know how old it was, but it was supposed to be valuable."

"I'll add it to the list." Dr. Sieck made shooing motions with her hands and said, "You two can show yourself out. I'll get you a report as fast as I can. And then..." She pointed at the two of us. "Then I want you to catch the guy who looted my museum."

We followed her instructions and scooted.

Chapter Thirty-Seven

"How did I do?" Brownie asked when we got into his car.

"You charmed her."

"That was easy—she charmed me first. But were my questions on point? Did I tell her enough without giving too much away? I was trying to be careful, but I might have revealed more than I should have." He exhaled sharply. "Am I doing this right?"

I reached over to pat his leg. "Brownie, there's no rulebook for this."

"It's just that this is a big part of your life, and I want to be a part of your life, and that includes this, and I think that sentence got away from me."

"You did fine," I said firmly.

"Good. Thank you."

By then we'd arrived at my house, and since Brownie had to work a shift at the zoo lights, he dropped me off with a quick-but-sincere kiss. Andrew and a grad student I hadn't met were working in the living room, so after I hung up my coat, I kept going until I reached Sid's attic.

"What do you think?" I asked as he reassembled himself.

"He did okay, for a rookie."

"I was talking about the information from Dr. Sieck, not Brownie's performance as a sleuth."

"We don't really have any information yet. I mean, she's just confirming what we'd already figured out about the thefts."

I started to argue with him but realized he was right. "Still, she might come through with something new once she goes through the database."

"I guess." He slouched across the couch, and while his bones were still firmly connected, I could tell he wasn't happy, but I didn't know how to cheer him up.

We had two grad students eating dinner with us that night. One was Andrew, who rarely seemed to leave our house, and the other was Mimi, who'd just begun work with Mom. Andrew was determined to bring the conversation over to his dissertation, of course, but Madison was just as determined to keep him from doing so and kept trying to draw Mimi out. Unfortunately, she was apparently so awed to be dining in the presence of two tenured professors that she could barely speak until Madison noticed her sweatshirt.

"Is that Dio Brando?" she asked.

Mimi brightened immediately. "You know *JoJo's Bizarre Adventure*?"

Introducing the dual topics of anime and manga instantly brought Mimi out of her shell. I could follow along, thanks to having watched some of the episodes with Madison's influence, and even my parents joined in out of general interest. That left Andrew out in the cold, though if I'd been feeling kinder, I could have pointed out that there was a Manga Classics version of *The Scarlet Letter.*

Finally, when there was a momentary conversational lull, Andrew got a chance to change the subject. He looked at me and said, "Do you have your riot escape plan worked out, Dr. Thackery?"

Several forks clattered to several plates.

"Excuse me?" I choked out.

"I heard that the Bostock strikers are going to fight it out with the scabs at the rally tomorrow. The scabs heard that if they can end the strike, they'll get tenure track jobs. And admin has planted ringers among the scabs—they're ex-Marines and such, not real academics."

"Where in the world did you get that load of sacrum?" I said.

"A lot of the grad students were talking online," he said. "Didn't you hear about it, Mimi?"

"I heard there was going to be a rally and that the Bostock

union is asking for other academics to come show support, but that's all," she said.

"Yeah, you're new in the department," he said condescendingly. "It takes a while to get hooked into the grapevine."

"Georgia," Phil said, "is this true?"

"There's supposed to be a rally tomorrow evening, and people are getting jumpy, but that's a long way from a riot."

"Feelings do run high around a strike," Mom said, her brow furrowed. "Perhaps you should stay away from the campus tomorrow."

Madison was looking concerned, too.

The last thing I needed was to cancel two classes at the last minute, especially so close to the end of the semester, and give the provost an excuse to fire me. Despite her protestations, I wasn't entirely convinced that she'd been pleased by my speech at the adjunct meeting. "I'll be fine, Mom. My classes are over by noon, then I'll have office hours, and I'll be gone long before anything happens. Which it probably won't."

"Andrew," Phil said, "do you intend to get involved?"

"Don't you think we should be there to defend our fellow academics, Dr. Thackery?"

"Both sides include academics," Madison pointed out.

"Technically, yes, but—" He stopped before he made it worse. "Maybe I better sit this one out."

"I think that's a wise choice," Mom said. "Now Mimi, can you explain what you mean by a magical girl?"

My cell phone rang just as we were finishing up dinner, and when I saw who it was, I said, "I'm sorry, I should take this."

"Go," Mom said. "We can clean up without you."

"I'll help," Mimi said, and Andrew reluctantly volunteered, too.

I popped into my parents' office and answered the phone.

"This is Georgia."

"Dallas Sieck here. I have a question for you. You sent me a batch of photos, and Brownie sent me another batch."

"Right."

"Which batch was taken first?"

"Mine." I did some quick figuring. "Brownie took his pictures yesterday or the day before, which was just over a week after I went to the museum. Call it eight days."

"Then you should know that sometime in those eight days, somebody switched a Queen Anne piecrust table with a laminate end table."

"Are you sure?" I heard the beginning of a *harrumph* and quickly said, "Sorry, of course you're sure. I'm just startled by this."

"As am I. This is terrible!"

"Honestly, it's not."

"Excuse me?" she said frostily.

"We've got some suspects for the thefts, but it's been nearly impossible to eliminate any of them over such a long timeline. Now we've got something more concrete."

"Oh. I suppose you're right."

"I know you collect Happy Meal toys, not piecrust tables, but do have any idea how a thief would sell something like that? Or really, any of the stolen items. Would eBay work?"

"That's an interesting question. I'll investigate further. But first I'll finish going through the inventory. I should have a tally for you later tonight."

"That would be great."

"Only if it helps. I'm counting on you and your colleague to stop this historical leak as soon as possible."

"We'll do our best," I said and hung up. Obviously solving Annabelle's murder was the primary aim, but I didn't have to be a historian to want to stop the theft of bits of history.

I zipped up to the attic and found Sid listlessly going through his files. "I've got a lead for you."

"Please tell me it's a good one."

"The thief has been active in the past eight days."

His eye sockets did that impossible widening thing. "How do you know?"

"The pictures Madison took at the museum don't match the ones Brownie took. A piecrust table was stolen between the time we were there and when Brownie went."

"Oh my spine and femur," Sid said. "Sit down while I…Just wait."

I sat while he clattered his way through screens and lists and more screens. It took half an hour, and right until the last minute, his bones were tense with anticipation. Then he sagged.

"Coccyx, coccyx, coccyx," he said.

"What?!"

"Before I couldn't eliminate anybody who'd helped clean the Nichols house. Now I've eliminated them all."

"That's not possible."

"We'd already eliminated the Hoarder Helper crew and the executor for not having access to Bostock. Sebastian Silva is dead. His cranky wife still doesn't drive, and I can't see her taking a table onto the bus. The former head of the Office of Development retired to Boca Raton, and his admin moved to Idaho. Then we get to the CSI cleaners, all of whom have long since graduated. None of them live in the area, and unless they're lying on social media, none of them have been in town recently. Any one of them could have stolen items ten years ago, but not a single one of them could have stolen that table Professor Sieck told you about. I don't know where to look now."

"Coccyx," I said, running my hands through my hair. "What about the girl who works at the museum?"

"She's what, in her twenties? You think she killed Annabelle as a tween? Chasing her down in battery-operated Barbie car?"

I swallowed the response I wanted to make. "Okay, maybe it's a gang of thieves. Or somebody's boyfriend or girlfriend, or a sibling, or…"

"Georgia, if we start widening the field that far, we may as well start looking at every student, every professor, every administrator, every employee of any kind. Which I could do—I'm not getting any older—but it doesn't make sense. The thief had to have been one of the people at the Nichols house. But it wasn't Annabelle, and it wasn't either of the other custodians. It wasn't the lawyer for the Nichols family, and it wasn't the development guy from Bostock or his assistant. It wasn't Deborah, and now we know it wasn't any of the student cleaners."

"Could somebody have been hiding in the house?"

"Sure, Georgia, a busload of thieves was hiding in the attic while all those people were wandering all over everywhere."

"You don't have to snap," I snapped.

"You don't have to be ridiculous."

"Well you don't have to be sarcastic, and you don't have to be—" I stopped. "Wait, what did you say?"

"I said you don't have to be ridiculous."

"Before that."

"I said a busload of thieves—"

"A bus. That's it."

"That's what?"

"Annabelle didn't have a car. How did she get to the Nichols house?"

"Deborah!" we said together.

Not that we meant that Deborah had provided transport. We just knew that my sister was the person to ask. It was late enough that I should have considered waiting until morning to call, but I was too excited, so I dialed her number.

"What do you need, Georgia?" she said wearily.

"I've got another question about your job at the Nichols house."

"Am I supposed to be surprised?"

"How did the cleaning crew get there?"

"They flew in on giant butterflies."

"Deborah…"

"Fine, let me think." I didn't count off the seconds, but I think Sid did. "Okay, now I remember. All of the Bostock people came together in a bus. Which was late most days, so I had to wait for them to get there before getting started."

"Like a city bus?"

"More like a shuttle bus. It must have belonged to the college—who else would have a stupid name like that on their bus?"

"Bostock? I've worked at colleges with worse names."

"It didn't say Bostock. It said Bus-Stock, with a logo of a bus with a creepy smile."

I was glad they'd changed that. "What about the driver?"

"Yes, Georgia, there was a driver. The creepy smiling bus did not drive itself."

"I meant did he help with the stuff in the house?"

"No, I already told you everybody who worked in the house. The driver didn't even help the cleaners load up the bus. And before you ask, I don't know his name, age, or shoe size. He was just a guy. I never even spoke to him."

"Anything you can remember will help."

She sighed. "College aged. White. Blond or light brown hair, I think, but he was wearing a hat most of the time. Average height, and as far as I could tell with the parka he was wearing, average build. That's it."

"That's more than we had before."

"I'm thrilled for you. Anything else, or can I go to bed now?"

"That's it."

"Don't make promises you can't keep," she said and hung up.

"The bus driver!" I said to Sid.

"The bus driver!" he replied.

Then came an impromptu dance party that was intense enough that Madison banged on the attic door to say, "Hello! Some of us are trying to concentrate."

"Sorry," I called back and threw myself onto the couch to catch my breath. "So how do we figure out who the bus driver was?"

Sid stopped short and plopped down next to me. "I have no idea."

Chapter Thirty-Eight

"Coccyx, Sid, I feel as if I'm riding a roller coaster."

"I'll take your word for it, but I assume you're talking about the ups and downs."

"Yeah, sorry," I said, resolving to come up with a way to get Sid onto a roller coaster. "Now what do we do?"

He made the sound of a deep breath. "I've got this. I'll check the Golden Pages to find out who was a part of Bus-Stock ten years back, and then figure out who is local and might have access to the museum and cross reference. And as soon as I get an updated list of what's been stolen, I can research where those items could have been sold and so on. It's spreadsheeting time!"

He did not, however, move a single bone in the direction of his laptop. Even when I received an email from Dr. Sieck a minute later that listed all the items she was sure had been stolen and replaced, he just nodded.

"Are you sick of spreadsheets?" I asked.

"I'm sick of useless spreadsheets. And don't say this is our process."

"I wasn't going to," I lied, but I was telling the truth when I added, "We would never be able to do any of this without your lists, and your spreadsheets, and your major Googling skills."

"I guess," he said, clearly not convinced.

Trying for a lighter note, I said, "Isn't there a rule forbidding pouting this time of year?" I hummed a few bars of "Santa Claus is Comin' to Town."

"I'm not pouting. You need lips to pout."

"True, but *you better not sulk* doesn't rhyme with *you better watch out*." He kept pouting. "It's late, and I should get to bed. Why don't you watch a video or read tonight? Do something fun. We'll brainstorm or skull-storm when I get back from work tomorrow."

"Wait, you're going to work tomorrow?"

"Don't tell me you believe this riot nonsense."

"It's all over the Bostock parents' Facebook page and the Bostock alumni page. Don't you think you should take it seriously?"

"Whatever happens will happen after I leave. I'll be out of there as soon my office hours are over."

"I still don't like it."

"I'm finding it hard to believe that there's going to be a riot of academics. Fighting over footnotes, sure, but this? It just sounds so unrealistic."

"Georgia? You're talking to an ambulatory skeleton. Reality isn't always what you expect."

"Try to picture somebody like my parents or Charles in a riot, and tell me how realistic that is."

"They'd riot in a heartbeat to protect you."

I just patted him on the skull and went downstairs.

I'd halfway expected Sid to see me off the next morning so he could warn me of danger another half dozen times, but he didn't appear, and I hoped he'd taken my suggestion to enjoy himself the previous night.

I kept on hoping until I was halfway to work and heard a tiny *bing* from the backseat, followed by a less quiet, "Coccyx."

I looked in the rearview mirror and saw that my emergency blanket was covering a lump that had not been there the night before.

From long experience, I knew that lump was the size and shape of a crumpled skeleton.

Chapter Thirty-Nine

"Sid, are you back there?" I said.

"Yes. I forgot to silence my phone."

"Why are you and your phone here?"

"I thought I'd hang around while you're in class so that if I get any useful information out of my ossifying spreadsheet, we'll be able to move on it instantly."

"Sid, I don't have any place to hide you. All I've got is a cubicle."

"That's okay, I'll stay in the car and work under this blanket. After all, I don't get cold, I don't breathe, and I can see in the dark. I've even got a couple of charger bars to make sure I don't run out of power. My rolling bag is in the very back in case you need to take me somewhere, and I've got some clothes to wear if I need to get out of the car. I've even got your spare car keys, just in case."

"You've been very thorough," I admitted. "How did you arrange everything?"

"I'm a meticulous planner, and I can move like a ninja when I need to."

"Madison helped you, didn't she?"

"Yep. She didn't want you on campus without backup."

"Charles and Brownie are going to be there." There was a painful silence, and so I added, "Of course, neither of them are the ninja type."

"That's what I thought. So, good plan, right?"

He really did seem to have covered all the bases, and I couldn't see any harm in him being there if he was willing to stay cooped up in the car for several hours. "Excellent plan. Thank you, Sid."

"You're welcome. Team Supreme, right?"

"Team Supreme." I reached into the backseat with my left hand made into a fist and a second later, felt a bony fist bump it.

Hoping my next sentence wouldn't erase that warm fuzzy feeling, I said, "I was planning to stop by the food trucks to get Brownie up to speed."

"I didn't think of that. Should I move further back?"

"No, I'll get out to talk to him."

"What, are you afraid I'll listen in?"

"Says the skeleton who made smooching sounds at me just a few days ago."

"Fair. Go ahead and talk to your hug muffin."

"My *hug muffin*?"

"Your sweetie pie. Your snookie-ookums. I've got more."

"Please keep them." We reached the food trucks just in time, and I parked and got out before Sid could start reciting his other euphemisms for Brownie.

The crowd around the coffee truck seemed surlier than it had been before, and some of the looks I got as I went around to the back of the truck were downright hostile. Brownie must have been watching for me because he had a cup of coffee and an egg-and-sausage breakfast sandwich waiting.

"I'd join you," he said, "but we're getting slammed. One of my cooks didn't come because he heard there's going to be a riot."

"I would love to know how this rumor started."

"Rumors grow in the corners of the mind, like mold."

"Are you quoting?"

"No, just short on sleep." As if to prove himself, he yawned.

"Have you got time for a status update?" I asked.

"On the case? You bet!"

I told him about Professor Sieck's call and how it had eliminated everybody, which then led to the shuttle-based epiphany. "I thought I'd quiz the shuttle bus driver when I go on campus and see if he has a list of former drivers we can look at."

"Sounds promising, but you'll be off campus before the rally, right?"

"That's the plan," I said. "You're not going, are you?"

"Nope. My mother heard the rumors from my missing cook, and I had to promise that we'd shut down early. Riot damage is expensive."

"Fair enough." I heard somebody calling "College Boy!" from inside the truck and said, "You better go. I'll talk to you later."

"You bet." After a quick kiss, he went back to the truck while I got into the car to eat my sandwich and drink my coffee.

"How do the strikers seem?" Sid asked.

"Testy. They keep looking around as if expecting wraiths to attack. It doesn't help that the weather is so gloomy. I forgot to check the forecast, but it looks like snow to me."

A moment later, Sid said, "They're saying snow starting just before four."

"That's when the rally is supposed to start. Maybe they'll cancel due to weather." I finished up my coffee. "Time to get to work."

The parking deck was considerably emptier than usual. I parked near the shuttle stop and told Sid which buildings I was going to be in so he could find them on a map, just in case. Apparently paranoia is contagious because I was feeling anxious.

When the shuttle bus arrived, I saw David was driving, which was a good sign. I was the only one on board, too, which was even better. "A wild professor has appeared," I said.

"I welcome her aboard," David replied.

As he drove, I said, "Hey David, can I ask you something?"

"I don't know anything definite about the rally, and we haven't decided about cancelling service."

"Thanks, but that's not it. I'm trying to track down one of the Bus-Stock drivers—"

"The what drivers?"

"Bus-Stock. Isn't that the official name?" I asked.

"Not since I've been part of the company. I think one of the drivers who was here when I bought in called it something like that once, but I thought it was a joke. I mean, what kind of lame name is that for a company?"

"What do you call yourselves?"

"Bostock Shuttles. It's a bit on the nose, but sometimes simple is best."

"Okay," I said, "then I'm trying to find one of the Bostock Shuttle drivers from years back. Do you guys have a company directory?"

"There's our Advisory Board, which is made up of the drivers who've graduated. They're always willing to give advice to the current drivers, especially the Founding Five. They'll drop everything to help out, even the one who's a VP with Prudential now."

"Would you be comfortable with sharing that directory?"

"Why do you want it?"

"I won't lie. One of your former drivers may have done something illegal."

"Like speeding illegal or hurting somebody illegal?"

"Seriously hurting somebody."

"Then I'll give it to you. If one of our drivers did anything serious, they should be punished. Good businesses need to be ethical, right?"

When we got to my stop, he parked long enough to pull up the list on his phone and email it to me.

"Thanks, David."

"You bet. And keep out of trouble, okay?"

As soon as I got inside, I forwarded the directory to Sid, along with an explanation, and informed him that he was not authorized to have a dance party in the car, no matter how excited he became.

When I arrived at my first class, I was wondering if I should have stayed home after all. A third of my students were missing, and the ones that were left were distracted and restless. I ended up letting them leave early, and the second class was a near repeat of the first. I still felt obligated to keep my posted office hours, even though I wasn't expecting anybody to show up, and I was correct. The only person I saw that whole time was Professor Lefebre, who walked by my cubicle without even glancing in my direction.

I texted Brownie to see if he wanted to have lunch, but when he didn't reply, I figured he was still busy at the trucks. Next, I called Sid to see if he'd made any progress.

"Yes and no," he said.

"What does that mean?"

"I went through the list of drivers and none of them could have both killed Annabelle and robbed the museum so recently."

"Is that the *yes* or the *no*?"

"It's—Don't get technical on me. The positive part is that a lot of the former drivers are on the alumni Facebook group, and I've been going through their posts. There are a couple of references to a driver that doesn't appear on the Advisory Board list."

"By name?"

"Only by his nickname, unfortunately, which is T.J. So in my alumna persona, I've posted a *whatever-happened-to-T.J.* note. My finger bones are crossed that I'll get a reply."

"Well, my office hours are over, so I'm going to head back in your direction."

"Good idea. The forecasters have moved the snow prediction up an hour and added a couple of extra inches."

"I'm on my way."

I packed up, bundled up, and went to the shuttle bus stop outside the building to wait. And wait. And wait. Nearly half an hour after I got there, another adjunct came by and said, "Didn't you hear? They shut down the shuttles for the afternoon."

"Without warning us?"

"Professor Lefebre told me there was a sign up at the student center," he said before going inside.

That would be the same professor who'd walked right past me without bothering to speak. Seething, I started walking toward the parking deck. I wasn't even halfway there when my phone rang. Though I expected it to be Sid checking on me, it was Dana Fenton.

"Is Brownie there?" she asked.

"No, not with me. Is something wrong?"

"I don't know. I tried to call him to see when the trucks are going to get out of there, but he didn't answer. I got a hold of one of the guys working with him, and he said Brownie told him he had to do something on campus. I thought maybe you and he were having lunch."

"I haven't seen him since first thing this morning, and he didn't reply to a text I sent a little while ago. Could he have left without your other people seeing him?"

"He hasn't got a car—he rode in one of the trucks."

Treasure Hunt got on the line and demanded, "Did you get him mixed up in that stuff with Sue?"

Before I could answer, I heard Dana say, "He got himself mixed up, and you know it. Now give me that phone back, you old fool." A moment later, Dana said, "Can you take a look around for him? We'll get there as soon as we can, but we don't know the campus."

"Of course. I'll let you know if I find him or hear from him."

"Ditto for me."

As soon as she hung up, I called Sid.

"That shuttle is really slow," he said.

"They cancelled service already even though the rally isn't until later."

"Not as late as it was. They've moved it up to try to dodge the snow. I just saw a post on the Bostock parents' group page."

"Coccyx! Look, Dana just called. Brownie's not answering his phone, and he's not at the food trucks, and nobody knows where he is. I'm heading back to look for him."

"Come get me first."

"Sid, I'm sorry, but I am not going to drag your suitcase all over campus."

"At least come get the car and move it closer. The place we went for that tour was right in the middle of campus, wasn't it?"

"That's for visitors only—adjuncts aren't supposed to park there."

"Georgia!"

I took a deep breath, realizing how rattled I was. "You're right, that's a good idea. I'll be there as soon as I can."

When I finally got to the parking deck, I saw that Sid, bless his empty chest cavity, had managed to turn the car on and switch on the heat before retreating into hiding. Despite the exertion, I was half-frozen after my long walk.

"Any word from Brownie?" he asked.

"Nothing," I said, checking my phone again for any missed calls, emails, or texts.

"I've got some news about our disappearing driver."

"Tell me on the way," I said and drove out of the parking deck.

"A couple of people remembered T.J. and said that he transferred to another college in the middle of the semester. That's odd, right?"

"It happens," I said, "but it's unusual. Students typically don't get any credit for the semester if they do that, which means they'll have to make up a lot of extra classes."

"I'm speculating that T.J. might be the dorm thief who was never prosecuted but had to leave Bostock in a hurry."

"Good thinking," I said, but I wasn't giving it much attention because I was too focused on driving as fast as I could without hitting anything. To get to the visitor center parking, I had to drive past the main entrance, and I saw the picket line was gone. "What time did they move the rally to?"

"Half an hour from now," Sid said.

"Ossifying pieces of sacrum! Couldn't they wait until tomorrow for their stupid yelling?"

One of Sid's arms slithered up the back of the seat and patted me on the shoulder. "We'll find him, Georgia."

"Coccyx, Sid, if I've gotten Brownie hurt or—" I couldn't even finish the sentence and tears were stinging my eyes.

"We're going to find him," Sid said. "Now give me your phone."

"Why?"

"I don't want you out there alone and I can't go with you while it's light out, so I'm texting Charles to meet you."

I handed the phone to him. "My password is—"

"Yeah, as if I didn't know." He typed in a text. "I told him it's an emergency and that you need him to meet you in the visitor's parking lot." A minute later, there was a ping, and Sid said, "He'll be there as soon as he can."

Almost anybody else would have asked for more information, but not Charles. He knew I wouldn't have sent a message like that if it weren't important.

He wasn't there when I parked, which gave me time to wipe my eyes and blow my nose. Sid continued to pat me until I said, "Here he comes."

"Stay in touch," Sid said and ducked back under the blanket.

I hopped out of the minivan and nearly ran to Charles.

"Georgia, what's wrong?"

"Brownie's missing!" I said more loudly than I'd intended and had to take a deep breath before I could explain.

"Have you called campus security?"

"Coccyx, I didn't even think about that."

"Of course not, you're distraught. I'll handle it."

While I resisted the urge to dash across campus yelling for Brownie, Charles stepped away to call the Bostock Security office. I could tell from his expression when he hung up that he wasn't happy with what he'd heard.

"Well?" I asked.

"I'm afraid that they're not overly concerned because he hasn't been missing very long. They might be more receptive at another time, but with the union rally starting at any moment, their attention is elsewhere. I apologize for wasting our time."

"No, it was a reasonable thing to do. I'm just not feeling reasonable."

"No matter. We'll take charge of the search ourselves. Where should we start?"

"I don't know. When I saw him earlier, he wasn't planning to come on campus. Something must have changed his mind."

"Am I safe in assuming that he's aware of your investigation?"

Oops. "I'm sorry, Charles. I shouldn't have told him without consulting you, but—"

"Don't give it a second thought. Brownie is entirely trustworthy. Now, in what direction was your investigation leading?"

I gave him a brief, undoubtedly jumbled, synopsis. "The last thing we discussed was trying to figure out who drove the bus for the crew cleaning the Nichols house."

"He could have gone to speak to one of the drivers."

"I told him I was going to do that myself, though I never let him know that I had, so…No, he wouldn't have duplicated my work without telling me."

"There is an extensive archive of the Bostock business reports in the library. Perhaps he went to see if he could find anything there."

"That makes sense. I should have thought of that, but I mostly rely on online research."

"Then let's try the library."

That meant another march across campus and I considered driving, but given the parking situation, it was faster to walk. Though the campus had seemed eerily quiet before, now I was seeing more and more people walking purposely toward the area of campus where the main administration buildings were clustered.

"I guess people are gathering for the rally," I said.

"So it would seem."

We finally reached the library only to find the door locked. A piece of paper taped to the door said *Closed Early Due To Rally*. It was stupid, but I peered in the window, just in case, but of course there was no sign of Brownie.

My phone rang again: Dana. "We can't get in," she said angrily. "The cops say the campus is closed to the public."

"That ossifying rally again," I said. "I've got Charles with me, and we're looking for him."

"We're going to ride around and see if there's a service entrance we can sneak in through. Call if you find him."

She hung up before I could answer.

I said, "Brownie's parents are here, but they can't get on campus because the police have it blocked off."

"Where shall we try next?" Charles asked patiently.

I tried to think, or at least to guess what Brownie would have been thinking, but before I could concoct anything, I heard a siren blaring.

A second later, an ambulance came tearing across campus and turned toward where the strikers had been going. I started walking that same direction.

"Georgia, there's no reason to think Brownie was injured," Charles said.

"I know," I said, but I didn't stop.

Charles caught up. "I'll escort you."

I nodded, saving my breath for walking faster.

We finally got to the edges of the crowd. The ambulance had already arrived, of course, and I could see it was surrounded by a tightly packed mass of people. Charles went in front of me to clear a path and got us close enough that I could see the figure on the stretcher being loaded into the back of the vehicle. It was a woman I'd never met. I went from fear to relief, then on to guilt for being glad somebody else was hurt instead of Brownie.

As the ambulance drove away, I tapped the shoulder of the man standing in front of me. "Excuse me. What happened?"

He didn't bother to turn as he said, "One of the scabs slipped and fell. No doubt she'll try to blame the union."

I hadn't realized I'd moved closer to the man than was polite until Charles gently pulled me back and in a crisp voice said, "That would be Dr. Hortiz, a single mother who was recently diagnosed with Parkinson's."

The man turned toward us and stammered, "What? I didn't realize…"

Charles deliberately turned his back on him and walked away, drawing me with him.

"I suggest we find a vantage point to observe the crowd," Charles said. "If Brownie is within earshot, he may also have heard the siren and come to investigate."

Since I had no better ideas, or indeed any idea at all, we fell back to the edges of the gathering and started making our away around. Since Charles was taller than I was by several inches, I relied on him to spot Brownie and took a minute to text Sid.

GEORGIA: *Anything?*

SID: *Nothing. Parents' list said somebody was hurt at rally. Heard ambulance go by. Where are you?*

GEORGIA: *At rally.*

SID: *!!!*

GEORGIA: *Charles is with me.*

SID: *BE CAREFUL!*

By that point, Charles and I had reached the front of the crowd and were within sight of a rickety-looking platform on which the union organizers were standing and using electronic megaphones to express their grievances. Their erstwhile adversaries, the provost and various other campus officials, were off to one side trying to look concerned but not angry as the union people played to the audience in front of them. Though a lot of the people in the throng were nodding along with the union's talking points, there were plenty of jeers from others. Outside the circle was a nervous-looking handful of Bostock security guards, looking as if they wished they really had hired the host of outside thugs the rumor mill had promised.

I admit that I wasn't paying much attention to the rhetoric. I was too worried about Brownie to give a splintered femur about either side of the strike.

Since my eyes were on the crowd, not on the platform, I saw the spark that nearly ignited disaster. One of the union picketers was waving his sign around, despite the crush of people, and when somebody jostled him, his grip wavered just enough for the sign's post to hit the person next to him. That person shoved the picketer into somebody else, who shoved at random, as far as I could tell. The shoving multiplied, and while some people were trying to get away from the confusion, others were trying to jump into the thick of it. The union organizer stopped her speech, the provost's party started backing away, security guards put their hands on their weapons.

Then, for no clear reason, one man punched another in the face, knocking him out of the crowd and onto the ground a few feet in front of the platform with blood streaming from his nose.

When Madison was a toddler and fell down or hit her head on something, there would be a timeless instant before she reacted. At that moment, I could never tell what was coming next. Would she laugh it off? Would she sniffle and call for me? Or would she howl in pain?

That's how it felt when that man fell. Everybody who saw him froze in place as if deciding on the appropriate response. Were we going to back off or would the real fighting begin?

During that millisecond of uncertainty, Charles slipped through the crowd, leapt to the platform, and took the megaphone from the startled union rep.

In the ringing tones for which his students adore his lectures, he said, "Colleagues! I call you all my colleagues because we all have the same goal: to seek knowledge and to share it." There were some murmurs and catcalls, but Charles ignored them. "We academics know that scholarship enriches the present, and it is a moment in history I want to share with you today. One of the finest triumphs of humanity over violence was the Christmas Armistice of 1914."

I saw the security guards helping the injured man up and trying to assess the damage to his nose, but he was listening as attentively as the rest of us.

"Picture it. Christmas Eve on the cheerless, icy-cold Western Front as the barrage of shells exploding and rifles firing slowly fades. With the dawn, German soldiers emerge from their trenches to extend a momentary olive branch by wishing their enemies a merry Christmas. Overcoming their fear and distrust, the British abandon their positions to return that greeting. Men who had been trying to kill one another just hours before exchange cigarettes and holiday treats. The next day, the bloody conflict continues, but for that one moment, there was hope and peace." He looked out at the crowd. "Colleagues, it's Christmas time, and though many of us don't observe the religious aspects, I hope we can all appreciate the cheer that the season brings. Or at least we can enjoy a few much-needed days away from our classrooms." There were some quiet laughs in response. "I ask you to set aside your differences for this brief respite, just as the German and British troops did so many years ago." Then he actually started singing "God Rest You Merry, Gentlemen."

It was incredibly hokey, and I couldn't believe it when people actually joined in. But they did. So did I.

Of course, since we were academics, by the second verse I was hearing spirited discussions about why the word was *You* and not *Ye* because *ye* is a subjection pronoun only, never objective; whether the carol dated to the sixteenth century or earlier; and if it was more properly "God rest you, merry gentlemen" or "God rest you merry, gentlemen." It would have been a perfect time for snow to start gently falling, but I suppose we couldn't have everything.

Chapter Forty

After the third verse, people started to wander off, and if we weren't all arm in arm, neither was it looking like a riot was about to break out. Security took the injured man to get first aid while the man who'd slugged him followed along apologizing profusely. Union organizers and administrators alike took Charles aside to shake his hand and tell him how awesome he was, which I totally agreed with. Later on, I was sure I'd look back at that experience fondly, but for the moment, I still didn't know where Brownie was.

I checked my phone and found messages waiting.

First up was a voicemail from Dana. "There were cops blocking every single entrance. We're going to camp out at the lot across the street. Find Brownie before my idiot husband breaks his neck trying to climb over the walls."

Next was a message from Sid.

SID: *ARE YOU OKAY?*

Sid must have gotten notification that I'd read his text, because my phone rang before I could respond.

"I'm fine," I said. "Charles stopped the riot."

"I think my ear holes must be blocked. *Who* stopped the riot?"

"I'll explain later. Have you got any more information or ideas about Brownie?"

"Nothing."

"Coccyx," I said for what seemed like the hundredth time that day. "I don't even know where to look. This campus is huge, and without the shuttle to get around…" Something about the shuttle was niggling at me. "Sid, Deborah said the bus at the hoarder house had *Bus-Stock* painted on the side, but my shuttle driver David said nobody calls it that anymore. When did they change names?"

"Hang on." There was a mighty clacking, and a moment later Sid said, "I checked the Golden Pages and found listings for eleven, ten, and nine years ago. It was originally called Bus-Stock Shuttles, and Deborah is right, the logo is heinous. The same artist must have drawn this dreadful cartoon of the six drivers who founded the company."

"Six drivers?"

"Yeah, why?"

"David also said something about the Founding Five. What happened to the sixth?"

"Let me enlarge the dreadful cartoon." After a few seconds, he triumphantly said, "Hello, T.J."

"What?"

"There are barely legible names under each of the figures in the cartoon, and one of them says *T.J.* Meaning that we have now successfully linked T.J. to the bus and the dorm thefts."

"That's amazing!" I said.

"Not as amazing as it might be. There's nobody with those initials in my files. Maybe I can go through old yearbooks and find somebody whose initials are T.J."

"Or T.J. something else," I pointed out.

"Come again?"

"T.J. could be a nickname for Thomas Jefferson, or it could stand for Thomas Jefferson Smith. Or he could go by a different version of his name now, like if Madison decided to switch to Maddie or Mad."

"Why do you fleshy people have so many names?" Sid grumbled. "I'll check my files, but with this many variations, it's going to take forever."

"I know, I'm just—" I had a flash of memory. The guide who'd taken Madison and me around campus had asked Madison what name she went by.

That reminded me that he was the first person I'd heard say the name Bus-Stock.

"Sid, look up the guy who gave us the tour of Bostock. Edward something."

More clacking. "Edward Alfred Humphries, Junior. Not even close."

"Another name for Edward is Ted, and Junior starts with J. Couldn't he be T.J.?"

"Yes!" I suspected the rattling I heard next was him doing a triumphant fist pump. "And his office is right here at the visitor center. I'm going to check it out. I'll call back."

I was still waiting when I heard somebody say, "Hello, Dr. Thackery. I don't know if you remember us, but we're the—"

"Yes, I know who you are, Mrs. Gleason," I said, hoping it didn't sound like I was talking through gritted teeth. I was starting to think they had a literal helicopter.

"Dr. Thackery," Mrs. Gleason said, "given the uproar of this demonstration, we think it only fair that you give our son Reggie extra time to finish his final paper."

Charles, who'd finished talking to the muckety-mucks, must have seen the flame in my eyes because he stepped over and said, "I'm sorry, this is not the time or place for such matters. We're in the middle of a crisis."

"We know, it's all over the parents' Facebook group. That's why Reggie deserves an extension. It's all been very distracting and upsetting. We saw a video of that man getting hurt!"

"There's already a video online?" I said. "It only happened ten minutes ago."

"The parents' group is very active," Mrs. Gleason said with a smug expression.

That's when inspiration struck. I said, "Mr. and Mrs. Gleason, may I tell you something in confidence?"

They nodded.

"I need to find somebody here on campus right away, but he's not answering his phone."

"Do you mean a student?" she asked.

"No, an employee. If you can help me locate him, I will give Reggie an extra week to get his paper in without deducting any points from his grade."

"You will?"

"If you can find him in fifteen minutes, he'll get two weeks."

"Who do you want us to find?" Mr. Gleason rumbled in the first words I'd heard him speak.

"His name is Edward Humphries," I said and went online to the Bostock site to find a photo. "He works in recruiting."

"Email me that link," Mr. Gleason said.

I did so, and after some serious tapping at their phones, they took off into the deepening dusk.

"Is Humphries man one who…?" Charles asked.

"I think so." My phone rang again, and I said, "I'll explain after I take this."

Charles politely stepped away to give me privacy.

"Anything?" I asked Sid.

"Humphries isn't answering his office phone, and the building is locked and dark. I don't think there's a basement, so there's nowhere he could have Brownie. I'm sorry, Georgia, I don't know what else to do."

"Me, neither, but I've got reinforcements."

"Who?"

"I told the worst pair of helicopter parents around that I'll give their kid an extension if they can find Humphries for me. I bet they're going to alert the Bostock parents' group to spread the word."

"I'll monitor the posts," Sid said. "You stay with Charles!"

"We'd cover more ground if—"

"STAY WITH CHARLES!" he bellowed.

"You're right, you're right. Keep in touch." I hung up, and though I was itching to do something, anything, it would have been crazy to run around looking under bushes, especially since Sid or the Gleasons could contact me at any moment. Besides, I needed to catch Charles up. So I took a few minutes to explain what we thought Edward Humphries, a.k.a. T.J., had done. I'd been finished long enough to reconsider that bush searching option when my phone rang again. I didn't recognize the number. "Hello?"

"Dr. Thackery, I don't know if you remember—"

"Yes, Mrs. Gleason, I know who you are. Have you found Edward Humphries?"

"I think so. One of the other parents said her daughter saw a shuttle bus that went right past her, even though she was at a stop, and she said it went to that old church on campus, but there's no stop there. She recognized Mr. Humphries driving because he gave her a tour of the campus just last year."

The museum! "Thank you so much!"

"I'm not sure Mr. Humphries is still there, and I realize that it's been seventeen minutes since we talked not fifteen, but—"

"That's close enough. Reggie's got two more weeks."

She started to ask if I meant from today or from his originally scheduled due date, but I hung up on her.

I texted Sid.

> GEORGIA: *They're in the museum! We're going there now. Will call you and leave connection open so you can listen in.*
>
> SID: *Go!*

After I dialed Sid's number and made sure he'd answered, I tucked my phone into my bra. It wasn't comfortable, but Sid would be able to hear what was going on, and I'd have my hands free. Then I said, "Charles, Humphries was spotted at the campus museum. Do you know the way?"

"Follow me!"

Charles had worked at Bostock longer than I had, and it showed. We soon left sidewalks behind and cut off a third of the distance I expected to have to trudge.

The museum was dark when we arrived, and at first I thought the Gleasons had failed us, but then I saw the shuttle bus parked on the slope to one side of the building, in the shadow of some trees.

I heard Sid's voice from inside my bra, and jerked, having forgotten that I'd left the phone there. "He's going to ram the building! I think Brownie is inside."

That's when I realized two things. One, while the headlights were off, there was exhaust coming from the shuttle bus's tail pipe, meaning that it was still running. Two, Sid was at the museum. Just for a second, I saw an impossibly skinny figure at the front door of the building before he slipped inside. Somebody else was moving around the shuttle.

"We've got to stop that bus," I told Charles, who hadn't heard Sid.

I'd never have gotten there in time, but Charles had longer legs and could move like a freight train. He was yelling, "Humphries!" as he barreled toward him.

Humphries looked up from where he was just about to pull something I later found out was a set of chocks from in front of the rear tires. He only got one pulled out before Charles tackled him.

With only one wheel blocked, the bus started lumbering toward the museum, lurching to one side. But it was slowed enough that it only crashed partway through the wall, striking the building's back corner instead of hitting it broadsides.

On the phone, Sid said, "He's in here—he's okay," and I ran for the open door and into the museum. Brownie was stumbling toward the front door with a thin line of blood running down his cheek.

"Georgia?" he said. "What's going on?"

That would have been the time to explain all the brilliant reasoning and ingenuity that had led to his rescue, while leaving out the Sid-related bits. What actually happened was me grabbing him, kissing him, crying, more kissing, and then more crying. He wrapped his arms around me and said, "I love you, too."

Chapter Forty-One

Bostock security people arrived a few minutes later, followed soon thereafter by the Pennycross police and Brownie's parents.

Treasure Hunt wanted to take Brownie to a hospital, and I thought that was a good idea, too, but Brownie refused to go without hearing more about what had happened.

Dana took a look at him and said, "He can wait," which settled it.

Since the museum was a crime scene and the heat was out of commission, it was decided that we should all relocate to the student center. Before we left, I looked into the exhibit room, and decided Sid had hidden in the big steamer trunk in the corner. Before I finally ended the phone call, I whispered my guess and the lid of the trunk lifted just a teeny bit in acknowledgement. We'd have to work out his retrieval later.

The students who'd been roused from their dorms by all the sirens must have been baffled by the procession. Pennycross cops led the way while Bostock security cleared the path. Brownie was leaning on me because he was still feeling a little woozy, and his parents were walking beside us protectively, with Treasure Hunt glaring at anybody who might get in our way. Both Charles and Humphries had been handcuffed, but while Charles maintained a dignified silence, Humphries was complaining to all and sundry that this was a mistake, that he'd done nothing wrong, and that he needed to call his father, his lawyer, and maybe his father's lawyer as well. Despite it all, the provost and various other administration personnel were trying to give the impression that this was just another lovely evening at Bostock College.

Once we got to the dining hall in the student center, Humphries pointed at Brownie and said, "That's the man! He's been stealing from the museum and was going to drive the shuttle bus into the building to cover his tracks. I was trying to stop him when his accomplice jumped me."

Treasure Hunt's face turned an angry red, and he snapped, "Typical towner—trying to blame a carney!"

"That man must be involved, too," Humphries said quickly. "It's a ring of thieves." While Treasure Hunt sputtered, Humphries looked around as if trying to decide who else he could accuse.

Before any of the rest of us could jump in to say what was really going on, Charles drew himself up and in a clear, cutting voice said, "Annabelle Mitchell."

Humphries froze for a second, then sagged so much that his police escort had to hold him up as they pulled him over to a corner of the room and sat him down.

Charles was taken to a different corner, while Brownie, his parents, and I were herded to a third. That's when we started the ludicrous amount of explaining to satisfy the police and Bostock personnel, or so it seemed to me at the time, but I later decided that I really wasn't at my best. It didn't help when Louis Raymond arrived with news to share.

Louis had found where Brownie had been left and pointed out that had the shuttle bus gone at full speed in the direction in which it was originally aimed, it would have almost certainly killed him. Of course I'd known what Humphries had intended, but for some reason, it didn't hit home until that moment. I don't know what my face looked like, but I know that somebody quickly gave me a metallic blanket, a cookie, and a bottle of water. I think that means I was very close to going into shock.

The only thing that helped was when Brownie said, "But that's not where I was. When I came to, I was right by the door."

In other words, Sid had carried him to safety.

While the Bostock people and most of the police were focused on the attempted theft and attack on Brownie, Louis kept looking at me speculatively and finally asked if I would like to give him a statement. I swallowed the rest of my water, then followed Louis to another room to explain as much of the connection between Humphries and Annabelle's body as I could without getting anybody else in trouble. He kept asking for more details, like why Charles was involved, and I finally had to say, "That should be plenty enough to put Humphries away and lay Annabelle Mitchell to rest, so that's all you're going to get out of me."

He shook his head ruefully. "You know, when I first met you, I thought you were the complete opposite of Deborah, but at times like this, I can definitely see the family resemblance." I'm not sure if it was a compliment or not.

Speaking of my sister, she and my mother showed up at some point and eventually convinced the people in charge that I needed to go home. Deborah insisted that she drive my vehicle back to the house because, as she put it, I looked like death warmed over. I agreed only on the condition that we not leave until we'd rescued Sid, but when we got to my minivan, he was already hiding under his blanket. I don't know how he managed to get out of the wrecked building and sneak across campus without being seen, but he did. Then again, what cop or security guard would have admitted seeing him?

It was snowing heavily by the time we got back to the house. Treasure Hunt had finally gotten his way, and he and Dana were taking Brownie to the hospital to be checked out, and since Charles had split his knuckles on Humphries's face, they took him with them, too. That meant it was only family at the house, so Sid could join in on the orgy of hugging.

When we went into the kitchen, I saw why Phil had stayed home. With Madison's help, he'd fixed enough sandwiches for a small army and had made hot chocolate from real chocolate, not a powder. I hadn't realized I was hungry until I saw the food, but once I did, I decided to let Sid tell most of the story while I ate.

"I think I've followed most of this," Phil said when Sid finished, "but I'm confused as to how Brownie got captured."

"He was really embarrassed about that," I said. "This afternoon he had a brainstorm about the guest register at the museum. Since the thief had to have visited more than once, presumably he'd have signed in repeatedly. Which wasn't a bad thought."

Deborah snorted. "Yeah, because thieves always sign in before burgling."

"Brownie's new at this," Sid said magnanimously. "And he wasn't totally wrong because Humphries did sign in multiple times when he first came to work at Bostock, but that was before he managed to get his own key."

"Why bother?" Madison said. "Anybody could pick that lock."

"What kind was it?" Deborah asked, and they diverted into technicalities for a minute until Mom spoke up.

"How did Humphries know Brownie was involved?" she asked.

"He'd hidden minicams inside the museum, so he knew everybody who'd gone in," I said.

"Including when you, Sid, and I were there?" Madison asked.

I nodded. "It's a good thing Sid stayed in the bag that day. The cameras didn't record sound. In fact, it was the cameras that caused the near-riot on campus."

"I don't understand," Mom said.

"From the way Brownie was examining the collection and taking pictures of the artifacts, it was pretty obvious that he'd figured out what was going on. If Humphries had just stopped stealing, he might have gotten away with everything, but he wanted one last, big score. So he started spreading rumors that the union rally was going to turn into a riot to distract everybody. Then, he loaded some of the best items still in the museum into his car. He figured that if he ran the shuttle into the museum, it would destroy a lot of evidence, and the police would chalk it up to riot-related violence."

"That's actually rather clever," Phil said. "Horrifying, but clever."

"Humphries went to the museum and told the student at the door she should head back to the dorm before the riot started. He was still picking out artifacts when Brownie showed up. I think he pulled the old hide-behind-the-door trick, and when Brownie came into the exhibit room, he hit him."

"I think it was with a cobbler's tool," Sid said.

"Ouch. I hope he's okay," I reached for my phone, but Deborah took it away from me.

She said, "The Fentons said they'd call when they know something. Stop worrying, and tell the rest of the story."

"That's most of it already. Humphries tied up Brownie and went on loading the stuff he wanted to steal into his car. Then he moved his car, broke into the shuttle garage, and hot-wired one of the buses, which he'd learned how to do when he was a driver. Luckily, he was dumb enough to let himself be seen, and that's how word got back to us. He positioned Brownie to stage the scene of him being a looter or something, and was just about to…" I decided to stop there.

Madison put her arm around me, and Mom patted my hand comfortingly.

"But why?" Phil asked.

"It had to have been the money," Deborah said. "The little creep must have realized he could make some easy cash, and when it looked like he was going to get caught, killed that woman to cover it up."

Later on we found out it was more complicated than that. Humphries's first student business had failed miserably, and he'd had to borrow money from his wealthy father, Edward Senior, to buy in to the shuttle bus company. The buses had been profitable enough that he could pay his father back, but he couldn't do that and spend money the way he wanted to. That's when the thefts began, first in the dorm rooms and then in the museum. After

Humphries got caught, Edward Senior bailed him out and moved him to another college. And then after graduation, he even helped Humphries find two high-paying jobs, both of which he was fired from. The last thing Edward Senior had been willing to do was use his influence and a large donation to get Humphries hired at Bostock. It turned out that much of the state-of-the-art equipment mentioned on the Bostock Difference tour had been paid for with that donation. I'd been appalled that a former thief could have been hired, even with a donation to sweeten the pot, but the current provost had never been told about the dorm thefts and nothing had been written down. Once he was back at Bostock, Humphries had promptly returned to stealing from the museum.

The simple answer was what Deborah said. It was all about money.

"And that's why he killed that poor woman?" Mom asked softly.

"Apparently Humphries noticed Annabelle was visiting the museum a lot because she did sign in, and since he'd seen her at the Nichols house, he decided he needed to get rid of her. He stole stuff from the dorm where she worked and planted pieces in her locker. That way, he figured nobody would believe anything she said about the museum. He'd gone by her house to see if she'd been arrested yet, and when he saw her walking down the street, he got the idea to run her down. He thought he was safe, even when he missed her, because she was sure to be arrested the next day. He didn't expect her to run and hide."

"How did he find her?" Madison asked.

"He saw her at the carnival. In addition to the on-campus route, the shuttles provide transport to local events like the Christmas Festival, and Humphries was in the parking lot when Annabelle left Fenton's. He was able to follow her back to the house without her spotting him, but had a schedule to keep so he couldn't go after her then. Instead he came back to the house the next day and strangled her. Having killed once, he was perfectly willing to go after Brownie, too." I teared up again.

Phil said, "But Sid and you saved him. I'm very proud of you both."

"Charles helped a lot," Sid pointed out.

"I'll tell him that I'm also proud of him the first chance I get. We should have him over for dinner before the holidays are over."

"Why don't you invite him for Christmas dinner?" Sid said.

I stared at him. "Sid, if Charles is here–"

"I know, I'll have to hide, but you know, I get you guys all the time. Charles is alone, and nobody should be alone on Christmas."

Everybody teared up a little at that, even Deborah, though she denied it later.

My phone rang, and when she saw it was Brownie, Deborah let me answer it to find out that he was indeed fine, with no concussion, only a headache and a few stitches in his scalp. I stepped into the hall for the next part of the conversation, ignoring an entire table full of Thackerys making smooching sounds.

After a few minutes, Phil called out, "Why don't you invite Brownie and his parents for Christmas dinner, too, Georgia?"

I did, Brownie accepted, and we made a few smooching sounds of our own.

Chapter Forty-Two

The next few days were a whirlwind. Of course, it's always hectic that close to Christmas, what with last-minute shopping, including a gift for Brownie. I found a newly published coffee table book about sideshow gaffs that Dana assured me he hadn't seen yet.

I also had to work in sessions with the police and various officials at Bostock. It turned out that Professor Sieck had found some of the places where Humphries had been selling pieces of the McClelland collection, so there was a good chance Bostock would get some of them back.

Plus I still had classes to teach and final papers to grade. Except Reggie Gleason's, of course. Knowing him, it would come in the very last minute of the last day of the two-week extension, but I was inclined to be generous. Somewhere in there, the strike was called off. No decisions had been made, but both sides had agreed to return to the bargaining table after the first of the year so they could work out their differences. I think the riot that almost happened had frightened everybody.

Almost before I knew it, it was Christmas Eve, and the house was filled with Thackerys and what Mom kept telling Phil was far too much food. Since my parents so often had grad students lurking about, we had a longstanding rule that Christmas Eve and Christmas morning were for family only. Any guests had to wait until Christmas dinner.

Another tradition was for Deborah to stay overnight on Christmas Eve. Back when Madison was younger, it was to make sure she could be there when Madison came running down the stairs to see what Santa had brought, but even now that Madison was usually the last one to wake up, it had stayed part of our holiday.

Since Louis and Oscar both had family in town, neither of them would be able to join us for Christmas dinner, so Deborah had a private gift exchange with them. I wasn't sure if she saw them separately or together, but I do know that they both did great jobs with their gifts. When she arrived on Christmas Eve, she was wearing a locket with a lock and key motif that Louis had given her, and she was so excited about Oscar's present that she didn't even wait to take off her coat to show it to us. He'd found a vintage story lock decorated with a lion's face and elaborate scroll work. "Now that is some serious craftsmanship," she said admiringly.

I did not let on that I had helped, nor did I feel guilty about giving him a leg up over Louis. After all, Louis got a murderer.

We had our traditional spaghetti dinner, followed by Christmas cookies, followed by the traditional argument over which Christmas movies we'd watch. As always, we ended the night with a viewing of *Emmet Otter's Jug-band Christmas.*

Sid was waiting for us on the couch when we came downstairs on Christmas morning, and he had even let Byron sit next to him. With the blinking colored lights from the Christmas tree, it would have made a perfect Christmas card picture for people who don't mind skeletons at Christmas.

Stockings were opened to reveal the usual crop of joke gifts and paperback books, and then presents were exchanged. If anybody wasn't happy with their gifts, they faked their appreciation extremely well. Madison was so happy with her Switch and games that she immediately texted her friends about them, which was a sure sign of gift-buying success.

Phil made omelets for breakfast, and in between eating, continuing to admire our gifts, and straightening up the house post gift-unwrapping, the day went by quickly. Our dinner guests were due at four, and we got Sid hidden by a quarter till, just to be sure.

"I still feel bad about you not being able to sit down with us for Christmas dinner," I told him.

"It's fine. I'll still be here watching. One thing, though. I was thinking of skipping the armoire and using the sugar skull bag instead. That way I can be on top of the armoire while you guys are in the living room and you can come up with some excuse to put me where I can listen in at dinner, too."

"Sure, if you'd rather." The bag wasn't as secure as the armoire, which he could lock from the inside, but I didn't think any of our guests were likely to reach into my bag. Anybody that did deserved to be bitten by a rogue skull.

Sid ran upstairs for the bag, then placed his usual subset of skull, hand, and phone inside. Afterward his headless skeleton put the bag in place, adjusting it a time or two, and clattered back to the attic. It's a testament to the oddity of my family that nobody stopped to watch. We just continued setting the table and getting dinner ready.

Charles was the first to arrive, looking both festive and dapper in a tweed suit paired with a red-and-white striped vest and a sprig of holly on his vest pocket. He kissed cheeks and shook hands, as appropriate, and gave a bottle of wine to my father, flowers to my mother, and boxes of chocolate to Madison, Deborah, and me. Byron just got a pat on the head, but he seemed satisfied with that.

About the time Charles finished greeting everyone, my phone buzzed and I took a look at the text on the screen. "Brownie and his folks are running late. They had to pick up our other guest."

"Who else is coming?" Deborah asked.

"I don't know." I was about to ask my parents who else they'd invited when my phone buzzed again with a text from Sid. I read it twice before saying, "That's right, I did ask if they wanted to bring somebody else from the carnival. I'm sorry I forgot to check with you guys."

"The more the merrier," Mom said. "I'll just set another place at the table."

Phil said, "You see, Dab, it's a good thing I bought the larger ham. We wouldn't want to run short."

Mom nodded, but I knew what she was thinking. He'd cooked so much food that we wouldn't run short if there was a blizzard and we were all trapped in the house until New Year's.

I stepped into the hall and texted Sid.

GEORGIA: *Who did I invite to dinner?*

SID: *Sue Weedon.*

GEORGIA: *Why did I do that?*

SID: *Because it's Christmas. You should be the one to greet them at the door.*

GEORGIA: *Why?*

SID: *Make sure everybody else is in the living room when she and the Fentons arrive.*

GEORGIA: *Why?*

SID: *Be sure to introduce everybody.*

GEORGIA: *WHY?*

SID: *Trust me.*

He didn't reply when I texted him for more of an explanation, but since he'd volunteered to forgo Christmas dinner, I figured the least I could do was humor him. Without letting Charles hear, I told my family how Sid wanted us staged. Deborah rolled her eyes, but she went along with it.

We got everybody in place just before the doorbell rang. Deborah was on the couch, Mom and Phil were sharing the love seat, Madison was on the floor with Byron, and Charles was in the armchair. And of course, Sid was watching it all from the sugar skull bag.

I opened the door. "Merry Christmas!"

Brownie gave me a kiss, Dana unbent enough for a hug, and Treasure Hunt, grinning widely, grabbed me in a bear hug. Then Sue came in. I knew it had to be her, but I'm glad Sid had warned me because I'm not sure I'd have recognized her otherwise. She looked like a completely different person from the overall-clad show painter.

Her hair had been colored and styled, and she was wearing both makeup and jewelry, but no glasses. When I took her coat, I saw she had on a dark red velvet dress.

"Thank you so much for inviting me," she said.

"My pleasure," I said. At least, it was Sid's pleasure.

Once I had the newcomers' coats hung in the hall closet, I led them into the living room. "Folks, I think everybody knows Brownie, and his parents Mr. Mannix and Ms. Fenton."

"Treasure Hunt and Dana are good enough for us," Treasure Hunt said.

"And this is Sue Weedon. Sue, my parents Dab and Phil Thackery. My sister Deborah and my daughter Madison. And this is my friend Charles Peyton."

Knowing Charles, I expected him to come forward for a formal handshake, and he did stand up, but then he stopped short and stared at her.

She was staring right back at him.

I don't know how long the silent tableau lasted, but it was lengthy enough to get awkward.

Finally Sue said, "Hello, Charles."

"Rose?"

I blinked. Rose? Rose was Annabelle Mitchell. Who was dead.

But Sue nodded. "It's me, Charles."

He stepped toward her like a man in a trance. "How? HOW?"

"It's a long story, but—"

Charles interrupted her. "I don't care." He took her hand in his and brought it to his lips. "Tell me I'm not dreaming."

"If you are, then so am I."

Treasure Hunt said, "You two know you're standing under mistletoe, right?"

They looked up and smiled the sweetest smiles. I don't know which one of them moved first, but I do know that their embrace lasted even longer than the staring had.

Chapter Forty-Three

It's likely that Charles and Rose or Sue or whoever she was would have kept kissing even longer if the timer hadn't gone off in the kitchen.

Phil cleared his throat, and when that didn't stir them, he did so again, more loudly. They broke apart, both of them looking extremely embarrassed.

"I suppose I owe you all an explanation," Sue said. Or maybe it was Annabelle.

"That's entirely up to you," Phil said, "but perhaps it can wait until I get the ham out of the oven."

The two of them stepped to the side, and Phil and Mom headed for the kitchen. After some pointed glances and nudges, the rest of us went into the dining room, and at the last minute, I grabbed Sid's bag. If we couldn't eavesdrop, neither could he.

"Mom, what's going on?" Madison asked.

"I don't know."

Treasure Hunt snickered. "Guess you didn't figure everything out, did you, Sherlock?"

Dana elbowed him. "Don't act like you figured it all out either. Now go out in the kitchen and see if Phil and Dab need help."

"I'm going," he said, and Dana followed.

"Did you know about this?" I asked Brownie.

"Not until this minute." Then Dana called him to help, too.

There were so many people in the kitchen and dining room that I decided I could be more useful staying out of the way and texting Sid, who still wouldn't reply. It wasn't until I threatened to put his bag in my parents' office, where he wouldn't be able to see or hear anything, that he finally promised to explain it all later. That satisfied me enough to find him a good vantage place on the sideboard.

Within a few minutes, the dining room table was fully laden with ham, tossed salad, mashed potatoes, baked macaroni and cheese, green peas, roasted Brussels sprouts, crescent rolls, and even more food. Phil and Mom were trying to decide on the polite way to ask Charles and Sue to join us when Dana called out, "You two want to eat or not?"

I don't know how they made it into the room, since they weren't looking at anything other than each other, but they somehow found their chairs, and we started passing platters and bowls around until everybody's plates were filled.

Sue waited until we were well into the meal before saying, "I really do owe you all an explanation," she said. "Especially you, Charles. I'm just not sure where to start."

He said, "Perhaps I can help. You all must know how Rose… Or should I say Annabelle?"

"Rose is fine," she said.

"Rose, then. You know why and where Rose went into hiding. As it happens, I was homeless at that time and was also squatting in the Nichols house. We met and began a relationship."

Rose took over. "I was desperate when we found out the house was going to be torn down, but then I saw that the Fentons' carnival was in town. I knew Sue Mitchell—the real Sue—had travelled with them in the past, so I called her. She told me she'd moved to another show, but that I should go to the carnival ask Dana and Treasure Hunt for a job and to tell them that she'd vouch for me."

"Not that I believed her," Dana said. "I didn't not-believe her, but I don't let just anybody stay on my lot without a reference, and it took me a while to get Sue on the phone."

"In the meantime, I'd returned to the house. I didn't see T.J., but he was at the carnival, driving a shuttle bus."

"T.J. is what Edward Humphries went by back then," I explained.

Rose nodded. "T.J. must have spotted me at the carnival or while I was walking back. If I'd been more careful, maybe—"

"Don't be a chump," Treasure Hunt said. "It was just bad luck. You can't fight bad luck. Sue would tell you the same."

"Only my bad luck rubbed off on her. After Charles went to work the next day, I packed my things and went to the carnival. I didn't know that after Sue talked to Dana, she caught a bus and rode all night to get to me. She arrived at the house after I left. T.J. was there, waiting for me." She swallowed visibly, and Charles squeezed her hand. "I told you that we were as close as sisters, but not why people thought we were sisters. Even after all that time, we still looked alike, and T.J. was one of those people who barely took notice of the custodians. He must have thought she was me because he—"

Dana interrupted to say, "We all know the next part. The thing is, we didn't find out Sue had come to Pennycross until her boss called that night wanting to know when she was coming back to his show. We went to the house, but there was nobody there but Charles, who we didn't know. No offense, Charles, but we didn't trust you until we met you years later."

"No offense taken," Charles assured her.

Dana continued. "We kept looking for Sue, and after a while, we figured she was probably dead. Only we didn't know where the body was or who killed her. Given what Annabelle told us, we weren't about to trust the cops, so we came up with the idea of Annabelle trading places with Sue."

"*Who* came up with that idea?" Treasure Hunt asked.

"Fine, *you* came up with the idea. You do get a good one every ten years or so. The plan was that once the police found Sue's body and caught the killer, Annabelle could come out of hiding and get her life back. Only they never found a body, never caught the killer, never discovered the thefts at the museum, never figured out squat.

I didn't see any reason for Annabelle to go back to her old life, not when she could stay with the carney."

Charles looked stricken. "But you never called me?"

"How could I, Charles?" Rose said. "I'd already gotten my oldest friend killed. I wouldn't risk your life, too."

"You didn't worry about risking our lives," Treasure Hunt muttered. Dana elbowed him sharply.

Rose went on. "I don't expect you to forgive me for putting you through this, Charles. I'm just glad I've had the chance to set things straight. It's been magical seeing you again."

"It will take time to forgive you," Charles said, then took her hand. "Please stay in my life long enough to give me that time."

The rest of us, even Treasure Hunt, suddenly became very interested in our food.

When the two of them remembered that they were at a table full of people, Rose said, "How did you figure it all out, Georgia?"

"Honestly, I didn't," I said, then left honesty behind. "I was doing a little Christmas matchmaking because I thought you and Charles might hit it off."

"Good deduction, Sherlock," Treasure Hunt said.

"Seriously, Dad?" Brownie said. "It took you all this time to pick a nickname for Georgia, and all you came up with was something as obvious as *Sherlock*?"

"I think it's rather appropriate," Phil said. "In *A Study in Scarlet*, the first appearance of Sherlock Holmes, Holmes deduces that the murderer is a cabby hiding in plain sight. Georgia caught a murderous shuttle bus driver. It's an excellent analogy."

"That's right, Professor, that's exactly why I picked it," Treasure Hunt said with a smirk.

I doubted I'd ever know if he was serious.

For the rest of the evening we ignored secret identities and crimes of all descriptions as we enjoyed what seemed to be a dozen different desserts before moving to the living room to sing Christmas carols. Treasure Hunt had a rather nice voice. As for

Brownie, I hadn't fallen in love with him for his singing anyway.

Charles and Rose were the first to leave. When he asked her if he could escort her home, she actually blushed as she accepted. After they left, Madison said, "Not to be a troublemaker, but who is she going to be now? Is she still Sue Weedon or is she Annabelle Mitchell again?"

Mom and Dana smiled knowingly, and Mom said, "The way those two were looking at each other, I think she'll be Rose Peyton before too much longer."

They turned out to be right. Charles accompanied Rose to the grand opening of the Carousel Restaurant on New Year's Eve, and precisely at midnight, went down on one knee to propose. He offered the ring he'd bought for her a decade before and had kept all that time. I'm told that the whole restaurant cheered when she accepted.

A few minutes after Charles and Rose left, the Fentons went, too, carrying a load of leftovers my father insisted on sharing. Brownie's goodbye kiss under the mistletoe was a chaste one because everybody was watching.

After that, I carried Sid's skull bag upstairs to the attic and found the rest of Sid's skeleton waiting for me in his favorite chair. He reached out for the bag with one hand, unzipped it, pulled out the skull, and popped it back in place before grabbing his other hand. Then he just looked at me. I'd expected him to look pleased with himself, even smug, but instead his connections were a little loose. I just didn't know why he would be upset, unless he was nervous about something.

Like knowing something I didn't.

"Hi," he said.

I sat down on the couch. "Spill it, Sid. How did you figure it out?"

"Would you believe while Christmas shopping?"

"Excuse me?"

"You know those paintings of the Nichols house I found on Sue's web site?"

"Right."

"When I was in your car at Bostock that day, I was looking at the site again, wondering if I should get a print of that picture for Charles for Christmas. Only I wasn't sure if a memento of his lost love would make him happy or sad. I'm not exactly an expert on affairs of the heart." He slipped two finger bones inside his chest. "No heart to be an expert with."

"Do you want me to drag out the Tin Man analogy again?"

"No, thanks. Anyway, I was checking out some of the other pictures when I found a close-up of another set of scenic panels Sue had painted for a different carousel. It was all historical scenes, and the clothing was like something out of Jane Austen."

"The Georgian era?"

"Right. One showed a woman in a flowing dress dancing with a man dressed in an impeccable evening suit. The woman's face didn't show, but the man's face was both clear and familiar. It was Charles."

"What?"

"Supposedly Sue had never met Charles, and Charles didn't recognize her name, either. So how had she known what he looked like? That got me wondering, but I kind of got distracted later on that day."

"Just a little."

"When I had a chance, I did some more digging and found Sue and Annabelle's college yearbook so I could look at their pictures. That's when I realized how much they looked alike. Around the same height, same build, same hair color. They were both in the art club—in fact, I found a picture of Sue painting the picture used for the cover of the yearbook. That's when I realized she was left-handed."

"So?"

"The carousel art site has pictures of our Sue Mitchell painting a carousel horse with her right hand."

"Couldn't one of the pictures have been flipped?"

"Nope, I checked for that. So if the live woman wasn't Sue, I figured she might just be Annabelle, and I hoped for a little Christmas miracle."

"Santa would definitely approve." Then I noticed he was still awfully loosely connected. "Sid, is something wrong?"

"I hope not. I just need to give you a Christmas present."

"You already gave me one." There had been a festive skull scarf for me under the tree that morning.

"This is different." He reached into his desk drawer and pulled out a flat package in bright red paper with a green bow to hand to me. "Here."

I pulled the paper off. It was a framed photo of Sid.

And Brownie.

Together.

I said, "This isn't Photoshop, is it?"

He shook his skull. "I told him."

"You told him?"

"I knew you were stuck, Georgia, and it was because of me. You didn't want to tell him about me unless he was a part of the family, and you couldn't add him to the family without knowing how he'd react to me. But the night we rescued him, I heard him telling you that he loves you, and I know you love him, too."

"You told him."

"Given the way his family kept Rose's secret all these years, I felt sure I could trust him to keep my secret, too, no matter how things turn out between you two."

"So you told him." I felt like a broken record.

"I called him one day while you were at work, got him up here, and we had a long talk. Then we took the picture."

"Which you did after you told him."

"I didn't tell his parents, if you're wondering. I thought that might be too much."

"You just told him."

"Georgia, you're stuck in a loop."

"I know. I'm just…I don't know what to say."

"Are you mad at me?"

"Sid!" I hopped up and hugged him as firmly as I could without cracking his ribs. "You risked everything to make me happy." I was crying, and though Sid is technically unable to cry, I was sure there was more wetness than I could rationally account for.

At some point, I noticed that one of his hands was busy typing something on his phone.

"What are you doing?" I asked.

"Nothing," he lied. "Keep hugging."

A second later, there was a tap on the door from the hall.

"Come in," Sid called out.

Given what had already happened, I shouldn't have been surprised when Brownie, who apparently hadn't left with his parents after all, climbed up the stairs.

"I take it that you told her," he said.

"I did." Without letting go of me, Sid held out one arm. "Now get in here!"

And darned if he didn't join us. If Brownie had any compunction about a three-way hug with a skeleton, he didn't show it.

When we finally broke apart, Sid said, "You two run along. I know you'll want some alone time."

I looked at Brownie, who gave me a smile and a wink. "Maybe later. I think I'd rather spend the rest of Christmas with both of my best guys."

Sid grinned as only he can.

Sid might have thought that I didn't believe in Christmas miracles, but I did—I just didn't think I needed another one. I'd had Sid in my life since I was a child. He was all the miracle I'd ever need.

Acknowledgments

With thanks to:

- My BFFs/beta readers Charlaine Harris and Dana Cameron, for unswerving support.

- My daughters Maggie and Valerie for doing their best to keep me up-to-date on nerd culture.

- The real Lauri Biegler, for her generosity in bidding for character naming rights.

- The Facebook hive mind for continuing to answer so many random questions with accuracy and speed.

- The teams at JABberwocky Literary Agency for keeping me on track.

- The team at Diversion Books for publishing enthusiasm.

LEIGH PERRY takes the old adage "Write what you know" to its illogical extreme. Having been born with a skeleton, and with most of her bones still intact, she was inspired to create Sid and write the Family Skeleton Mysteries. *The Skeleton Stuffs a Stocking* is the sixth in the series. As Toni L.P. Kelner, she's published eleven novels and a number of short stories, and has coedited seven anthologies with *New York Times* bestselling author Charlaine Harris. She's won an Agatha Award and an RT Booklovers Career Achievement Award and has been nominated for the Anthony, the Macavity, and the Derringer awards. Leigh lives north of Boston with her husband, fellow author Stephen P. Kelner. They have two daughters, a guinea pig, and an ever-increasing number of books. You can visit Leigh online at LeighPerryAuthor.com.